Laura Martin writes historical romances with an adventurous undercurrent. When not writing she spends her time working as a doctor in Cambridgeshire, where she lives with her husband. In her spare moments Laura loves to lose herself in a book, and has been known to read from cover to cover in a single day when the story is particularly gripping. She also loves to travel—especially to visit historical sites and far-flung shores.

HER RAGS-TO-RICHES CHRISTMAS

Laura Martin

MILLS & BOON

First published in Great Britain 2019
by Mills & Boon, an imprint of HarperCollins*Publishers*
1 London Bridge Street, London, SE1 9GF

Large Print edition 2020

© 2019 Laura Martin

ISBN: 978-0-263-08622-5

MIX
Paper from
responsible sources
FSC
www.fsc.org
FSC C007454

This book is produced from independently certified FSC™ paper to ensure responsible forest management. For more information visit www.harpercollins.co.uk/green.

Printed and bound in Great Britain
by CPI Group (UK) Ltd, Croydon, CR0 4YY

For Mum and Dad, and that
trip around Australia a decade ago.

Chapter One

Crouching down, George Fitzgerald took a handful of earth and let it trickle through his fingers. The earth here wasn't like anywhere else in the world—and he'd stopped off in many countries during the long voyage back to Australia. It was thick and fertile and smelt of home. It felt good to be home, good to have the warmth of the sun on his face and the sound of the sea behind him. Three long years he'd been gone and now he was eager to get back to his farm, to get back to a normal life.

Sydney had changed in the time he'd been away. There were more buildings, more people, and as he walked away from the port he felt an optimism for his country that he hadn't for a long time. It was as though people had finally realised this fledgling colony was here to stay and one day might be more than just a place to send those England had sentenced to transportation.

George was just crossing the road, heading north-west to start the long and dusty journey out of Sydney and back to his farm when he heard a scream so piercing it made him stop in his tracks. Five seconds passed and then ten, then there was another cry, even more desperate than the last. Another and another passed in quick succession, each followed by a loud sob.

Quickly he ran down the street, dodging the children playing and the women bustling through the town, rounding the corner just as he heard another agonised scream. He slowed as he came up against a small crowd, gathered around watching the spectacle in front of them, muttering uneasily. This time the crack of the whip was unmistakable, coming just a fraction of a second before the woman's cry of pain.

George took in the scene. Tied to a post was a young woman, her age difficult to tell as her head was lolling forward, her face covered by thick tresses of hair. Her dress had been ripped at the back, exposing pale skin crisscrossed with the marks of the whip. Some of the lashes had broken the skin and blood dripped down in crimson droplets. The guard brandishing the whip had a serious expression on his face, but as he drew back his arm for another lash George could see he was relishing the power he held over the woman tied in front of him. She would get no mercy from that quarter.

Before the rational part of his brain could stop him, George sprang forward, parting the crowd and placing himself between the guard and the woman. He shot out a hand, grabbing the whip just before the guard could flick it, stopping it in mid-air. His hand was wrenched forward, but he managed to stand his ground, planting his feet firmly and bracing his shoulders.

For a moment the guard just looked at him with surprise.

'Move away,' he growled after a few seconds.

'She's had enough,' George said, his voice calm and his manner polite, but he knew the guard would see the steel in his eyes.

'What business is it of yours? Move away.'

'I can't do that. She's had enough,' George repeated.

With a snarl the guard yanked at the whip, trying to unbalance George and send him sprawling into the dirt, but George had a good hold on the leather now and pulled back just enough to show the guard he wasn't going to be shifted easily.

'I'll whip you, too, don't think I won't.'

George had no doubt the guard would go through with the threat in a fit of anger.

'Go fetch someone from the Governor's office,' he instructed a young lad standing at the front of the crowd. 'There'll be a coin in it for you.'

He watched as the boy scurried off, then turned his attention back to the man in front of him. The guard still hadn't moved, but every so often would pull on his whip, trying to unbalance George from a distance. He wanted to check on the woman hanging from the whipping post, but did not dare turn around and take his eye off the threat in front of him.

There was a murmuring in the crowd and out of the corner of his eye he saw people step aside as a couple more guards pushed through, coming to investigate the commotion.

Within seconds he was surrounded by four large men, doing their best to tower over his six foot two frame, but failing.

'Gentlemen…' George said, knowing they were nothing of the sort. 'Please step back. Someone from the Governor's office will be here shortly to sort this mess out, but I wouldn't want any of you to get hurt before he arrives.'

One of the guards laughed mirthlessly. 'Let go of the whip, or you might find you are holding on to it with a broken arm.'

George sighed, cursing the protective instinct that had pushed him to interfere. He was a good fighter and strong from years of working on the fields. He had no doubt he could land a few punches if it came to it, but he was outnumbered five to one and that meant he could expect a pretty good beating. Perhaps a black eye or two. What a welcome back home he was receiving.

Smoothly, he dropped the whip for a fraction of a second, using the guard's surprise to un-balance him, catching hold of the leather further down and yanking forward, pulling the first guard so he crashed into the body of one of the others. Ignoring the shouts of outrage, he swung his body round, landing a couple of punches on the jaws of two of the other guards before he felt them catch up to what was happening and pile on top of him. George was buried under the bodies and fists of five men, gasping for air and wondering if this foolhardy rescue would be his last when he heard a loud voice calling for order.

Slowly the men on top of him rose, not missing the opportunity to get in one or two more sneaky jabs on the way up.

George lay on the ground, looking up at the brilliant blue sky, contemplating if the dull ache in his chest meant one of his ribs was broken. He was out of breath and he could feel a warmth on his cheek which he suspected meant his eyebrow had been split open.

'Mr Fitzgerald, if I'm not mistaken,' a cultured voice said. 'Australia's prodigal son returns.'

George looked up, seeing only a silhouette against the sun, but took the proffered hand to pull him out of the dirt.

'Colonel Hardcastle,' George said, recognising the man who was now the Lieutenant Governor, second only to the Governor of New South Wales in status and rank. Hardcastle had been in Australia for almost a decade and George had known him from social and bureaucratic events before he'd taken his trip to England. The Colonel was a good man, if a little eccentric.

'Tell me, what on earth did you do to anger so many of my guards?'

'He interfered with the execution of my duty, sir,' the first guard rushed to say.

'Hmm. Mr Fitzgerald?'

'He's not wrong,' George said with a shake of his head. 'If his duty was to whip this poor woman half to death.'

All eyes turned to the woman still hanging lifelessly from the post a few feet away. Colonel Hardcastle stepped over to her, lifting her head as he crouched down as if to satisfy himself she was still breathing.

'She's a thief, sir,' the guard said helpfully. 'I caught her stealing. The punishment is whipping, fifty lashes.'

'How many lashes has she had?' Hardcastle asked.

'Only six, sir.'

George watched as the other man's eyebrows raised. To rip open her back in such a fashion with just six lashes spoke of the whip being wielded with an almighty force.

'I think she's had enough,' Hardcastle said. 'Where is she working?'

'The laundry, sir.'

Again Hardcastle looked surprised. To get a place somewhere like the laundry the woman tied to the post must have been so far a well-behaved convict. The worst jobs, mainly those in the factories, were saved for the troublemakers, the best for those who followed the rules and toed the line.

'What did she steal?'

'Bread, sir.'

Hardcastle crouched down in front of the woman, shaking his head in regret.

'Well, that'll be her post gone now. Untie her, take her to the cells.'

George knew he should stay quiet. It was only his status as one of the wealthiest local landowners that had saved him from being whipped himself, but even so he couldn't find it in himself to keep his mouth shut.

'I'll take her,' he said quietly. As soon as the words left his mouth he regretted them. He had no need for a convict worker, not a domestic at least. He always could use an extra pair of hands in the fields, but the petite woman tied to the post wasn't going to be much help there. He was thinking with his heart again, not his head, feeling sorry for the woman who had been whipped so harshly. It was no doubt down to spending so much time away from his farm— soon he would need to start thinking like a business owner again.

'I've got a need for a servant,' Fitzgerald said. 'I was going to put in an application, but I will take her instead. It'll save you the trouble of punishing her further.'

Hardcastle seemed to consider the proposition for a moment, regarding Fitzgerald with his keen blue eyes. Then he shrugged. 'If you wish. File the paperwork in the next couple of weeks.' He turned to the guards. 'Cut her free, Mr Fitzgerald will take her from here.'

With a slash of a knife, one of the guards cut the woman free, sending her tumbling into the dust. George could see she'd recovered from the faint, but her movements were stiff and her head still bowed. Slowly the crowd began to disperse, muttering at the odd conclusion to the day's events. George wasn't sure if they were disappointed there hadn't been more violence or glad for the woman's relatively light punishment in view of what the guard had planned for her.

'Can you stand?' George asked softly as he moved over and crouched down next to the woman.

He felt the air in his lungs being sucked out of him as she slowly lifted her head, fixing the bluest pair of eyes on his he'd ever seen.

Without answering she began to rise to her feet, wincing in pain as the remnants of her dress brushed against her shredded back. George reached out a hand to help her, but she stiffened at his touch, glaring at him from under her long eyelashes until he backed away.

As she rose she had to hold her dress to her body to stop it slipping down and George quickly shrugged off his jacket, placing it gently over her shoulders.

'What's your name?'

Ten seconds passed, then twenty. He knew she wasn't mute after hearing her screams not ten minutes ago, but right now she didn't look as though she would answer him.

'I'll not be your whore,' she said eventually.

'Excuse me?'

'That's why you saved me. So I could be your whore. I'll not demean myself in that way.'

George had never been lost for words before in his life, but found his mouth opening and closing in surprise.

'Thank you for your intervention, but I will take my chances at the factories.' She began to hobble away, every step the pain evident on her face.

'Stop,' he called out, wondering whether to assure the young woman he hadn't asked the Lieutenant Governor for her just so she could serve him in the bedroom, or to point out that it didn't much matter what she wanted—she'd been assigned to his farm. 'I think there's been a misunderstanding.'

He could see the anxiety in her expression, the naked fear as her eyes darted over him. Alongside that there seemed to be a hint of anger, directed at him even though they'd only just met. He moved a fraction closer, spreading his hands out in front of him to try to make himself look less intimidating. 'I merely wished to employ you on my farm, nothing more.'

'Why?' she asked, still looking mistrustful, but standing her ground, her eyes narrowing.

George hesitated. In truth, he didn't know. She was nothing to him, a stranger, yet he'd risked a whipping for getting in between her and the guard's harsh but lawful punishment. And now he'd lumbered himself with a convict worker he did not need.

'Call it Christmas charity,' he said with a shrug. 'My good deed for the year.'

'It's not Christmas for another month.'

'Then I'm banking it for later.'

They stood five feet apart, both regarding the other for a long minute. Then she gave a gracious nod, as if she were a queen and George a lowly servant requesting a favour.

'You don't touch me,' she said, thrusting out her hand and stabbing a long and dainty finger in his direction.

'On my honour.'

She inclined her head once again and allowed him to guide her along the street, the most unlikely of couples.

Chapter Two

'It doesn't need to be anything fancy—just a shirt and trousers will do. Anything's better than that shredded old dress.' Alice listened to the voices outside the door for a moment before sinking fully under the water, revelling in the warmth and watching the bubbles rise to the surface in a neat little stream. It had been agony for the first few seconds in the bath, the open wounds on her back throbbing and stinging as the water came into contact with them, but she knew the importance of getting them clean. Open sores like that could fester. She'd seen more than one person's wounds start swelling and weeping after a whipping on the transport ship on the way over to Australia and that could be fatal.

Now though, after her body had got used to the sensation of the water against her open flesh, the bath was soothing and she silently gave thanks for having the opportunity to bathe before the journey ahead.

Rising up to the surface, Alice could hear the argument still going on outside the door.

'I'll not dress a woman in a shirt and trousers. It's not right. It's not Christian.'

'Whatever you can find,' said the deep voice in reply. Her saviour. Mr Fitzgerald. A man with kind eyes, eyes that it would be all too easy to trust. Alice snorted—she wouldn't be trusting him any time soon.

With a sigh, she rose up out of the water, letting it drip from her body before she stepped out of the bath. She grabbed the towel from where it had been hung within easy reach and began to pat down her body, grimacing as she laid the soft material against her back. Six lashes, that was all she'd had, and the guard had made sure every single one would leave a scar. He'd ripped open her back with the first lash and continued the damage with the next five. It wasn't the first time she'd been whipped, but it was the most painful.

Alice heard the door click open and the landlady slipped in, brandishing a dress that was going to be much too large. Her own coarse grey sack of a dress lay shredded on the chair, stained with her blood and ripped past repair. However, looking at the garment the woman was holding in her hand, Alice wasn't sure this would be much better.

'It's a little large, my dear,' the woman said, her deep Yorkshire accent making Alice think of home. 'But it'll protect your modesty well enough. Now let's have a look at that back of yours.'

With a series of tuts and sighs the landlady helped her dress, leaving the material loose at the back so it wouldn't stick to the open wounds. Alice peered in the steamed-up mirror, noting the wet strands of hair hanging around her face, the pink skin on her sunburned nose and the freckles that had appeared on her cheeks these last few months. The dress hung off her, inches too long at the bottom and sitting all wrong around her hips. She looked like a child playing dress-up in her mother's clothing.

'You'll do, child,' the landlady said, looking at her with her hands on her hips. 'I'm sure Mr Fitzgerald will sort you out with something that fits once he gets you home.'

Home. The very word sent a slither of dread

into her core. *This* was exactly what she'd been avoiding for the nine months she'd been in Australia. Most of the other women she'd been transported with, and many who'd arrived after her, were settled with a man by now. Either the freemen, landowners, workers—any of the men who had the right to select a convict woman to be theirs, as a wife or something more lurid—or with other convicts, men who promised to look after them in this frightening new life.

Alice had resisted both. Her life was little enough her own as it was, she didn't want a man controlling what few choices she did have. She'd made that mistake in England, saddled herself with a man who'd promised her the world, slowly reduced her to a shadow of her former self, then led her into the situation that had resulted in her arrest and transportation.

Now it would seem that she didn't have a choice. Of course she was grateful to Mr Fitzgerald for stepping in when he did, but what would be the price?

'Come, dear, he's waiting for you. Eager to get back home, I would think.'

Alice smiled weakly, allowing the landlady to usher her out of the room. Mr Fitzgerald had insisted she get cleaned up and a change of clothes before they headed for wherever it was he lived. Alice was grateful; she felt much more human now she'd washed the blood from her back and the dirt from her hands.

As she descended the stairs she saw him sitting in the corner of the tavern, feet up on a stool and hands behind his head. There was no one else in the room, it being so early in the day, but even if there had been he would have commanded attention. He was a tall man, with broad shoulders and strong arms. Arms that hadn't hesitated in defending her.

She saw the moment he noticed her, watched the flicker of amusement in his eyes as he took in the dress made for a woman three times her size. Suddenly she felt self-conscious. She looked a state with her sunburned skin and her loose and tousled hair, but then she rallied. Perhaps he would be less inclined to force her into his bed if she continued to look quite so unattractive. For a moment Alice wondered if she was being uncharitable with her suspicions, but she couldn't help it. Time and time again since her sentencing men had tried to take advantage of her—she couldn't trust Mr Fitzgerald even if he had been kind to her.

'Are you feeling fit enough to travel?' he asked, standing. His movements were lithe and fluid, despite his size, and Alice was surprised to find him in front of her before she could blink.

'Yes, sir,' she said, looking at the ground. She was in a fix, there was no denying it. It would be foolish to run off here, with so many guards patrolling the city overseeing the work gangs of convicts. One shout from the man in front of her and she'd be dragged back to the whipping post. Still, the idea of leaving everything she'd known for the past nine months behind made her feel queasy.

'After you.' He took a step back and extended his arm, inviting her to go ahead of him. Alice blinked a couple of times, unused to anyone displaying manners like this, then stepped forward.

'I'll call in next week and settle the bill,' Mr Fitzgerald called over his shoulder to the landlady. She nodded graciously and Alice wondered what kind of influence he must have if he could walk away with just the promise of payment some time in the future.

Outside there was a cart, loaded up with a cou-

ple of large trunks and space up front for two. Mr
Fitzgerald paused in front of it, holding out his
hand to help her up. Alice brushed past him, ignoring the hand, and hauled herself up on to the
seat. Once she was settled she squeezed herself
over as far as she could go, but the seat was small
and as he climbed up his body brushed against
hers. She closed her eyes and took a deep breath,
trying not to let the panic of being in such close
proximity to someone overwhelm her.

'Comfortable?' he asked, looking at her shrewdly.

'Does it matter?' she asked, trying to focus on
the road in front of them rather than the man sitting next to her.

Mr Fitzgerald shrugged, seemingly unper-
turbed by her brusqueness.

They set off through the streets of Sydney,
heading west at a sedate pace. The sun was high
in the sky even though it was still an hour or two
before midday and it beat down relentlessly. If
their journey lasted any longer than half an hour
no doubt she would turn pink on any exposed
bits of skin. She'd been in Australia for a few
months shy of a year now, but this was the hottest
month yet. In England at the end of November
they would be getting ready for snow, but here

the temperatures just kept creeping up. It would be strange to have Christmas in the sweltering heat rather than the dull coldness of a December in England.

"Will you tell me your name?" he asked quietly, his eyes fixed on the road ahead of them.

"Alice," she offered. "Alice Fillips."

'Tell me about yourself, Alice,' Mr Fitzgerald said as they made their way out of Sydney. The road ahead was dusty but clear and he had relaxed back into the seat next to her, holding the reins casually in one hand.

She looked at him, her eyes narrowed. Although many of the men she'd met on the transport ship and since arriving in Australia weren't this subtle, there had been a couple. A couple of men who'd tried to trick her with kindness, to make her let down her guard so they could slip in and take advantage.

'What would you like to know, sir?' she asked, her voice flat.

'Do I detect a Yorkshire accent?' he asked after a moment.

'Yes, sir. I grew up in Yorkshire, just outside of Whitby. I moved to London when I was sixteen.' She kept her answer short, her voice terse, trying to discourage any more questions.

For a moment she felt a pang of homesickness, not for the crowded streets of the capital where she'd spent her years as an adult, but for the carefree life she'd left behind in Whitby. At the time the rolling Yorkshire countryside had seemed dull and Alice had been eager for any opportunity to get away; now she would give almost anything to be back there safely with her sisters.

'And how long have you been in Australia?' he asked, glancing over at her. Alice shifted. Of course he would want to know about her crime. Whatever his motivation was for rescuing her from the whip and taking her into his home, he would want to know what kind of woman he'd taken on.

'Nine months,' she said. 'I spent a year of my sentence in gaol in England, then nearly a year on board the transport ship. I have just over two years left to serve.'

He nodded and Alice waited for the inevitable query as to her crime. The seconds ticked past and it didn't come. Mr Fitzgerald was just sitting there, surveying the road ahead, and by the expression on his face he couldn't care less what she'd been convicted of.

'Don't you want to know what I did, sir?' she asked, her tone challenging.

He shrugged. 'If you want to tell me.'

She frowned. Everyone wanted to know what crimes had brought people to this country: the woman she'd worked for in the laundry, the stern couple who'd provided her lodgings. It was expected that she divulge her crime over and over again and now this man didn't seem overly bothered by what she'd done. It was unsettling.

'You're taking me to your home, but you don't want to know what crime I committed?' she asked eventually. It felt wrong, suspicious.

He looked at her, a smile fighting to gain control of his lips. 'Five years,' he said with a shrug. 'If they only sentenced you to five years, it couldn't have been anything too terrible.'

It was true the murderers and the violent criminals weren't often the ones who found themselves aboard the transport ships to the other side of the world, and especially not for a mere five-year sentence. Most of Alice's fellow convicts were thieves, pickpockets or men who'd stolen from their masters or forged documents. They still could be violent and cruel, but the crimes were not often the most heinous.

'I like Yorkshire,' Mr Fitzgerald said after a few minutes' silence. 'Very dramatic scenery. The moors, the cliffs.'

'You've been?' Alice cursed herself for the instinctive question. The last thing she wanted to do was encourage conversation. She wasn't even sure why she was surprised. Most people in Australia hadn't been born there. The man next to her could have started life anywhere in England.

'Recently. I've just got back from my very first visit to England. I travelled a lot—given the distance, it might have been my only opportunity.'

It felt strange to be sitting next to this man making small talk. Although she wasn't a slave and had some rights, she had been given to him as a convict worker, required to follow his rules and do what he said or risk the harsh punishments dealt out to those convicts not seen to be toeing the line. Still, she could use the opportunity to get some information on the man who'd rescued her. It always paid to know those you were forced to be close to.

'You sailed to England?' she asked, feeling her heart hammering in her chest. It seemed impossible—although ships did leave for England, no one she knew had ever been aboard one. Probably some of the guards went home after their stint in Australia was up, but even most of those chose to stay and make a life for themselves in the colony. And the convicts... Well, everyone dreamed of going home, but a passage was far too expensive. That was the harshest part of the sentence they'd received for their crimes. Five years in prison for theft was one thing if your family and friends were waiting for you when you were released, but once you'd been transported to the other side of the world it was likely you'd never make it home again.

'I did. I'd only just disembarked the ship this morning when I heard you screaming.'

Alice shifted uncomfortably in her seat. The wounds on her back were throbbing and as the temperature rose little beads of sweat were forming and trickling down into them, making the pain worse.

'But you said it was your first visit to England?'

'It was. I was born here. My parents made the journey while my mother was pregnant.'

'But they weren't...' Alice hesitated—most

people settled in Australia were ex-convicts or guards, but a few families had decided to make the colony their home out of choice '...convicts?'

Mr Fitzgerald laughed and Alice saw the way his eyes crinkled, the flash of white teeth and something tightened inside her. Pushing away the feeling, she looked down at her hands, focusing on the chapped skin, cracked from all the time spent working in the laundry.

'No, not convicts, just dreamers,' he said fondly. 'My father believed Australia to be the land of opportunity and for him it was true.' He paused, looking at her with a broad smile. 'You're very adept at that,' he said.

'At what?'

'Deflection. I still know next to nothing about you.'

Alice hadn't even realised she'd done it. Keeping as much of herself private as possible had become second nature to her over the past few years. The less people knew about you, the less ammunition they had to hurt you with.

She opened her mouth to answer, but was cut off by Mr Fitzgerald pulling on the reins and abruptly jumping down off the cart. She peered after him, trying to work out what had made him stop so suddenly. Inside her chest she could feel her heart hammering and a coil of icy dread snaking through her stomach.

'What are you doing?' she asked, her voice shrill.

'Come here,' Mr Fitzgerald said quietly.

She glanced at the reins, wondering how far she would get if she grabbed them and rode off. There was no reason for Mr Fitzgerald to stop the cart out here in the middle of nowhere. No *good* reason.

Alice shuddered as she remembered the men on the transport ship, the arms holding her down, the warm breath on her neck. She would never let another man have the opportunity to attack her again, even if it meant committing another crime to get out of the situation.

Mr Fitzgerald glanced back at her, frowning slightly, but then turned away again, his attention focused on something at the side of the road. Alice hesitated. It could be a ploy, a way to distract her, but as he moved to one side she saw him crouch down next to something brown and furry.

Carefully, trying not to open the wounds on her back any more, Alice stood and climbed down from the cart, too, crossing to where Mr Fitzgerald had knelt down by the side of the road. They'd left Sydney behind them and were now on a dusty road winding through farmland on the Sydney plain. It was the furthest Alice had been from the city since her arrival in Australia and as she walked across the road she was struck with the beauty of the land sprawling out in front of her.

'She's injured,' Mr Fitzgerald said as Alice crouched down beside him. 'Looks like the work of a dingo.'

'A dingo?'

'Large native dog. They're a pest to livestock, vicious, too, and they love kangaroo meat.'

Peering over his shoulder, Alice saw the kangaroo. It was large and would have been almost comical looking if it wasn't for the blood matted in its fur. She could see it wasn't breathing, there had been no movement since they'd hopped down from the cart, and she wondered what exactly Mr Fitzgerald was hoping to achieve by stopping.

'Come here, little one,' he murmured, leaning forward and lifting a brown little bundle out from the kangaroo's pouch.

'A baby?' Alice asked in surprise.

Mr Fitzgerald nodded, handling the small animal with care as he stroked its furry little head.

'It's all right,' he murmured. 'I've got you. We'll keep you safe.'

Alice watched as he stood and shrugged off his jacket, wrapping the baby kangaroo in it before holding the bundle out to her.

'I c-can't...' she stammered.

'Of course you can. I've got to drive the cart.'

'What if I hurt it?'

'Did you have any animals growing up?' he asked.

Nodding, she remembered the beautiful collie her older sister had brought home one day. 'A dog.'

'And did that dog ever have puppies?'

'A couple of litters.'

'Think of this just like a puppy. He just needs a little love and attention, handle him carefully but he is a sturdy little joey.'

Alice reached out and took the little animal, feeling its warmth through the fabric of Mr Fitzgerald's jacket. Carefully she set it on her lap once she'd climbed back aboard the cart and gently stroked its fur. At first she could feel him trembling, but after a few seconds the kangaroo seemed to relax under her touch and snuggled in deeper on her lap.

'Time to go home,' Mr Fitzgerald said, urging the horse forward. His hand brushed against her thigh as he rested the reins down and Alice stiffened. She glared at him, trying to work out if it had been deliberate or not, but he seemed oblivious, staring out into the distance as if he were soaking up the view for the first time.

Chapter Three

'Mr Fitzgerald,' Mrs Peterson's delighted voice called out from the doorway of his house and George could see the older woman had to hold herself back to stop running to embrace him.

'You are a sight for travel-weary eyes, Mrs Peterson. I am glad to be home.'

'We've missed you, sir. We've missed you sorely.'

George hopped down from the cart just as the lumbering form of Mr Peterson rounded the corner, a bright smile lighting up his face.

'You should have sent word. I'd have been at the docks to meet you if I'd known you were coming.'

The couple had been convict workers assigned to his father's farm many years ago. They'd served out their sentences, found companionship in one another, and stayed on as live-in servants for well over twenty years. When George's parents had passed away, there had been no question of the Petersons going elsewhere, and for the past eight years they had looked after his home and him with devotion.

'You know what these ships are like, there's no telling how long the crossing will take.' George had split his return journey into shorter voyages, stopping off for a few weeks in various ports along the way to see a little of the world before his return home. He had sent a few letters on ahead of him, but hadn't specified the date he would be making the final crossing to Sydney.

He watched as the Petersons looked Alice over, taking in her bedraggled appearance and ill-fitting clothes.

'This is Alice,' he said, reaching up to take the bundle containing the orphaned joey from her lap before helping her down from the cart. He was pleased to see she didn't recoil at his touch this time as she had in Sydney, although she did slip her hand from his as soon as she was steady on the ground. 'She's had a rough morning.'

Mrs Peterson looked her over, appraising her, then nodded her head. 'Let's get you settled,

Alice, then in a couple of days we can find you some work to do.'

He watched as the two women moved inside, Alice's petite figure dwarfed by Mrs Peterson's. At least she was in safe hands now.

'Let me take that for you,' Mr Peterson said, gently taking hold of the bundle and peering inside. 'Bringing home more waifs and strays, I see.'

George nodded, his eyes following Alice as she moved stiffly through the kitchen. She still looked wary, her eyes darting backward and forward as if always trying to find a way to escape, but he knew he just needed to give her time. Who knew what horrors and degradation she'd suffered on the transport ship from England, or indeed, who had tried to take advantage of her during the nine months she'd been in Australia? He knew life for the male convicts was tough, especially for the first few years of their sentence, but the female convicts were at risk of even more exploitation. It was by far enough to explain her fear and even anger—no one liked to feel helpless.

'I'll take care of this little creature,' Mr

Peterson said. 'You reacquaint yourself with your home.'

Alone, George stood back and took in the view. He'd missed home, missed the picturesque sun-scorched fields and the hazy blue mountains in the distance. Missed his beautiful house with the veranda built in the perfect orientation to enjoy the sunsets. Missed the sense of purpose when he rode out over his land, designating each area for cattle or crops, always on the lookout for new opportunities. He'd enjoyed his trip to England, but he was mighty glad to be home.

After a minute he walked inside the house, using the kitchen door as he always had as a boy. Inside he could hear Mrs Peterson chatter-ing away to Alice, telling her about the farm and their lives here. Turning away from the women, he moved through the house, running his fin-gers over the furniture, reacquainting himself with the space. He'd lived here all his life—the house had been built by his father when his par-ents had first settled in Australia almost thirty years earlier. It was large, but still managed to have a comfortable feel about it.

'Fitzgerald,' a loud voice called from outside. 'You're home, you sneaky reprobate.'

With a grin on his lips George raced through the house and back out through the door, slowing only as he came up to the two men he thought of as his brothers.

He embraced Sam Robertson first, receiving a hearty slap on the back from him before he moved on and hugged Ben Crawford.

'We had word your ship had docked,' Robertson said. 'We've been on the lookout for a week, but you managed to sneak through.'

'It's good to have you home,' Crawford said, with a broad smile that must have matched George's own.

They made their way into the house, the two men flopping down into chairs and making themselves comfortable. Although it was George's home, both Robertson and Crawford had spent much of their youth there, taken in by George's father after they had saved George from an attack by a poisonous snake while working on the farm. They had their own homes now, their own vast and successful farms, but they still came back to the Fitzgerald house regularly and George knew they still saw it as the home of their childhood.

'We were getting worried you were never coming back,' Robertson said, swinging back on the chair so only the back two legs were on the ground, shifting his weight so it balanced without toppling.

'It's a nine-month voyage,' George said with a mock serious expression. 'Some of us didn't want to rush our time in England and set off back home two months after arriving. How is the fair Lady Georgina?'

'Just plain Mrs Robertson now,' Robertson said, and George could see the happiness on his face. 'Beautiful and blooming, we're hoping for a sister for little James in a few months.'

It felt strange to be talking of wives and children. His friends' lives had changed so much these past couple of years and here he was back home to the same life. It was a good life, there was no denying it, but George knew his friends had moved on to the next stage while he remained in the same place.

'And the new Mrs Crawford?' he asked.

'Not so new any more. We've been married for near on two years,' Crawford said. 'And Frannie is expecting again, too.'

'It seems we have much to celebrate.'

'How about you, Fitzgerald? You didn't bring a bonny English lass back home with you?'

George laughed. 'You two escaped with the two fairest women in England, I wasn't about to settle for third best.'

From somewhere else in the house George could hear raised voices, stern words getting louder as the argument became more heated. He frowned. Mr and Mrs Peterson bickered, just like any couple who had lived together for so many years, but he'd never heard them argue before.

'I'd better...' he started to say, getting up from his chair, but didn't get any further as Mrs Peterson burst into the room, dragging Alice behind her. 'What is all this noise about?' George asked, looking at the two women's dark expressions. Mrs Peterson's face was red with fury while Alice's remained stony.

'Begging your pardon, sir, I'm sorry for making a scene, especially with your guests here,' Mrs Peterson said.

'Don't mind us,' Robertson murmured, his eyes flicking from the older woman to Alice, then looking at George with an amused question in his expression.

'She can't stay,' Mrs Peterson said with more

dramatic flair than George had seen in the entire time he'd known his housekeeper.

'I'm sure we can sort this out,' George said, wishing momentarily for the free life he'd been living while away. He might not have a wife and child, but he did still have responsibilities here.

'She's been saying the most terrible things, sir, most wicked.'

He regarded Alice, who was standing up straight despite the pain she must have been feeling from her wounds, resolutely not looking at him, her expression that same mix of anger and fear she'd had ever since he'd helped her up from the ground near the whipping post.

'Please excuse me,' George said, a little annoyed to be pulled away from his friends at the moment of their reunion, but curious as to what the young convict woman could have said to upset his normally unflappable housekeeper.

He strode out of the room, turning back to see Alice having to be chivvied along by Mrs Peterson. With a shake of his head he wondered what he'd got himself into.

'Would you sort some tea for Robertson and Crawford?' George asked his housekeeper. She looked momentarily surprised, as if wanting to stay and defend the man who towered over both her and the new convict worker, but then rallied and bustled off down the corridor, murmuring under her breath.

'Congratulations,' George said after a minute. 'I've never seen Mrs Peterson that irate before.' He shook his head. 'And I really tested her boundaries when I was a lad. What did you do?'

'I merely spoke the truth,' Alice's reply came tersely.

'I may be a man who seems to have time on his hands, Alice, but I would prefer it if you didn't talk in riddles and told me straight out what upset Mrs Peterson.'

'I called you a vile lecher.' There was defiance in her eyes, but underneath George saw an unmistakable flash of fear.

He nodded slowly, tapping his fingers on the banister. 'In the six hours that I've known you, tell me what is it that I've done to be given that label?'

She looked at him with a stony expression, but just shook her head.

'Was it when I rushed in to save you from a whipping? Or when I volunteered to take you in as a convict worker to save you from a worse punishment? Or when I insisted you get cleaned up before we journeyed out here?' George's voice was completely calm, despite the bubble of irritation he felt rising up inside him. He struggled to suppress it. His father had always had infinite patience with those he helped and George knew he could do worse than emulate the man, in his kindness at least.

'Why did you save me?' Alice asked. 'Why step in and risk a whipping yourself, or worse? Why volunteer to bring me back to your home?' There was pent-up emotion in her words and George wondered not for the first time what had brought her to this life. Despite professing not to be interested in her crime during their ride to his home, he did want to know what had led her to the path she was on now.

He shrugged. 'It seemed like the right thing to do.'

She laughed a bitter, mirthless laugh that cut right through him.

'So I had the good fortune to be saved by the only decent man in Australia? Tell the truth. You wanted a young, willing and grateful woman in your bed, just like every other man in this god-forsaken country.'

'Look at me, Alice,' George said, waiting for her eyes to reach his. Not for the first time he noticed their intensity, the deepness of the sparkling blue, and he realised she must have had it hard being a pretty young woman in a country filled with men. 'Do I look like I need to force a woman into bed with me?'

As he watched her eyes flicked over him, taking in first his face and then his physique, until she shrugged rebelliously.

'No one does anything for nothing,' she muttered.

'Yes, they do,' he said firmly. 'Now the problem arose when Mrs Peterson showed you to your room?'

She nodded. 'There's no lock on the door.'

'And you thought that was so I could sneak in at the stroke of midnight and have my wicked way with you?' He saw her redden at his directness and was pleased to be finally getting a reaction from her that wasn't suspicion or anger. 'Come with me.'

Without checking to see if she was following, he took the stairs two at a time, pausing only when he was outside the room Mrs Peterson had seen fit to give to Alice. It was a generously proportioned bedroom with a view over the farm and to Sydney in the distance. Furnished with a bed, wardrobe and writing table, it was homely and comfortable—no wonder Mrs Peterson took offence when Alice refused to settle herself in.

'You're right, there's no lock,' George said, 'just as there isn't a lock on my bedroom door, or any of the bedrooms. Not...' he held up an admonishing hand '...that I'm inviting you to find out. I find a chair wedged under the handle like this...' with a flourish he closed the door, took the back of the chair and propped it under the handle, demonstrating that the door could not be easily opened '...does the job.'

Alice was staring at him, blinking every few seconds as if she couldn't quite believe what she was seeing.

'I understand you don't trust me, Alice, and I don't think anything I can say will reassure you that I didn't bring you here for nefarious purposes, but my father always used to say that deeds spoke louder than words. Hopefully with time you will come to trust me.' He paused, wondering exactly what had happened to the young woman in front of him to make her quite so distrustful. 'Can I give you a word of advice, though? I wouldn't say anything bad about me to Mrs Peterson. For some strange reason she thinks I'm more virtuous than all the saints combined. If you want to have a moan about me, find someone more neutral.'

He turned, resisting the urge to delve into Alice's past. Perhaps one day she would want to tell him a little about what had brought her to this point in her life, or perhaps not.

'Sorted?' Crawford asked as George walked back into the room.

'Who knows?' George shrugged, wondering if Alice would be climbing out the window, risking being caught as a runaway just to avoid spending a night in his house.

'Who is she?' Robertson asked. 'And what is she doing here?'

'I ran into her when I got off the ship,' George said, sitting back down with his friends. 'One of the guards was whipping her, lashes that were far too brutal.'

Crawford grinned. 'You saved her?'

George rubbed his jaw, remembering the punches he'd received when he'd refused to back down.

'I politely asked them to desist with such a cruel and unnecessary punishment.'

'How many were there?'

'Five.'

Robertson studied his face carefully. 'Looks like they got a couple of good punches in.'

'I would have been tied to the post alongside Alice if Colonel Hardcastle hadn't turned up.'

'Our new Lieutenant Governor,' Crawford murmured. George could hear the approval in his voice.

'Hardcastle agreed to release Alice to me as a convict worker for the farm.'

George saw Robertson and Crawford exchanging looks and shook his head.

'Just like one of your injured animals,' Robertson said with a grin.

'Neither of you would have left her there,' George said with conviction. 'Not to that brutality.'

'It looks like you're going to have your hands full,' Crawford said.

He wasn't wrong. George had imagined Alice slotting into the life on the farm, taking up her role as a housemaid, perhaps helping with the kitchen garden, but that seemed a long way off for now. He shrugged. If things didn't work out, he could just send her to look after one of the properties he owned further afield. Whatever happened, he would be able to rest easy, knowing he hadn't abandoned her in her hour of need.

Chapter Four

Alice padded down the stairs, her footfalls silent on the thick rug that covered the wooden steps. Down below her she could hear the voices of the three men, laughing and talking as they had been for the past two hours. She'd made her peace with Mrs Peterson, apologising for her outburst and promising to keep her opinions to herself from now on. The older woman had been mollified and a few minutes later had brought Alice a few dresses to try on, clothing that fitted her better than the huge sack she'd travelled from Sydney in.

Now that she wasn't in fear of her dress falling down to her ankles with every step, she was feeling curious about her surroundings and had decided to explore a little. It wasn't as though Mr Fitzgerald had instructed her to keep to her room and Mrs Peterson had told her to take a few days to get settled before she started on the work of a housemaid.

Quietly she made her way down the hall, feeling like a thief as she trailed her fingers over the polished furniture and the collection of ornaments that seemed out of place out here in the middle of the Australian countryside. They would look more at home in an English manor house.

The kitchen was at the end of the hallway, a large room that still managed to feel homely despite its size. At one end the door was open to the outside and Alice looked around guiltily before placing her foot over the threshold.

'Don't be a fool,' she muttered to herself. 'It's not as though you're running away.'

Running away would be the worst thing she could do. Although she felt uncomfortable with her new circumstances, she knew she would be so much worse off if she was branded a convict runaway. She'd never known another convict woman who had dared. The men who tried to gain their freedom by heading off into the wilds of the countryside were always caught and brought back, their punishments ranging from a hundred lashes to being shipped off to one of the other penal colonies in Australia. Somewhere disease-ridden and much less civilised than Sydney. She shuddered at the thought.

Outside the sun was so bright it made her blink rapidly as her eyes struggled to adjust and the heat was much more noticeable than in the cool of the house. Over to the left was a little kitchen garden, with a vegetable patch and plants climbing up stakes. She could see Mr Peterson's bent form as he worked at picking whichever of the vegetables flourished in this climate.

To the right was a large enclosure with twenty or so cows huddled up one end and a little further away were horses grazing on the patchy grass behind a sturdy fence. With a hand shielding her eyes from the glare of the sun, Alice stopped for a moment and properly appreciated the view. Nine months she'd been in Australia and all she'd seen up until now was Sydney. The ramshackle buildings, the dusty streets, the weary faces. Out here was different. Out here she could see why some people seemed to fall in love with this country.

'Beautiful, isn't it?' a low voice said beside her.

Slowly she turned, finding Mr Fitzgerald standing a fair distance from her.

She nodded, watching as he moved closer, wary of his proximity, but noting how he stopped an arm's reach away. She couldn't fault his behaviour. Yet. She'd known men who bided their time before.

'I've stopped off in many countries on my way back to Australia,' he said, looking out over the rolling hills in front of them, 'and none of them is half as beautiful as here.'

It must be a wonderful thing to have a home you loved so much. Not since she'd left Yorkshire had Alice felt that way. The smog-filled streets of London weren't exactly inspiring and she hadn't seen anything but splashing waves and the rocking hull on the transport ship.

They stood in silence for a few minutes, Alice willing the man beside her to go away and leave her in peace, but he seemed happy just to stand there with her, looking out over the rolling fields.

'Is this all your land?' she asked eventually, motioning to the expanse in front of them.

'As far as the eye can see. When my father first came out to settle here he bought a small farm and planted crops. He was purely an arable farmer for well over a decade. Then he began to anticipate the demands for more than just simple crops and branched out. Now the majority of the land I own is taken up with cattle, although we do still grow a selection of crops.'

'And how about those?' she asked, pointing in the direction of a small enclosure that housed a few kangaroos happily hopping around in the sun.

She watched as his face lit up with pure joy and wondered what sort of charmed life this man in front of her must have had to still be able to feel such a thing.

'Come on, let me introduce you,' he said, reaching out to grab her hand, but remembering her previous reactions to him just in time. Quickly he adjusted his behaviour and beckoned for her to follow him. He strode over to the fence and with a single movement vaulted over the wooden struts, turning back to assist her. Alice paused, eyeing the animals with uncertainty.

'They're one of the gentlest creatures I've ever met,' he said, holding out his hand to help her over.

She hesitated for just a moment longer, then hitched up her skirts and climbed the fence, hopping down on the other side, resolutely refusing to take his hand even when she wobbled a little at the top. With amazement she watched as the biggest of the kangaroos hopped comically over to Mr Fitzgerald and began nuzzling him.

'They're your pets?' she asked.

'No, definitely not. They're wild animals, but these three—' he motioned to the three kangaroos now surrounding him '—I found injured in various ways over the years and brought back here to tend to their wounds. Once they'd recovered they didn't seem to want to venture back into the wild, so they stay here.'

'Like the little one you found this morning.'

'Exactly. When he's grown—if he survives, of course—I'll try to release him, but who knows if he'll go.'

She watched as he shrugged off his jacket in the heat before crouching down to get on the level of the kangaroos. Softly he stroked one after another, murmuring greetings and apologising for his long absence. The animals were larger than she'd imagined when she had first heard of the strange lolloping creatures that were native to Australia. The biggest of the three came up to her shoulder in height and had a rotund belly and large feet protruding out underneath it. They seemed friendly enough, but Alice hesitated in reaching out and stroking one—she'd never been very good with animals.

'Try it,' Mr Fitzgerald said, taking her hand gently and placing it on the kangaroos fur. 'Hetty here is the gentlest creature in the world.'

'Don't,' she hissed, pulling her hand out of his. He backed away slightly, but didn't reprimand her or try to force the issue.

Alice felt as though her whole body was stiff and on edge, her instincts telling her to run, to get out of arm's reach at the very least.

'I think Hetty likes you,' Mr Fitzgerald murmured.

Slowly Alice felt herself relax as the kangaroo cocked her head to one side and watched her out of big brown eyes. Tentatively she reached out a hand and placed it on the animal's back. The fur was soft but short, more like a donkey or a horse to stroke than a dog, but as she stood there petting the animal Alice felt a peculiar peace come over her. A peace she hadn't felt for a long time.

'Shall we check on the little one we found earlier?' Mr Fitzgerald asked as the kangaroos hopped off to find some shade.

It was a strange offer, but she was fast learning Mr Fitzgerald was a strange man. By rights they should be worlds apart, he a wealthy and respectable landowner and she a convict worker, but he spoke to her as though she was a house guest rather than a maid. She could understand it more if he'd come from the same beginnings, but unlike a lot of men who owned land in Australia Mr Fitzgerald wasn't an ex-convict, he hadn't ever lived the life she lived. It made his compassion even more perplexing.

Don't be a fool, she told herself silently. It wasn't compassion. It wasn't anything more than trying to gain her trust.

She watched as he vaulted back over the fence, noticing not for the first time the strength in his arms and the chiselled contours of the muscles of his torso. Mr Fitzgerald was an attractive man, the sort of man she would have once lost her head over.

'Come on,' he said, looking back over his shoulder with a wide smile, the sun glinting off his bright blue eyes and making the neat-trimmed beard on his face appear golden.

This time he waited on the other side of the fence, standing back to allow her to climb over herself. Alice winced in pain as the skin on her back stretched and immediately he stepped forward, but one pointed glare was enough to stop him from touching her.

Leading the way back to the kitchen, he softened his steps as they crossed the threshold. Alice hadn't noticed the small bundle in the corner on her way out, but now they crossed quietly over to it.

'Looks peaceful, doesn't he?' Mr Fitzgerald said, crouching down and motioning for her to join him.

'Will he live?' Alice asked as she tentatively reached out a hand to stroke the soft brown fur.

'I think so. He looks about five months old, so not so young he can't survive without his mother. Hopefully with a little milk and a few days to adjust he'll start to thrive soon.'

The little kangaroo looked up at her with blinking eyes and Alice felt a rush of affection for the animal. They'd both been saved this morning.

Carefully Mr Fitzgerald reached down and scooped the young joey into his arms and held him out for her to hold.

'He won't bite.'

Alice still hesitated.

'He's lost his mother. A little affection will go a long way.'

Placing the bundle in her arms, Mr Fitzgerald took a step back and Alice found herself wondering why this man in front of her didn't have a wife and a brood of children. Looking down at the kangaroo in her arms, she felt a tug of regret at the loss of her own family. Not for Bill, the good-for-nothing scoundrel who had led her into trouble in London, but for her parents and her sisters. People who she would probably never see again.

'Have the gentlemen, your friends, left?' she asked, grasping for a subject of conversation to distract herself from her maudlin thoughts.

'They have, although I'm sure I will see them again before the week is out.'

'You seemed very close,' she murmured, knowing she was being presumptuous, but Mr Fitzgerald's easy manner was hard not to emulate.

'They're like the brothers I never had. Friendship is a wonderful thing…' He paused, looking at her in that perceptive way of his. 'I'm sure you've found that during your time in Australia.'

Alice looked away, blinking to try to disguise the tears in her eyes. There should have been comradeship between the female convicts, but it just wasn't the case. Many of them had suffered atrociously on the transport ship and as soon as they'd arrived had set about looking for a man to protect them. Alice hadn't wanted that and that had made her stand apart from the rest of the women.

'No,' she said quietly. 'It hasn't been like that.'

He regarded her for a moment and not for the first time Alice felt as though he was seeing past the hard exterior she projected to the world. The thought made her uncomfortable.

'I should go and see if Mrs Peterson needs any help,' she said quickly, rising to her feet and placing the baby kangaroo back in Mr Fitzgerald's arms.

Hurrying off, she chided herself for being a coward. It was herself she was running from, the strange urge she had to relax, to allow herself to let down her guard when she was with Mr Fitzgerald. She didn't know if it was the cheerful smile, the mischievous twinkle in his eyes or the kindness he'd shown her, but something made her heart beat faster whenever he accidentally brushed against her, even though his interest was the last thing she wanted. Shaking her head, she tried to put him out of her mind. She would do better to remember the trouble men had brought her in the past and continue in her mistrust, even if Mr Fitzgerald was relentlessly kind.

Chapter Five

'If you don't hold your tongue, I will come over there and give you a thrashing, open wounds or no.' Mrs Peterson's irate voice rang through the house, causing George to pause and put down the papers he was reading. It had been almost a week since he'd returned home, a week since Alice had first stepped over the threshold into the farmhouse, and it had been far from the most peaceful week of his life.

He listened for Alice's reply, hearing a low murmur, but not the words.

'I've never heard such vile rudeness.' Mrs Peterson's voice rose again and with a groan George hauled himself to his feet. There was at least one altercation a day between Alice and his housekeeper. And even in between the sharp words there were long periods of sharp silence.

'Is there a problem?' he asked, striding into the kitchen.

'She has got to go,' Mrs Peterson said, crossing her arms in front of her chest and breathing heavily.

'I'd be delighted to,' Alice said, flashing a look that contained a challenge in his direction.

'No one is going anywhere. Alice, join me in my study, please. Mrs Peterson...' He looked at his fuming housekeeper and gave her his most winning smile. 'Whatever you've got cooking smells delicious.' It was the truth—wafts of spices and fruit, mixed with the unmistakable smell of gingerbread baking, took him back to the Christmases of his youth.

George turned, not waiting to see if Alice followed, and made his way back into his study, sitting down heavily in the comfortable leather-lined chair behind his desk.

'Sit,' he said, motioning to a chair facing him.

Alice sat, looking defiant.

'I really don't know how you do it,' he said quietly. 'Mrs Peterson can be a bit prickly, but I've never actually seen her angry before.'

Alice shrugged, a non-committal gesture that hid a world of pain.

'I know what you're doing.'

Her eyes darted up to meet his.

'You think if you make a nuisance of yourself I'll send you back to Sydney. The thing I can't understand is why. It's comfortable here, the work is easier than the laundry, you're safe and you're not under the direct scrutiny of the guards the whole time. Surely here is better than where you were?'

'Yes, sir,' Alice said, her voice emotionless.

'Is there something you're missing in Sydney? Or someone, perhaps?'

'No.' The denial was hard and fast and George was inclined to believe it.

'I want you to be comfortable here, Alice.'

'Why?'

'Because everyone deserves a little humanity and I think you've experienced barely any at all these last couple of years.'

'No one does something for nothing.'

He looked at her, feeling regret that such a young woman had been brought down to feel this way. Once Alice would have been trusting and content with the world—her attitude now was a testament to the suffering she had endured.

'Let's make an agreement,' he said, waiting for

her to look up to continue. 'Give it one month. If you're still not happy here in one month, then you can return to whatever post they will give you in Sydney. I'll arrange it. I give you my word.'

She eyed him suspiciously.

'The only thing I ask for is that you give life out here a chance. You look for the positives, stop riling Mrs Peterson and see if this is some-where you would like to spend the last few years of your sentence.'

'And if I decide not to stay, you'll let me go?' Alice asked.

'On my honour.'

She sat thinking for a moment, then nodded. He even saw a hint of a smile under the prickly façade.

'This is your home, at least for the next month, and if you decide you want to stay for a couple of years, I want you to be comfortable. And I want you to stop provoking Mrs Peterson. Can you do that?'

'I can try.'

Pulling on the soft leather, George changed his boots for the pair he used when out riding the vast distances around his farms. It felt good to be home and he was eager to get out and continue reacquainting himself with the land he loved so much.

Out of the corner of his eye he saw the swish of material as Alice padded silently around the house. He could tell she felt awkward, unsure of her position, but he hoped in a couple of days Mrs Peterson would have found her some work she could take charge of and make her own. There had been an uneasy truce between Alice and Mrs Peterson the last couple of days since he had taken Alice into his study and made the agreement that she would make an effort to see Mountain View Farm as her home for the month before they decided on the longer-term plan.

It felt strange to have another person in the house. For a long while before his trip to England it had been just him and the Petersons and it was odd to wake up and find someone else walking through the otherwise empty halls.

Throughout his childhood his parents had always had at least a few convict workers doing the manual work in the fields alongside the regular workers and the free-men they hired seasonally as the demands of the farm increased. Only once had they had a female convict worker. With a frown George put that memory from mind. He wasn't his father, he wasn't the same man and he didn't have to make the same mistakes.

His parents had enjoyed living a life without too many servants, just a housekeeper and a cook and a maid, and he had happily survived with just the Petersons for the past eight years.

Still, Alice was here now and hopefully before long she would have slotted into life at Mountain View Farm.

As he stood up he saw Alice come walking out of his study with a book open and her eyes skimming over the words. For a second he felt his breath catch in his chest. Today for the first time she was dressed in a dress that more or less fit her. The light blue cotton clung to the curves of her chest and waist before skimming out over her hips into a full skirt. It accentuated her figure and George felt the first stirrings of desire. A very inappropriate desire.

His eyes travelled upwards to the neat curls of her hair. The past week her hair had remained the untamed frizz it had been whipped into after the bath in the tavern in Sydney, which had been followed by a long and dusty cart ride to the farm. She must have begged a bath from Mrs

Peterson the night before and the results were astounding. Today her hair looked like spun gold with just a hint of red, smooth waves that fell way past her shoulders.

She looked up, surprise registering in her sparkling blue eyes, and then gave him a tentative smile.

George felt as though he'd been punched in the gut and struggled to make his voice sound normal as he greeted her.

'Good morning, Alice,' he said, wondering where the scruffy convict he'd rescued over a week ago had gone.

'Good morning, Mr Fitzgerald,' she said, hesitating a moment and then dipping into a little curtsy. Her manner was still often skittish and fearful, but over the past few days a lot of the anger she'd had when she had first arrived had ebbed away. 'I hope you don't mind, sir, but Mrs Peterson said I could borrow a book or two.'

'Of course. No point the books gathering dust when someone wants to read them.'

He glanced at the cover of the book, expecting to see one of his mother's awful adventure stories, but instead was surprised to find a book about botany in her hands. She was clasping it to her chest and unwittingly George's eyes travelled from the rough leather of the book to the rather smoother skin that peeked out above the neckline of her dress.

Get a hold of yourself, he silently chastised himself. He was being exactly the lecherous sort of man Alice had been afraid of. Exactly the sort of man he had always vowed never to be.

'Botany,' he said, forcing his eyes back up to her face. 'Are you interested in it?'

She shrugged and he fancied he saw her blush a little, just a hint of colour on her cheeks.

'I don't know anything about it,' she admitted, 'but when I flicked through it looked interesting.'

'That book there is focused mainly on plants of England, or at least western Europe. There are no comprehensive guides to the flora of Australia yet.' He thought of the hundreds of samples of plants he'd collected over the years, some dried and pressed and kept meticulously in his study, some planted from seed and nurtured in the private garden around the side of the house. One day there would be a book on the flora of Australia and he meant to contribute to it.

Mrs Peterson bustled out from the kitchen and

stopped for a moment, looking between them before smiling.

'Are you off out, Mr Fitzgerald?' she asked, reaching for his jacket from the hook on the wall and passing it over to him.

'Just off to inspect some of the fields, take a look at the cattle,' he said. 'Mr Williams is due later today to hand things back over to me. If he arrives before I return, will you make him comfortable?'

'Of course, sir. I've got a lovely batch of biscuits about to pop in the oven. I'm sure I can distract him with a cool drink and a biscuit or two if you're late.'

Mr Williams was the very capable man he'd left in charge of his farms for the duration of his trip to England. George had been away almost three years and a lot could change in that time and he was eager to start getting control of everything again. He was sure there had been no major disasters—for the past two years Robertson and Crawford had been back home and they would have kept an eye on everything for him. They hadn't mentioned anything going wrong so he was confident Mr Williams wouldn't have any terrible news for him.

'Thank you, Mrs Peterson.' He took a step towards the door and hesitated. Knowing he would regret the offer, he still couldn't stop himself. 'Would you like to come and see some of the farm?' he asked Alice.

She blinked in surprise and George found himself smiling. He liked how she wasn't able to hide when something shocked her, her eyes reacted before she had time to take hold of herself.

'This is to be your home for the next couple of years if you decide to stay with us,' he reminded her gently. 'Perhaps you'd like to see a little of where you'll be living.'

'That's very kind, Mr Fitzgerald,' Alice said, 'but I wouldn't want to hamper your progress.'

'Nonsense,' he said. She would hamper his progress, of course she would. He doubted a woman of her background would know how to ride, at least not proficiently, but he realised he didn't regret the offer all the same.

'I would like to see a little more of the countryside,' she said, looking at him as if she couldn't quite believe she was saying the words. He knew she still distrusted him, so for her to agree to ride out alone with him was certainly a step in the right direction.

'Wonderful.' He looked at her appraisingly. The dress did much for her figure, but he doubted it would be the most suitable thing for a trip into the countryside. 'Can you ride, Alice?' he asked.

She laughed, the first proper laugh he'd heard pass her lips. 'Of course.' Seeing his look of surprise, she continued. 'My family had a horse up in Whitby. We lived a little out of the way so it was necessary for getting into town.' Alice looked down at herself and shrugged, 'I can't ride in that fancy way, though.'

'Side saddle?'

She shook her head, 'We only had a normal saddle, so that's all I can do.'

'I don't think that'll be a problem.' He leaned in closer and lowered his voice, 'One of the best things about Australia is how you can ride for a good couple of hours and not see another soul. No one is going to be judging you.'

They stepped outside, George trying to ignore the disapproving look from Mrs Peterson. She'd been with the family for years, having been transported well over two decades previously for some long-forgotten crime, and she was very protective of him. She was also quite old fashioned in her ways, thinking the servants should stick to below stairs, metaphorically, of course, and the masters above. This sort of mixing was out of the question.

'Wait,' Alice said, stopping so abruptly his body almost collided with hers. She turned and rushed back inside, leaving him staring after her. It gave him a moment to get control of himself, to regain his equilibrium and promise himself he would not look at Alice with anything other than mild, friendly interest.

She came back out, brandishing a bonnet.

'I found it in my room.' She grimaced 'I may as well try to protect my skin from any further damage in this sun.'

From her colouring he could tell she should have naturally pale skin, but exposure to the strong Australian summer sun had pinkened her nose and cheeks and there was a smattering of freckles dotted about as well. The ladies of London he'd spent the last couple of years socialising with would be aghast at such colouring, but it wasn't uncommon among the women here. The summers were hotter and everyone spent more time outdoors, it was no surprise both the men and women of Australia had more of a tan on their faces.

Outside Mr Peterson had saddled a horse and left it tied to a fencepost ready for him and it was the work of a couple of minutes to get another horse ready for Alice. She watched him as he tightened the strap to secure the saddle, before looping over the bridle.

'Mrs Peterson tells me you're English nobility,' Alice said, her eyes following his every movement. 'I've never known an English lord to saddle his own horse.'

'I'm no lord,' George said, shaking his head. 'My father was the younger son of a baron, a destitute baron. He inherited no title and no money. We have ties to the nobility, but I view myself as a farmer, a landowner, nothing more.'

His identity was important to him and he certainly did not feel as though he'd fitted in with the lords and ladies of London society during his recent stint in England. Their customs had seemed too rigid and old fashioned and he'd returned to Australia knowing even more than ever that this was where he wanted to be.

Holding out a hand, he wondered if she would take it. Alice had thawed in her attitude towards him since their initial interactions, but she still seemed skittish and he wasn't sure if she would allow him to help her up on to the horse.

Stepping forward, she hesitated for a long moment before grasping hold of the saddle and placing her foot in his hand, allowing him to boost her up and then steady her while she found her seat. In the process of mounting her skirt had hitched up and caught around her thighs, exposing one of her calves. Trying not to look, George tugged at the material, covering her up again, his fingers accidentally brushing against her soft skin as he did so. Alice stiffened beneath his touch, brushing him away.

Without another word he turned and led her horse out of the stables to where his was waiting.

'Good morning, Kareela,' he said, stopping to stroke the horse's nose. Three years he'd been gone and there was still recognition in the animal's eyes. Quickly he mounted, feeling the satisfying pull of muscles he hadn't used for a long time. The voyage home had taken him an entire year with lengthy stops in various countries and in that time he'd only ridden twice. It felt good to be back on horseback and he urged Kareela forward with a gentle nudge of his heels.

They took the track out that they'd arrived on,

George choosing a sedate pace to let Alice get used to riding again after so long.

'Just over a week ago I was stuck in the laundry all day long,' Alice murmured, 'and now I'm here.'

The laundry would be a grim place to work, although not the worst convict job in Sydney by far.

'Via the whipping post.'

She nodded, flinching at the memory. 'They were determined to get me somehow,' she murmured.

George frowned, not understanding the comment.

Alice shook her head and smiled as if determined to put something out of her mind.

'Did they set you up?' he asked. Robertson and Crawford had both been convicts and before they'd landed jobs on his father's farm they'd spent a couple of years doing the backbreaking work of road building in Sydney under cruel and malicious guards. Their stories did not make you feel confident in the humanity of the men sent to guard the convicts and inflict the punishments if someone stepped out of line. George could well believe a particularly nasty guard would set someone up for a whipping for their own amusement.

'Not exactly.' She shook her head. 'I stole the bread I was whipped for.' He thought she wasn't going to elaborate for a moment, but then she sighed. 'Just not for myself. For one of the other women's sons. He's only six and has a terrible chest. All skin and bones and his mother was struggling to feed him. So I took a little extra bread to try to feed him up.'

'And they whipped you for that?'

'It's all about control, isn't it?' she said with a hint of anger in her voice. 'They stop seeing us as living, breathing humans with a heart and a history and see us as criminals who shouldn't have any rights and just need to be controlled.'

'I think transportation is one of the harshest punishments, aside from hanging, of course,' George said quietly. 'They take your freedom, but they take so much more than that. They take your future, or at least the future you'd envisaged. They rip you away from everyone and everything you've ever known and ship you to a strange country where even the smallest misdemeanour is seen as a rebellion against the authorities.'

'But perhaps we deserve it,' Alice said quietly.

George looked at her, but she'd turned her face away, staring off into the distance. He couldn't imagine this young woman doing anything so reprehensible that she deserved to be transported for her crimes.

You don't know her, he reminded himself. He didn't know anything about her, not other than what she had chosen to tell him. It was a timely warning. She might seem sweet and kind, she might look like an angel from heaven, but something had led her to being convicted and sentenced to transportation and although he knew there were many miscarriages of justice, she'd never protested that this was the case for her.

Chapter Six

Alice watched as Mr Fitzgerald leaned over the well, supporting himself on his forearms and leaning out far more than could be safe or sensible.

'Are you sure that's safe?' she called, not wanting to distract him at a crucial moment, but equally not wanting him to fall down the old stone well.

'It's dried up,' was the reply, distant and echoey as he spoke into the well. Instead of standing back up, Mr Fitzgerald proceeded to lean out even further, gripping the wooden strut above his head that had a hook to attach a bucket and rope to.

'If it has dried up, stand up,' Alice muttered, feeling the unwelcome clamouring of her pulse around her body. She felt nervous of confined spaces and even just imagining the man in front of her plummeting into the narrow well made her feel on edge and out of control.

'This well hasn't been dry for twenty years,' he said, leaning so far his feet were almost off the ground.

'For the love of—' Alice said, her words cut off by the loud crack as the wooden strut Mr Fitzgerald was holding on to splintered. She leaped forward, not knowing what she was planning to do. It wasn't as though she would be able to hold Mr Fitzgerald's weight and pull him out of the well, but she dashed to him all the same.

He'd toppled over, the momentum of his body after the wooden strut had given away flipping him over completely, but as Alice nervously peered into the well she saw his face grinning up at her.

'You should be dead,' she muttered, eyeing first the snapped wooden strut and then the plummeting depths of the well below him.

'You almost look concerned for me, Alice,' he said as he started to pull himself up.

She *had* been concerned. Although she'd lost some of her humanity during the past couple of years, it would seem her compassion was still burning away under all the fear and desire for self-preservation.

'Do you need a hand?' she asked. Her heart was still hammering away in her chest even though Mr Fitzgerald seemed unconcerned. And he was the one dangling out over the fifteen-foot drop.

He flashed her another smile and with an almighty heave pulled himself up over the lip of the well and rolled forward on to solid ground.

'There's no need to show off,' Alice said, trying to hide her profound relief that he was out of the well and no longer in danger of falling into its confined space.

'I thank you for your concern,' he said, standing and brushing himself off. Although he'd saved himself quite spectacularly she was amazed to see he wasn't more shaken up by the incident. He might have pulled himself from the well easily, but when the wood had splintered and snapped he'd been in real danger of falling all the way to the bottom and ending up a mass of broken bones.

'That was foolish,' Alice said, knowing she shouldn't speak to her employer in that way, but unable to help herself.

He shrugged. 'Perhaps a little, but I needed to

make sure the well itself has actually dried up rather than something falling down and covering the water.'

'And has it?'

Mr Fitzgerald grimaced. 'Yes.'

Alice knew next to nothing about farming. Her father had been a clerk and although they'd lived out in the countryside they had only owned a horse and a couple of pigs. As soon as she'd been old enough Alice had left the rural way of life behind, fleeing to the big city for what she'd hoped was a life of excitement and opportunity. Even since arriving in Australia she'd stayed in Sydney, never venturing into the countryside until Mr Fitzgerald had scooped her up just over a week ago. She didn't know how serious it was that the well had dried up—if it was a minor inconvenience or a major disaster—but from the look on Mr Fitzgerald's face it wasn't something to be taken lightly.

'Surely it's dry because we haven't had much rain,' Alice said quietly. Mr Fitzgerald was staring off into the distance with a troubled expression on his face.

It was November and back home it would be one of the wettest and coldest months of the year.

Alice had always hated November with its grey skies and short, dull days, but now she was stuck in Australia she often found herself daydreaming about the dreariness of the English weather. At least if she was under an overcast November sky it would mean she was back home.

They both looked up at the cloudless sky. Thinking about it, Alice realised it hadn't rained for weeks—no wonder everywhere was so dry and dusty.

'Probably,' he said. 'Although these are old wells, they tap into the aquifers…' He paused, noting her expression. 'It means that they don't rely on the rainwater to fill up.'

'But surely some of the water comes from the rain?'

'It depends if the wells are covered or not. The groundwater, the water you get in the wells, is cleaner, purer, than the water that falls as rain or flows in the rivers. It's been filtered by the rocks over years and years.'

'I don't understand why the well would run dry, then,' Alice said, frowning.

There was a long pause as Mr Fitzgerald looked out into the horizon. 'Neither do I,' he said, 'but I know someone who might.'

* * *

George swung himself back up on to his horse, pulling the hat that had fallen back across his shoulders back on to his head. The sun was ferocious this time of year and he knew that his skin had lost some of its natural protection, some of the deep tan, in the time he'd been away from Australia. The last thing he wanted was to get burnt.

Glancing across at Alice, he saw her pink cheeks and nose and couldn't help but smile. Now they were shielded under the large bonnet she'd brought with her, but no doubt her skin was still adjusting to the strength of the sun here.

In profile, with her blue eyes staring out over the dusty fields, she looked beautiful. Unlike the ladies of London he'd been socialising with these past couple of years she wore her hair loose, the gold-red strands curling around her shoulders in natural waves. In the sunlight it glimmered like a precious metal and George had the urge to reach out and check it was real.

'Would you like me to take you home first?' he asked. The ride would be long and the sun was especially hot. It was a lot to ask of someone to be out in the heat for such a time.

Immediately she shook her head, then seemed to consider a moment.

'Where are we going?' she asked.

He had to hide a smile. Alice was suspicious and untrusting, but for a moment she'd put her welfare in his hands out of choice rather than necessity. It might have only lasted a moment, but it was a start.

'To see a man who knows more about this land than anyone I've ever met.'

She frowned for a moment, as if considering her options.

'You mean an aboriginal man, don't you?' she asked eventually.

He nodded. 'Djalu is one of the wisest men I know.'

'Is he dangerous?'

George smiled, thinking of the wizened old man who didn't know how old he was, but told everyone he must be over a hundred.

'No, not dangerous. Not dangerous at all.'

'And he can speak English?'

George nodded. It had amazed him, too, the first time he'd met Djalu, to hear clear and fluent English coming out of a mouth that had such a different native language.

Alice seemed to consider for a moment, as if weighing up her options, then nodded. 'I would like to come.'

He felt inordinately pleased and had to school his face into a neutral expression to stop the pleasure showing on it. Perhaps it was the loneliness that had sneaked up on him during the long voyage home or perhaps it was the knowledge that his two closest friends had moved on somewhat with their lives, but he found he was enjoying Alice's company more than he should. He needed to remind himself she was a convict worker, nothing more. A convict worker who already thought the worst of everyone. He needed to keep his distance.

They rode over the dusty fields, sticking to the perimeters of those that were used for crops, only riding through the centre of the large open spaces George had cultivated for his thousands of cattle. As they rode in the distance they saw some farm workers, toiling away in the beating sun, but no one close enough to greet.

It took an hour and a half to reach Djalu's house, a neat wooden hut with a fresh coat of paint on the door. The old man himself was sitting in a comfortable-looking chair just outside the door in the shade of a eucalyptus tree.

'Australia's prodigal son returns,' Djalu said in greeting, a wide smile stretched across his face. 'I was worried you might have found something to keep you away. Especially when those two convicts came back two years ago.'

Although he, Robertson and Crawford had all set sail together for England, circumstances out of their control had meant both George's friends had cut their trips short and boarded ships for Australia long before George had been ready to come home.

'Mudga dhurdi,' George said in greeting, causing the old man to open his mouth wide and begin guffawing with laughter.

'Your pronunciation hasn't improved in your absence,' Djalu said with a shake of his head. George saw the old man turn his gaze on Alice and waited as he looked her up and down, smiling genially all the time. 'Your wife is far too pretty for you,' he said after a few moments.' He turned to Alice. 'You're far too pretty for a rugged old man like him.'

'She's not my wife,' George said at the same instant that Alice spoke up.

'I'm not his wife.'

Djalu looked at them both for a long moment, then shrugged. 'It is a shame. Fitzgerald is always alone.' He turned his attention back to George. 'It is not good to be alone in this world, my friend.'

It would not do to point out the old man was alone. Over the years George had found out a little of his history. It wasn't pleasant or comfortable. Djalu had always lived in the area, travelling and living off the land as the native people of Australia had been doing for centuries. His stories told of how he'd been there when the first fleet had arrived, been dazzled and awed by the arrival of a shipload of Englishmen. Then in the smallpox outbreak that followed he'd lost his wife. Disease after disease, new to his tribe, had ripped everyone he had ever loved from him within ten years of the English landing at Botany Bay.

'Would you care for some bark tea?' Djalu motioned for George and Alice to sit, pointing at the only other available seat, a roughly hewn wooden bench that would only just fit both of them.

Alice hesitated for a moment, glancing at George, then perched herself on the very edge of the bench. George sat down next to her, doing everything he could not to touch her, but his legs brushing against her anyway. It was warm even in the shade of the tree and George shrugged off his jacket, rolling up his sleeves and running a hand around the back of his neck to try to cool himself. Next to him he could feel the heat coming off Alice's body and he wondered how uncomfortable she must be in the tight constraints of her dress. An unbidden image of her loosening the ties at her back and letting the dress drop down to her hips popped into George's mind. In it she was looking over her shoulder at him enticingly.

George almost laughed—he couldn't imagine Alice ever looking at him like that. He glanced across at her, hoping she couldn't sense the subtle change in his demeanour. He needed to stop having these inappropriate thoughts, otherwise he was just as bad as she'd imagined him to be. Just as lecherous as all the other men who'd tried to take advantage of her. Just as bad as his father.

'Mr Fitzgerald won't bite you,' Djalu said, frowning at the stiff way Alice was leaning away from George. 'He's a good man, not like those brutes on the ships.'

George was always amazed at how perceptive the old man was. In just a few short minutes he'd analysed Alice's behaviour and come to the correct conclusion.

Glancing at him, Alice gave a wary smile, but George could tell she was looking to see if he'd taken much notice of Djalu's comment about the ship. Feeling the first stirrings of anger, he wondered what she'd been through on the transport ship, wondered just what she'd had to suffer during the long months at sea.

'I knew a woman a long time ago,' Djalu said as he poured out the steaming liquid. 'She was one of the early female convicts. Never said exactly what had happened on the transport ship over here, but she once told me that she had lost all faith in human nature during the voyage.' His voice was quiet, soothing, and Alice was looking down at her hands, staring at the redden skin, chapped from her work in the laundry.

As he watched a fat tear dropped from one of her eyes and fell on to her fingers. She brushed it away quickly, not looking up so she wouldn't have to meet his gaze, and in that moment George vowed to himself that he would do whatever it took to show the woman next to him that there were good people in the world.

Djalu handed over the two cups and Alice murmured her thanks, still staring down at her hands.

'Look at me,' the old man said, 'talking about things I have no business prying into. You came here with a question.'

'The well at the edge of bottom field has dried up,' George said. 'I understand it has been a dry couple of months, but even so…'

'Not just a dry couple of months,' Djalu said. 'It has been a dry few years.' He shrugged, 'There's been rain, a little here, a little there, but nowhere near as much as there should have been.'

'The water table has dropped,' George said, feeling the beginnings of dread start to form in his stomach. Everything he did, from growing crops to keeping cattle, needed water. And although Australia was warmer than England, during his lifetime they'd never had too many issues with rainfall and water supply. Whenever he thought of his land, the rolling fields interspersed with corpses of trees, it was green and verdant in his imagination. Not sun scorched and dusty as it was now.

'We may have rain in the next few weeks,' Djalu said with a shrug, ever the optimist.

'Have you ever known it to be this dry?'

George watched the old man as his eyes moved leisurely from side to side as if he were reliving the years of his life in his mind.

'From 1770 to 1773,' he said after a minute. 'It was worse then. Three years with hardly any rain. We had to move around much more than usual to survive.'

'But the land recovered?'

'It recovered. Just like it will this time. But whether that will be in a few months or a few years it is hard to know.'

George nodded slowly. They would have to wait out the drought and, in the meantime, come up with ways to keep the livestock watered and the crops growing.

'Thank you,' he said to the older man. George stood and Alice followed, but Djalu held up a hand, motioning for them to wait for a moment.

'I have something that might interest you,' Djalu said. He ambled inside his house, coming back out after a few moments, handing George a delicate stem with a brilliant red, strangely shaped flower on it. 'The desert pea plant,' he said. 'I thought you could add it to your collection. I found it on one of my trips out into the desert.'

'Thank you.'

They remounted their horses and only when they'd waved goodbye to Djalu from a distance did George speak. He'd seen how uncomfortable Alice had been when his old friend had mentioned the horrors some women endured on the transport ships and he hated the haunted look in her eyes even as she thought of it now.

'Djalu is a good man, dependable,' he said slowly. 'He knows this land better than anyone else I know.'

Alice nodded.

'And he's seen people come and go, from his own tribe and others, and settlers and convicts.'

Again Alice nodded, but still didn't speak. George tried a different approach.

'Do you recall the two men who visited the day you arrived at Mountain View Farm? Robertson and Crawford.'

'Yes.'

'They're my two closest friends. Two good men...' He paused, looking over at Alice. 'They were both convicts when I first knew them.'

He saw the surprise register on Alice's face. Although most of the ex-convicts who'd served out their sentence settled in Australia and made a life for themselves, not many were as successful as Robertson and Crawford. Between them they owned at least five thousand acres and probably had bought more land in the time he'd been away.

'They were transported as young boys, worked for a couple of years building roads in Sydney and then ended up as convict workers on my father's farm.' He thought back fondly to the days of their youth when the three of them had run wild around the Australian countryside, looked on indulgently by his father.

'Robertson was ten when he was convicted and Crawford twelve, they were only children. They don't often talk about their time on the transport ship, only to say it was the worst part of their entire sentence, worse even than the back-breaking manual labour of building roads.' He paused and saw the pain behind Alice eyes that she was trying to hide behind a stony expression. 'I just want you to know that you're safe now,' he said quietly. 'You have a job here for as long as your sentence lasts. There's no one to force you to do anything you don't want to, no one to take away what should only be yours to give.'

For a moment he thought Alice wasn't listening, she was perfectly still on the back of her horse, looking more like a statue than a living, breathing woman. Then she turned to look at him and he saw the tears glinting in her brilliant blue eyes.

'I'm not sure if I can believe you're real,' she said quietly.

George smiled, waiting for her to say more.

'It feels like this is all a dream and at any moment I'm going to wake up and be pulled back to that whipping post and my awful life in Sydney.'

'I won't let that happen, Alice.'

She regarded him again and he saw one of the tears roll out of her eyes and on to her cheek. He wanted to lean across the gap between them and wipe it away with his thumb, but he knew he couldn't do something so intimate. Alice raised her fingers to her face, drying off the tears and shaking her head ruefully.

'I don't cry,' she said, a rueful tone to her voice. 'Even on the transport ship I didn't cry.'

'Did someone hurt you on there?' George asked. The last thing he wanted was to make her live through her nightmare again, but he had the feeling she was about to start opening up to him.

She nodded, looking down at her hands where they grasped the reins.

'They don't separate the men and the women,' she said quietly. 'I'd heard rumours when I was in gaol, waiting to be put on the transport ship, but I didn't quite believe them. When we were thrown down the hatch into the bowels of the ship I couldn't believe my eyes.'

'Someone attacked you?' George asked gently. He knew it wouldn't have just been someone, there would have been a pack mentality.

'They did. As soon as the guards had closed the hatch and we were left on our own it began.' Her voice had gone quiet as if the pain of re-membering was too much for her. 'There were ten women. Two were old, too old to be of in-terest. But as soon as the ship began moving all eyes were on the rest of us.' She shuddered and George felt the urge to gather her in his arms, but he knew physical contact was the last thing she would want while remembering this horri-ble ordeal.

'There was this one man, he had such an evil look in his eyes—' She broke off for a moment.

'He kept staring at me and moving closer and closer. He whispered that he would look after me, save me from the other men.'

George felt a hot surge of rage at the idea of Alice suffering like this. She might have committed a crime, but no woman deserved to be punished so awfully.

She shook her head. 'I probably should have accepted.'

'You didn't?'

'I had a long piece of wood I'd sharpened to a point while I was in gaol, just in case the rumours about the ships were true. When he...' She swallowed, composing herself before continuing. 'When he put his hands on me I stabbed him in the stomach as hard as I could.'

George blinked in surprise. It hadn't been how he'd feared the encounter would end.

'Did he die?'

Alice shrugged. 'I don't think so. He lashed out a couple of times and then was pulled back by some of the other men. Later that day when the guards came to give us our rations he was taken up on deck to have his wound seen to. I saw him at a distance after that, but he must have been put in one of the other compartments.'

'Did anyone else try to…?' George asked.

He saw the pain flash before her eyes and knew there must have been some other incidents.

'Mostly I gained a reputation as someone to be left alone,' she said and George had to wonder at the significance of the mostly. 'But I did have to sleep with one eye open.'

'Not a pleasant crossing, then?'

'Without a doubt the worst experience of my life.'

They rode on in silence for a moment, both lost in Alice's recounting of her time on the transport ship.

'I meant what I said,' George said quietly. 'You have a safe place here with me for the remainder of your sentence. Mrs Peterson can use your help and you won't need to worry about your safety.'

'Thank you,' Alice said quietly, raising her eyes up to meet his. In that moment George felt something squeeze inside his chest and he knew he needed to look away, but the intensity of her gaze was difficult to break. 'It's the kindest thing anyone has ever done for me.'

Chapter Seven

Alice watched as Mr Fitzgerald swung himself down from his horse and took a step towards the muddy pool of water. The sun was high in the sky now and even through the layers of her clothes she could feel the intensity of its heat on her skin. She envied the way Mr Fitzgerald had shed layers, taking off his jacket as the temperatures had risen, now to be dressed in just a cool cotton shirt and his trousers.

As if they had a mind of their own her eyes danced over his body as he walked away from her, taking in the strong muscles of his legs, the broad, strong back and the arms that looked as though they could lift her without any problem at all. He was a physically fit man. An attractive man. A man she couldn't tear her eyes away from.

'Inappropriate,' she murmured to herself, too

quiet for Mr Fitzgerald to hear, even though she knew her protest was too little too late.

The man in front of her was attractive with his kind eyes and warming smile and the body she could just imagine running her hands over, but that wasn't the only reason she was feeling like a giddy schoolgirl in his presence. There was a kindness to him, a generosity, that she had never experienced before. He'd rescued her for no other reason than he believed that to be the right thing to do. He'd promised her a safe home for the duration of her sentence, promised she wouldn't need to live in fear again.

It was impossible not to fall for him just a little. Even after everything she'd been through.

Alice watched as he crouched down near the edge of the muddy pool, watched as the shirt stretched across his back and found herself imagining lifting it off over his head and running her hands over his chest. Quickly she closed her eyes, trying to banish the thought, but it lived on in her imagination.

It's impossible, she told herself. There were so many reasons nothing could happen between them, not least he'd made it clear nothing would happen. Mr Fitzgerald had looked aghast at the idea of abusing his authority and power over her. For as long as she was in his employ, his convict worker, he wouldn't even notice her that way.

Trying to suppress a bubble of hysteria, she clamped her lips tight. Of course he'd never consider her anyway, even if he wasn't bound by his strict moral code. She was a convict girl and even before that she'd been many rungs below him on the social ladder. Before her conviction she'd even been working as a servant, that was how low she'd been brought.

Bill, she thought with disgust at the man who'd promised her the world and instead taken everything from her. That was another reason she was probably finding Mr Fitzgerald so attractive. He was the opposite of Bill in every way. Mr Fitzgerald's blond hair and blue eyes were as light as Bill's features were dark. And Mr Fitzgerald was kind, generous, always thinking of others, whereas Bill was the most selfish person she'd ever known. Of course at first he'd been charming, giving her enough compliments to make her feel like the only woman alive, but once he'd persuaded her to leave her family and everything she knew behind he'd changed. And he'd changed her.

'There's something stuck in the middle,' Mr Fitzgerald called, looking back over his shoulder at her.

Alice slipped down from the horse, tying her gentle mare to the same tree Mr Fitzgerald had looped his reins over.

'Look,' he said as she came to stand beside him. He raised an arm, brushing her side gently as he did so and sending a tingle of excitement through her at the contact.

She peered out into the muddy pool, looking at where he was indicating. It was difficult to see, there were logs and debris sticking up out of the mud, from where they would normally be positioned on the floor of a much deeper pond.

'Next to that log,' he said. Alice felt her breath catch in her chest as he moved in even closer so she could see exactly where he was pointing.

Trying to concentrate, she peered out, eventually making out a scruffy, muddy ball of fur in the middle of the mud. Every so often it would struggle a little, but even she could see the movements were weak and without real purpose.

'What are you doing?' she asked as he began to untuck his shirt from his waistband.

'It's muddy,' he said simply. 'There's no need for me to spoil a good shirt.'

'You're going out there?' She eyed the swampy ground, trying to distract herself from Mr Fitzgerald's movements as he pulled the shirt off over his head.

'Of course,' he said, turning to her.

It was impossible to *not* look. Her eyes moved downwards taking in the tanned chest covered in light hairs, further to his toned abdomen, so taut she could see the muscles defined clearly, rippling as he moved, and lower to the waistband of his trousers. For one giddy moment she thought he might shed those as well and she found herself leaning in closer involuntarily.

Control yourself, she cautioned as one hand started to rise up to touch the impossibly perfect skin over the muscles of his torso. He was her employer, a man who had assured her in no uncertain terms that he harboured no attraction to her whatsoever. With an effort she managed to turn the movement into a gesture for him to hand over his shirt.

'I'll only be a minute,' he said, flashing her one of his smiles.

She watched as he waded into the mud. Probably just a few weeks ago it would have been a little pond and in the winter after the rains a cool and refreshing pool, but now it was pure mud, and within a few steps Mr Fitzgerald was submerged up to his knees. She could hear the squelch with every step and saw the effort it took him to lift up his feet in turn to progress towards the middle.

A couple of minutes later he'd reached the middle and was bending down over the little creature.

'He's alive,' he shouted back over his shoulder, a grin on his face. She'd never known a man so invested in the welfare of wild animals before. Most would have ridden on by rather than ruin a good pair of trousers for some creature stuck in the middle of a muddy pond.

Alice watched as he scooped up the little bundle and held it to his chest. From this distance, with the animal covered in mud, it was impossible to tell what it was, but she knew it wouldn't matter to Mr Fitzgerald. Mrs Peterson had told her he had a love of all living things, from the plants he collected and collated, hoping one day to publish a guide to botany in Australia, to the waifs and strays he rescued while he was out on his farm or further afield.

'You included,' she murmured to herself. That was probably how he saw her: a stray, wounded animal who'd needed rescuing. It shouldn't matter—in fact, Alice should feel pleased that was how he viewed her—but there was a little part of her that wanted him to see more.

Quietly she snorted. Only a few days ago she'd been warning him to keep his hands to himself and accusing him of the most heinous of intentions. Today she couldn't tear her eyes from his half-naked body.

Slowly Mr Fitzgerald began to make his way back to the edge of the pond, slipping and sliding in the mud, more unsteady than he had been on the way out now he had the little creature in his arms.

He was only six feet away when he stumbled, his foot going deeper into the mud than it had before. The sudden change in depth unbalanced him and Alice watched helplessly as his one free arm wheeled round and round as he tried to keep his balance. She was certain he would fall over, worried he might submerge beneath the thick mud he'd been wading through, but somehow he managed to regain his equilibrium and stay on his feet. Looking up at her, he grinned.

'Lucky escape,' he said, taking a moment to steady himself before he started towards her again.

She saw him pull his leg from the mud, or at least try to. The muscle contracted, but his thigh didn't move. Bending down, he used his free hand to pull at the leg, but still it wouldn't come free.

'It would appear I'm trapped,' he said, looking down slightly bemused at his predicament.

Alice eyed up the mud.

'Don't come in,' he said, 'Go get help. Mr Peterson will get me out.'

'Don't be silly,' Alice said. 'It's an hour's ride back to the house and it'll be another hour for Mr Peterson to get to you. You can't stay there for two hours.'

Deftly she slipped off her boots, turning her back to Mr Fitzgerald to unroll her stockings and place them neatly inside the tops. She considered her dress, but there was no way she could strip down to her undergarments, so it would just have to get dirty. From her time spent in the laundry she knew with a little soap and a lot of rubbing any stain could be removed from clothing.

'Don't do it, Alice,' he said. 'You might get stuck, too.'

Scrunching up her nose at the feel of the soft mud between her toes, she took a step into the pond. The surface was warm, heated by the sun, but as her feet sunk deeper into the mud it rapidly became cooler. She slipped almost immediately, but managed to steady herself, taking small steps as she held her dress up to save it from the worst of the mud.

'You're going to get filthy,' Mr Fitzgerald said, watching her pick her way towards him.

'Nothing a good soak in the bath won't cure.'

'Don't get any mud on your back.'

Alice grimaced at the thought of the dirty mud seeping into the wounds on her back. She could feel the sting in her imagination.

'I'm not planning on rolling around in it,' she said.

'Nor was I.'

A giggle slipped out of Alice's mouth as she looked up and saw the mud-covered figure in front of her. He was caked in the thick brown mud up to his waist, but where he'd been struggling to free his leg more had splattered up his torso, with a fleck or two on his face, speckling his neatly trimmed beard.

'Don't laugh, Alice.'

She clapped her hand over her mouth, trying to claw back the sound, but it managed to escape. Giving in to it, she laughed out loud, glad to see in a few seconds her laugh had been infectious and Mr Fitzgerald was smiling along with her.

'That's the first time I've seen you properly laugh,' he said.

'You've only known me just over a week.'

'Don't you think you should be laughing more than once every week?' he asked, then waved a mud-covered hand. 'I don't mean that judge-mentally, it's no comment on your character. It's just sad that circumstances have conspired to subject you to such trials in life that laughing is a rare occurrence.'

She'd reached his side now and stopped, shrugging. 'Many people would think a convicted criminal shouldn't be in a position to laugh, to have fun.'

'Many people are idiots,' Mr Fitzgerald murmured.

'How shall we do this?' Alice asked, gesturing to his leg.

'Perhaps if I could lean on you it will give me the momentum I need to pull it out of the mud.'

Resigned that she was going to finish this little episode covered in mud, Alice let go of her skirts where she'd been holding them at knee level. Immediately they began soaking up the moisture and felt heavy around her legs.

She held out her arm, feeling Mr Fitzgerald's strong fingers gripping her gently.

'Are you ready?' he asked.

Nodding, Alice braced herself. Slowly he began to put his weight on her, pulling at his leg at the same time. She felt it shift slightly and widened her stance to give a better base so she didn't slip.

'Nearly there,' Mr Fitzgerald said.

His leg came free all of a sudden and with a rush of movement he hurtled into her. Together they tried to keep their balance, toppling backward and forward until the momentum was too much and they went crashing down into the mud. Alice landed on top of Mr Fitzgerald, her body pressed closely to his, and immediately she was aware of every part of him. He'd landed on his back, the arm holding the little creature out to one side, his free arm instinctively coming up to encircle her.

'I'm so sorry,' Alice said as she slipped and slid, trying to get purchase so she could get to her feet and off the man whose body she was just a little too aware of.

'My fault,' he said, trying to push himself up to help her, but unable to get anywhere in the slippery mud.

He paused, holding her still on top of him and waited for Alice to fall still as well, then he looked into her eyes. It was the first time she'd made proper eye contact with him and she felt the breath being sucked out of her body. His eyes were an intriguing shade of blue, with hints of green fanning out from closest to the pupil. They were kind eyes, eyes that were surrounded by a pattern of tiny lines he could only have got from smiling so much.

Time seemed to slow and Alice imagined herself lowering her lips down to meet his and brushing the gentlest of kisses there. She knew it was wrong, knew it could never be, but her body wanted it all the same.

'Let's think about this,' he said softly. He was

looking into her eyes, holding her by the waist so she wouldn't slip off him. It was the most intimate of positions and Alice wished that they could stay that way for just a few seconds longer. 'If I give you this little one and put you down on the ground,' he said, his fingers seeming to burn through the fabric of her dress and imprint themselves in her skin, 'Then I think I can stand. Once I'm upright I will get you out of here.'

She nodded, not trusting herself to speak.

Gently he passed her the mud-covered creature, then slid her off his body, placing her in the mud. Alice felt the coolness of the water seeping through her skirts, but knew it couldn't be helped. Once they were out of the pond the heat would dry them in no time.

He stood, slipping once or twice, but managed to keep his feet. Then with a strength like none Alice had ever seen before he pulled her upright, surprising her by scooping her into his arms and carrying her across the rest of the pond. Once on dry land he set her on her feet and took the little furry animal from her.

'Are you injured?' he asked, looking her over with concern.

Alice shook her head, unable to speak. She felt

bereft of the closeness they'd shared and felt like a fool for even thinking it.

'That didn't go quite as I planned.'

'Really?' she managed to ask, shaking her head. 'I had scheduled a mud bath into my afternoon.'

He grinned, then looked down at the little animal they'd saved from the middle of the pond.

'What is it?' Alice asked.

'A koala. Beautiful creatures. I've got no idea how this one ended up in the middle of the pond, though.'

'Perhaps he was thirsty and searching for water.'

'Perhaps. Koalas get most of their water from the leaves they eat,' Mr Fitzgerald said. 'They don't often frequent their local ponds or rivers.' He shrugged, 'I suppose it doesn't matter.'

'Is he hurt?'

She watched as Mr Fitzgerald studied the animal, wiping some of the mud off with his hands.

'I can't see anything obvious. Let's get him home and cleaned up, then I'll take a closer look.'

'Mrs Peterson was right about you,' Alice said as they remounted their horses. 'You can't stand to leave anyone in need without trying to assist.' She paused. 'It's rare to find that in a person.'

'You're going to make me blush, Alice,' he said in mock embarrassment. 'And you paint me as far more saintly than I really am. I'm just a man who loves his fellow creatures.'

They began the ride home, uncomfortable in the muddy clothes as they began to bake in the sun. Alice kept finding herself stealing glances at the man beside her, remembering how he'd felt beneath her as he'd held her in the mud, recalling the enchanting blue-green of his eyes and wondering what it would be like to have his body pressed against hers in an altogether different situation.

Chapter Eight

George felt as though he were made of stone as he slipped from his horse and handed the reins to a bemused-looking Mr Peterson. On the hour-long ride back to the house the mud had hardened and, although some had fallen off with his movements, there was still a thick layer on both his skin and clothes. Looking across to Alice, he had to suppress a smile. She wore the mud well, sitting regally upon her horse as if she were wearing the finest silks, not a layer of smelly pond grime.

'I dare not ask...' Mr Peterson said, darting a look towards the kitchen where no doubt his wife was already shaking her head at the mess.

'This little koala was stuck in the middle of a half-dried-up pond,' George said.

'And you and Alice thought you'd go in and

join him?' Mr Peterson said, his voice thick with disbelief.

George grinned. When he'd been in England he had hated the obsequious way the servants had spoken to their masters. The class differences were so much more pronounced there. Although he employed Mr and Mrs Peterson, and as such expected them to work hard and be polite to his guests, he would hate if their interactions with him were limited by a subservient attitude. He much preferred the gruff sarcasm of Mr Peterson and the admonishing sighs of Mrs Peterson.

'That's two strays in a week,' Mr Peterson said, looking at the little animal. 'Three if you count her.' He motioned to Alice.

George looked up at her. In truth, she looked a mess, as he no doubt did. The dress that he had so admired her figure in earlier that morning was completely caked in mud as was what was exposed of her skin. There were even flecks of mud on her face, little splatters as far up as her forehead. Beneath the bonnet that was still perched obstinately on her head her hair had become matted by the mud and the golden-red tones of earlier that day looked decidedly more dull than they had when they'd set out on the journey. In short, Alice looked as though she needed a long soak in a hot bath.

So do you. He tried to suppress the image of sinking into a bath alongside Alice, of her wrapping those slender limbs around him as they submerged together.

George coughed to cover his momentary lapse of good sense. Ever since her soft body had landed on top of him in the mud he'd been struggling to forget the way she'd felt as she'd pressed against him. How the curve of her waist felt beneath his hand, how the swell of her breasts had pushed against his chest. Those few seconds had stretched out and now George knew he wouldn't be able to look at her without thinking completely inappropriate thoughts.

'I'll ask my good wife to get the water heated for the bath,' Mr Peterson said, handing back the koala to George. 'No doubt she'll have something to say about it.'

'It will take a while,' George said as Mr Peterson walked back into the house, shaking his head and muttering at the same time. 'Why don't we get this little one cleaned up.'

Leading the way into the kitchen, he commandeered the sink, giving Mrs Peterson his most winning smile as he set Alice to heating some water for the koala's bath while Mrs Peterson did the same for theirs. Once the sink was filled, he tested the temperature and gently lowered the frightened little animal in. Immediately the water turned a murky brown, thick with the mud and debris from the pond. The koala clung to his hand, looking up at him with big frightened eyes and George found himself murmuring soothing sounds to try to calm the little creature.

'You're good at that,' Alice said from behind him. She was peering over his shoulder, watching as he gently cleaned the mud from the animal's fur.

'Giving muddy things a bath?' he asked, unable to help himself.

'Soothing frightened animals,' Alice said, giving him an admonishing stare.

'Hmm,' he said, unable to think of anything sensible to say as images of Alice sinking down into the bath filled his head. Alice closing her eyes and letting her head drop back as the water washed over her. Alice submerging completely under, only to come up, her skin pink and glow-ing. Alice standing, the water rolling from her body, as she stepped out of the bath.

He swallowed. He'd always been cursed with a vivid imagination. Right now he could see every inch of her in glorious detail.

Behind him he felt Alice shift, moving closer so he could feel the tickle of her breath on his neck. The sensation sent jolts through his body right to his very core and he knew he was very close to doing something stupid. Something like turning round and kissing her.

With his free hand he gripped the edge of the sink. He was being ridiculous. He barely knew the woman. True, she was pretty and he enjoyed her company despite their rocky start, but she was the one woman in the whole of Australia who'd made it perfectly clear she didn't want anything to do with men. That she expected them to act on their lusts and subsequently didn't trust them. She was the last woman he should be fantasising about.

She leaned past him, reaching out to rub a little mud off the koala's head, her hand brushing his arm, and George almost groaned.

He closed his eyes, took a deep breath and

pushed away all thoughts of the woman behind him. He'd promised himself he would make her feel safe again and the first rule to that was not to feel anything but a fatherly benevolence to her.

'That's better,' Alice said softly, scooping the koala from his hands and wrapping it in a towel Mrs Peterson had laid out.

After a moment he turned around, watching as she gently rubbed the koala dry, smiling down at the little animal, pleasure lighting up her face.

'Bath's ready,' Mrs Peterson said, her voice breaking through the contented silence that had been between them.

'You go first,' George said, holding out his hands to take the koala. Later he would check the little animal over for wounds and injuries, but right now it would be scared enough being in a strange place.

'Oh, I couldn't,' Alice said, although he saw the flicker of temptation in her eyes.

'You need to keep those wounds on your back as clean as possible,' George said, motioning for her to go. 'It's only a bit of mud, I can wait another half an hour.'

'If you're sure...?'

'I'm sure.' He watched her follow Mrs Peterson from the room, his mind once again flooded with images of her stripping down and stepping into the bath.

Alice took a deep breath and sunk under the warm water, holding the air in her lungs for a long as possible before letting a slow stream of bubbles erupt from her mouth. She felt wonderfully clean now, the mud had washed off easily and Mrs Peterson had left her a bar of soap that smelt like honey. Alice had lathered it into her skin and her hair, knowing the scent would linger for days.

Sitting up, she heard the door open and saw the bustling figure of Mrs Peterson walk into the room with a clean dress in her hand.

'You look better,' she said, giving Alice an appraising look.

'I could hardly look worse.'

'No, quite.' The housekeeper still hadn't warmed to her entirely after Alice's shaky start. 'Mr Fitzgerald is always getting into scrapes like this,' she said as she began fussing around the bathroom, 'but have a care to remember your place.'

'My place?'

'Yes, dear. You heard me. You're not his friend. You're not his equal. You're a convict worker, a servant. Mr Fitzgerald might be very lax with his social hierarchy, but right is right and you need to act appropriately.'

Alice smiled her blandest smile. 'Of course.' She wasn't about to fight with the older woman, who was, in her own way, right. Mr Fitzgerald *was* her employer, nothing more. Even if Alice already knew how his blue-green eyes dazzled in the sun and how his face lit up when he spoke about anything to do with nature. She might know these things, but she had no right to.

This response seemed to throw Mrs Peterson and with Alice's meek manner the older woman lost some of the fire in her eyes.

'You'll find your way, dear,' she said a little more kindly. 'It just will take a while to settle.'

A while to settle. Right now she found it hard to think beyond the next few days, weeks at the most. For so long she'd been focused on survival, she hadn't spent any energy getting to know her surroundings, getting to know Australia.

'Don't be long,' Mrs Peterson said. 'Mr Fitzgerald is downstairs looking like a creature who's spent all day wallowing in the mud.'

Alice nodded, allowing herself thirty more seconds of relaxation in the warm water before standing and beginning to dry herself.

'You'll need to be careful of those wounds,' Mrs Peterson said, eyeing Alice's back dubiously. 'All that mud can't have been good for them.'

'At least they're clean now.'

'Hmmm.'

The older woman slipped out of the bath-room, mumbling something to herself that Alice couldn't hear. As she patted herself dry Alice tried to strain and look over her shoulder at the healing gashes on her back, but she could only see a hint of red; she wasn't flexible enough to make out more.

'A bath a day, I've never heard such a thing,' Mrs Peterson grumbled as she poured the last of the hot water into the tub, motioning for Alice to step in. Ever since Alice had ridden out with Mr Fitzgerald and ended up caked in mud in the half-dried-up pond he had insisted she have a bath every day to clean the wounds on her back. She'd only half-heartedly protested, saying it was too much trouble, but in truth she was pleased to sink into the warm water every day as she was petrified of the wounds festering.

'Now let me have a look at that back of yours,' Mrs Peterson said.

Alice was used to little privacy. Growing up, she'd been the middle sister, there was always someone to share your bed, always someone to know every aspect of your life. And since her conviction privacy had been stripped away as completely as if the judge had condemned her to a life to be lived without it. Still, she craved it. Craved a knock on the door before someone entered, a request rather than an order to show her wounds.

Knowing that was an impossible dream, she leaned forward, wincing as the water dripped down and the air began to dry the wounds across her back.

Mrs Peterson tutted and shook her head, and out of the corner of her eye Alice saw the woman's concerned expression.

'They look like they might be festering,' she said, biting her lip.

For a moment Alice closed her eyes and blocked the rest of the world out. A festering wound was the worst possible outcome—when a wound putrefied it could take your life. She'd known strapping men felled by what at first had seemed only a small injury, their health quickly ebbing away as the fever took hold.

'It'll be that mud. You really shouldn't have got them dirty.'

Alice opened her eyes. She didn't know what to say. There was a chance the woman was wrong, but she felt panicked all the same.

'Get out of the bath,' Mrs Peterson said, 'Get dressed, but leave your back open. I'll get Mr Fitzgerald to look at it. He will know what to do.'

Alice nearly spluttered out loud at the idea. He had seen her back ripped and bare immediately after she'd been whipped, but then she'd been in no fit state to protect her dignity. Now she couldn't let him see her exposed and vulnerable. It was out of the question.

'I can't…' she said.

'Hush,' Mrs Peterson said. 'It's only a back. And yours isn't particularly pleasant to look at. You've nothing to worry about.'

Before Alice could protest further Mrs Peterson was out of the door, closing it softly behind her.

Standing, she let the water drip from her body,

trying to twist to look over her shoulder at the wounds at the same time. It was impossible and after a few moments Alice abandoned the contortions and set to drying herself off.

It was two hours later that Alice uncomfortably loosened the ties of her dress and shrugged the fabric from her shoulders. She kept hold of the front, ensuring the dress didn't slip down entirely and completely destroy her dignity, but still she felt the warm air hit her bare skin and felt very self-conscious.

She heard footsteps behind her, two pairs, but kept her head facing the wall in front of her.

Even without looking she knew the moment he entered the room. There was a subtle shift in the air, a faint scent of his soap, and then the soft footfalls as he moved towards her.

Alice felt as though all the air had been sucked from her lungs as he placed a gentle hand on her shoulder. She knew his eyes would be on her skin, looking at the ugly wounds criss-crossing her back, and she had the urge to wrench up the fabric to hide it from his eyes.

'Oh, Alice,' he murmured, his voice filled with concern.

'Is it bad?'

'Have you seen it?' he asked.

She shook her head. She was torn between wanting to know the damage and feeling too scared to look.

Reaching out, he took the small mirror from the wall where it hung by the door. It was only the size of a dinner plate, but the glass was clear and of good quality and looked as though it had been recently polished. He held it up by her shoulder, angling it downwards so if Alice turned her head she would be able to look at her back.

He must have seen her hesitating for he placed a reassuring hand on her arm, squeezing gently.

With a deep breath Alice looked back, taking in the red, raw wounds that criss-crossed her back, and she had to stifle a cry. She took a moment, closing her eyes and breathing deeply before she looked again.

The very top wound, the one that came up to her shoulder blade in a deep diagonal line, was redder than the others. The surrounding skin looked swollen and angry and the wound itself had a thin yellow crust around the edges.

'It's festering,' she said, her voice completely flat.

'I think so,' Mr Fitzgerald agreed quietly.

They both knew what that meant, what risk a wound like this carried. Things would go one of two ways. Either her body would fight it, would find the strength to prevail, or some time in the next few days she would become feverish and rapidly decline.

'Send for the doctor,' Mr Fitzgerald said, gently taking the mirror away.

'Yes, sir.' Mrs Peterson nodded.

Alice felt a hint of surprise, although from what she'd seen of her employer these past days she shouldn't have expected anything less. Many of the men who employed convict workers didn't see the convicts as human beings, more like numbers on a sheet of parchment or animals to be worked to the breaking point. Of course there were exceptions, but even the kinder ones would mainly baulk at the expense of calling the doctor out for a worker.

There had been no hesitation on Mr Fitzgerald's part, though, and she felt the tears spring to her eyes. The past few years her luck had gone from bad to worse, first when she'd been taken in by Bill and his promises of a wonderful life in London, and then things had gone rapidly downhill from there. Now was the first time in years she felt that something positive was happening to her and she couldn't quite believe it was real.

'Thank you,' she said, turning her head to look over her shoulder at Mr Fitzgerald.

'We will get you better,' he said with more conviction than she felt. With gentle fingers he pulled up the fabric of her dress, making sure he didn't graze any of the wounds. Alice wanted nothing more than to sink into his arms, to bury her head in his shoulder and allow him to wrap her up safely, but she knew that couldn't happen. He was kind to her, but it was in the same way he was kind to the stray animals he found. There was no ulterior motive underneath it. In some ways that made Alice glad—it was oh, so nice to have her faith in human kindness restored—but in many other ways it made her pine for what she knew could never be.

Slowly she turned to face him, smiling nervously. He was still standing close, closer than he should, and she wanted to reach out and draw him to her.

As they stood there facing one another, he raised his hand, his fingers reaching out as if he were about to cup her cheek, but when he was about halfway through the movement he paused, a momentary uncertainty flashing across his face. Then his hand dropped back to his side and he stepped away.

Alice felt the hope and confusion flare within her and quickly suppressed it. He was looking to reassure her, nothing more, and had decided the movement was inappropriate. Probably because of her outbursts when she'd first arrived, the accusations she'd made towards him.

Closing her eyes at the shame of the memory, she bit her lip, trying to use the pain to bring her back to the present. She'd been so scared, so worried that she might have finally ended up in a situation where she was entirely at a man's mercy, she hadn't stopped to find out what sort of a man he was.

'Two weeks ago, when I first arrived...' she said quietly '...when I accused you of trying to take advantage of me...' she swallowed, not daring to look up '...of trying to force your way into my bed, that was unacceptable. I'm sorry. I was scared and I lumped you in with all the other men I'd met, all those that did try to take advantage. It was wrong of me.'

He smiled at her and she saw a hint of sadness in his eyes. 'No need to apologise, Alice.

I can't imagine what these last few years have been like for you.'

'I know you're not like that,' she said, her eyes meeting his, trying to convey all the emotions that were hurtling through her in a single look.

Without another word he turned and left the room, leaving Alice staring morosely after him, wondering at the feelings he had awakened in her. Feelings that she thought she was incapable of experiencing ever again after her last failed foray into a relationship.

Chapter Nine

George paced up and down the hall, unable to undo the frown that he knew was darkening his face. Upstairs the doctor he'd summoned from Sydney was examining Alice. He was a man George had seen on a couple of occasions before. Once when his mother had taken ill and died a few weeks later, and again when his father had begun coughing up the blood that had signalled the start of the illness that would claim his life. All in all, not very cheerful meetings. Now he was afraid the medical man was about to deliver more bad news.

There was a sudden knock on the door, the unexpected noise making George spin around sharply. He strode over to it and flung it open with more force than he meant to.

'Whoa there,' Crawford said from his position on the doorstep.

'My apologies,' George said, retrieving the door from where it had bounced off the inside wall. 'I was distracted.' He motioned for his friend to enter and led the way into his study, the room he felt most comfortable in.

'What's got you so distracted?' Crawford asked, his expression shrewd.

'Alice, the convict worker I picked up in Sydney,' he said, trying to keep his voice neutral. For some reason he didn't want his friend knowing just how much she'd got under his skin these last few days. 'I told you she was being whipped when I found her? Well, the guard was not sparing any force and her skin was ripped to pieces, and now it looks like the wounds are festering.'

'Poor girl,' Crawford murmured. They all knew how serious a wound like this could be and George knew Crawford had been whipped when he was serving his sentence for theft.

'The doctor is with her now.'

'Hmm.'

George shared Crawford's sentiment. Doctors were useful for certain ailments and their potions and powders had their limited uses, but for something serious, something like an inflamed wound, there was little they could do.

Looking at his friend, George tried to forget what was going on above his head and focused on the man in front of him.

'Was today a social call?' he asked.

'I was ordered here,' Crawford said with a smile. 'My lovely wife has instructed me to invite you to dinner tomorrow evening. Nothing formal. Just me and Frannie, Robertson and Georgina and you, of course.' He paused, drumming his fingers on the arm of the chair for a moment. 'Why don't you bring your Alice?'

'My Alice?'

Crawford grinned, a mischievous glint in his eyes. 'Your Alice,' he repeated.

He let it go, knowing any protest would only play further into Crawford's hands. 'Wouldn't your wife mind?'

Although both Crawford and Robertson were both ex-convicts, their wives were from rather a different stock. Lady Georgina was the daughter of an earl and Crawford's wife, Francesca, had been the widow of a viscount and lined up to marry an earl before she'd run off with Crawford.

'Frannie? Not at all.' He grinned. 'She can't

exactly have a problem with convicts. She married one after all.'

'A rather uncouth one at that.'

'True. So what do you say? Will you bring your Alice?'

'I'll ask her. She's a little strong minded, so I doubt I'll be able to convince her if she doesn't want to. And I'll get an earful from Mrs Peterson for it.'

'Ah, dear Mrs Peterson,' Crawford said, leaning back in his chair. 'Still as protective of you as your own mother?'

George nodded. Mrs Peterson had been their housekeeper when Crawford and Robertson had first been taken in by his father. The woman had initially been cool towards the two scruffy convict boys, but their charm had soon won her over. Now she fussed over the grown men as if they were still half-starved little lads. It was George, however, whom she had always had the softest spot for and he knew that she would always see it as her place to protect him from the world. Even though he was now thirty-one, over six feet tall and could probably lift the older woman with one arm. He smiled indulgently. He knew he was lucky to have her, even if her temper could be fierce if she thought someone was doing him wrong.

'She watches Alice like a hawk,' he said.

'Perhaps not a bad thing. What do you know about the girl?'

'Not much. She's not very forthcoming on her origins, but that's hardly surprising. When I first brought her here she was rather prickly, but that's subsided pretty quickly. I think she was just scared I would turn out to be like all the men who've tried to take advantage of her over the past year or so.'

Crawford grunted and George noted the far-away look in his friend's eyes. Neither Crawford or Robertson spoke much about their time on the convict ships or the first few years of the sentences that they spent digging roads in Sydney, but George had gleaned a little here and there and it hadn't sounded pleasant at all. He knew Crawford would be thinking of that now, probably sympathising with the woman upstairs who had been through it all so much more recently.

'She's pretty,' Crawford said. 'From the little I saw of her, I could tell that.'

'She is,' George agreed. It was no use denying it. Alice *was* pretty, especially once she'd washed the grime from her skin and lost a little of the haunted look from her eyes. Probably in a few weeks when she'd had a sustained period of three healthy meals a day and gained a little softness, she'd be even prettier.

Crawford regarded him for a second, then shook his head ruefully. 'Robertson and I were certain you'd come back from England married.'

'Really?' George was surprised. Of course there had been women he'd spent time with in England, but marriage hadn't ever entered his head despite his two friends coming back from the other side of the world with brides on their arms. 'Well, don't start getting any ideas about Alice. We're not for each other,' he said with a finality that must have made its mark as Crawford just nodded amiably.

He knew he was an anomaly. To anyone looking in at his life he *should* be married. He was wealthy, influential and knew he had a face that was pleasant enough. What was more important to women out here was the ability to provide, a reassurance that they would finally be looked after, and he was certainly in a position to give that. Yet he was still single.

George grimaced. Of course he'd like a wife,

a woman to share his life with, a woman to fall into bed with at the end of the long day. An image of Alice curled up, her head resting on the pillow next to his, popped into his mind uninvited and George had to quickly push it away.

What so many people didn't understand was the unique position he held here in Australia and as such the difficulty in meeting someone he would feel comfortable sharing his life with. As a free settler he was in a position of power over so many, a position that could so easily be abused, and George had been so desperate not to do just that that it ruled out well over half of the female population in one swoop. Of course there were the daughters of the landowners, robust farm girls who were pleasant enough, but despite their fathers' best efforts to align their daughters with the man who owned the largest cattle farm in Australia, no one had caught his interest.

Shaking his head, he knew that wasn't the only reason. Once he had thought the most important thing in life was finding the right woman to spend it with. He'd looked up to his parents' seemingly happy marriage and wanted to emulate it. Just as he had wanted to emulate his father in so many ways. That was until he'd realised it was all a lie. His father, the man who everyone knew for his generosity and virtue, had begun an affair with their female convict worker. He'd destroyed the partnership he'd shared with George's mother and also dashed the respect George had felt for him.

For a long time he hadn't been able to look at his father in the same way. George hated him, for how he hurt his mother and for the seeming double standards. After years of preaching about equality and kindness, he had abused his position of power and treated the convict worker poorly.

He would not make the same mistakes. It had made George distrust relationships, made him realise that even the seemingly strongest unions had flaws when you got close.

'I'll leave you to it,' Crawford said, standing and making his way to the door. 'I need to ride over to Robertson's to extend the invitation and I'm sure you're anxious to hear what the doctor has to say about your Alice.'

'Until tomorrow evening,' George said, following his friend out of the room and pushing away the thought of his father at the same time. Neither Crawford nor Robertson knew about the affair with the convict worker—both still thought George's father to be a saint.

He watched Crawford ride off into the distance, a cloud of dust billowing behind his horse and giving George a stark reminder of just how dry the land was. Although his farm had survived while he was away, it hadn't exactly prospered and with the drought they could be looking at harder times ahead. In the next few days he would have to get out further afield and see things for himself. Mr Williams had visited him a couple of times, giving him a detailed overview, but there was nothing like being out on the land yourself.

Once Crawford had disappeared over the horizon George went back inside, heading directly for the stairs and taking them two at a time. He paused outside Alice's room, hearing the deep voice of the doctor, wondering if he should go in, but resisted the temptation to knock. Privacy was one thing Alice would have lacked these past few years. It was the least he could afford her now.

'Thank you, Doctor,' Alice said as she pulled on her dress.

The doctor was an elderly man with a shock

of white hair, a thick beard and moustache that drooped down over his lip like a wilted leaf. He spoke with a soft drawl that Alice had heard once or twice before, from people who came from Devon or Cornwall, somewhere in the west of England, although his was hardened as if it had soaked up the rougher accents of the coarse convicts hailing mainly from London and the south.

He barely acknowledged her, packing up his bag and letting himself out of the room even before she was fully dressed. Resting her forehead in her hands, she took a deep breath, trying to take in everything the medical man had told her. Then she rose and made her way to the door. It would be pointless to sit and stew on his words, what would be would be and spending the next fortnight worrying would not help matters in the slightest.

'I'd send her back,' Dr Whittaker was saying, his voice void of any concern for his patient.

She waited to hear Mr Fitzgerald's answer, curious to find she didn't feel apprehensive at all. It wasn't that she didn't mind if she stayed or was forced to return to Sydney, to the laundry and the guards and the awful life she'd led—of course she minded. It was that she was quietly confident that Mr Fitzgerald wouldn't even contemplate that as an option.

'He's one of the few good men in this country,' she murmured to herself. And he was. In just a short time he'd restored her faith in humanity. He'd shown her that not everyone was out for what they could take from you, not everyone was selfish and cruel.

'That's not an option,' Mr Fitzgerald said calmly and she could just imagine his cool, confident stare and unwavering determination as he spoke.

'Then you'll have to wait and see. One of the wounds is inflamed, but only mildly so at the moment. Either her body will fight it and she'll survive or a fever will take hold.'

'Is there anything we can do to improve her chances?'

There was a pause before the doctor spoke again. 'Rest, good food, a little light exercise, nothing strenuous. These would be the things I'd be advising for a *normal* person. But the patient is a convict worker and I am a realist. You won't be wanting to rest her and lose out on money. So just work her as usual and either she'll survive or she won't.'

Alice felt the sadness well up inside her and manifest as a thick lump at the base of her throat that made it hard to swallow. So many people were like the doctor, so many people saw her life as worthless now, just because of one mistake she'd made as a foolish nineteen-year-old girl.

She heard Mr Fitzgerald murmur something under his breath, then the chink of coins as he paid the doctor for his time. Slinking back into the shadows, she waited for the medical man to leave before she quietly knocked on the door to the study.

'Come in,' Mr Fitzgerald's voice called. He was standing by the window, looking out over the fields as she entered, turning only after a couple of seconds. As he spun to face her the light from the window bathed him in a golden glow, glinting off his hair and beard and making him seem other-worldly for an instant.

'The doctor told you what he saw?' Alice asked quietly.

'He did.'

She nodded, trying to fight back the tears. A few months ago she hadn't cared if she'd lived or died, but now she felt as though she were coming out of the darkness. Now she wanted to live.

Wordlessly Alice bit her lip, knowing the tears might begin to fall if she tried to say anything more.

Mr Fitzgerald stepped forward and gently took her hand, holding it as softly as he might a china doll, and waited for her to look up at him before he spoke.

'You will survive this, Alice,' he said, with a quiet conviction in his voice that almost persuaded her on the spot. 'A little rest, some good food and careful bathing and those wounds will get better every day. You're young and healthy, there's no reason this will get the better of you.'

'You should send me back,' she said quietly, knowing she was pushing for a reassurance he shouldn't need to give her, but wanting it all the same.

'I meant what I said earlier. You have a home here for the remainder of your sentence, whether you are up to working or not.'

'I should work, no matter what the doctor said.'

He smiled at her, a flash of something in his blue-green eyes that Alice was beginning to recognise whenever he was making a plan.

'I have a very important job for you,' he said, letting go of her hand and stepping away to his desk. Alice followed him, wondering what it could be. 'Tell me, back home did you celebrate Christmas?'

Memories of the family gathered around the fire on cold Christmas Days, merry and laughing, exchanging presents and singing songs, assailed her. It was memories like this that made her realise how foolish she'd been wanting to escape the monotony of country life. Her couple of Christmases with Bill in London had been much more grim, not occasions to celebrate.

'We did,' she said, forcing her thoughts to the happier times at home with her parents and sisters.

'Carols and good food and the exchanging of gifts?' he asked.

'All that and more. My sisters and I would decorate the house with mistletoe and sprigs of holly and my father would save up all year for the finest joint of meat from the butcher.'

'You have fond memories?'

She nodded, revelling in the warmth she felt as she remembered her mother's smile at the family being gathered together on Christmas Day each and every year.

'So do I. It was one of the traditions my parents

were keen to bring over with them from England. We always celebrated. We'd go to church, of course, but we'd have a family celebration as well. My mother would decorate the house and we would all exchange gifts. Mrs Peterson would always cook a feast of a Christmas dinner. Christmas time holds some of my happiest memories.'

'What job do you want me to do?' Alice asked, intrigued.

'I want you to prepare the house for a wonderful Christmas celebration. Decorate the drawing room, consult with Mrs Peterson on the menu, see what elements of an English Christmas you can bring into this stifling Australian December.'

'Mr Fitzgerald,' Alice said softly, 'that's not work. You should be setting me about polishing the furniture and changing the sheets, not enjoying myself preparing the house for a Christmas celebration.'

He looked at her with mock-admonishment. 'Who is the master of this house?' he asked. 'If I want to set my convict worker to finding an Australian substitute for holly, then who is anyone to protest?'

Alice smiled, she couldn't help it.

'The doctor said to rest. This way I still get some work out of you, but you're not doing anything too strenuous,' he said more seriously. 'And I like Christmas, it's one of my favourite times of year.'

'If you're sure…'

'I'm sure. You've got four weeks until Christmas. Four weeks to prepare the house and recuperate from your wounds. After that I promise I'll let you attack the dust on the furniture.'

Alice felt a thrill of anticipation at the idea of her job for the next few weeks. Mr Fitzgerald had said it was one of his favourite times of year—the very least she could do was make it as special as she could for him.

'You have an invitation,' he said nonchalantly as she turned to leave.

'An invitation?'

'Crawford and his wife invited me to dinner and asked if you would come along.'

She blinked, lost for words. Surely they knew she was a servant, even lower than a servant. Convict workers weren't invited to dinner by wealthy landowners, it just didn't happen.

'I… You… I…' Alice stammered, unsure what to say.

'It's your decision,' he said with a shrug, picking up some papers on his desk. 'If you feel up to it tomorrow, then let me know.'

Alice knew she should take her leave, but was so astounded by the invitation she felt rooted to the spot.

'Do they know I'm a convict?' she asked eventually.

'Yes.'

'Oh.'

'You don't have to decide now,' he said with a smile. 'Think about it and let me know tomorrow.'

Nodding, Alice left the room, utterly perplexed as to why Mr Fitzgerald's friends would invite a lowly convict worker to dinner, and unsure whether she should accept or politely decline.

Chapter Ten

George awoke suddenly. He had been sleeping fitfully, his body not yet adjusted to the sweltering heat of the Australian summer, and twice already he'd made his way downstairs for a glass of water. It wasn't thirst that awoke him this time though, but a low, keening wail, a noise that sent shivers through his body.

Sitting up, he listened intently, waiting for the sound again, wondering if it had been a fleeting figment of his dream. Thirty seconds ticked past, then a minute, the silence of the middle of the night pervading the room, and then suddenly the wail started up again.

At first he thought it might be an injured animal. Perhaps some predator had got into the enclosure where the kangaroos were kept or even a wild animal had been attacked out on the farm, but as he listened intently he realised with a sinking heart that the noise was coming from inside the house.

He sprang out of bed and was halfway to the door when he remembered he was completely naked. Normally this didn't matter. The Petersons had a little cottage half a mile away they retreated to every evening so he was used to being the only occupant of Mountain View House. But not any longer.

Quickly he pulled on a pair of trousers, leaving his top half bare as he heard the low wail again and hurried from the room.

He hesitated outside Alice's door, wondering if she had placed the chair underneath the handle as he'd suggested on her first day in his home. With a shrug he knocked, not expecting an answer. There were two reasons Alice could be making such a noise as the one that had woken him. The first, and most preferable, was that she was in the middle of a bad dream. The second, which he was fearing, was that the wound on her back had festered and she was feverish and delirious.

There was no answer. George tried the door, surprised when it opened easily, no sign of a chair to keep unwanted interlopers out. It was dark in the room, but the moonlight shone in through the window, giving just enough light for him to see Alice's silhouette curled up on the bed.

'Alice,' he called out, not wanting to startle her if she was just having a bad dream.

She mumbled something incomprehensible under her breath, falling silent for a few seconds before the low moan started up again.

'Wake up, Alice,' he said, stepping closer.

There was no reply. Quickly he crossed the room, laying a hand on her shoulder and feeling his heart sink as his hand came away slick with sweat. She was burning up, her skin on fire, and even in the darkness of the room he could see her eyes were half-open and unfocused as she succumbed to her delirium. He felt the crashing weight of worry and guilt, the knowledge that it was his fault her wounds had festered, his fault she was now fighting for her life.

'Please, Bill, no,' she muttered, thrashing her head from side to side.

'Hush, Alice,' he murmured, crossing to the window and throwing it open. Although the night outside was sweltering he could feel a slight breeze through the open window and knew it would cool her skin a little. It wouldn't be enough, though.

'I don't want to do it,' she called out. 'Please don't make me.'

'You're safe, Alice,' he said, wondering if he was speaking the truth. She might be safe from Bill, whoever he was, but she had a new enemy now. The fever that had taken over her body in such a short time.

Carefully he peeled back the sheets that covered her, trying not to notice the way her nightdress clung to her and instead keeping his eyes on her flushed cheeks and half-open eyes.

'No, Bill.' She was shouting now. 'Please don't. We'll find the money another way.'

'Hush,' he said, sitting down on the edge of the bed and taking her into his arms. Gently he stroked her hair, murmuring soothing noises in her ear as he rocked her backward and forward as if she were a small child frightened by something out of her control. At first she was stiff and unyielding in his arms, but slowly she softened, sinking into him and seeming to take comfort from his presence.

The mutterings subsided as she fell into a fitful sleep, but every so often she would stiffen and whimper in his arms.

'Lavender's blue, dilly-dilly, lavender's green. When you are king, dilly-dilly, I shall be queen. Who told you so, dilly-dilly, who told you so? 'Twas my own heart, dilly-dilly, that told me so.'

He sang quietly, the words of the song his mother had sung to him as a boy whenever he'd been ill or injured low and melodious. It seemed to have a calming effect on Alice and her intermittent whimpers quietened as he sung and her body relaxed further. After a few repetitions he felt her breathing deepen and become more regular as she fell into a restful sleep.

George had sat perfectly still, his arms wrapped round Alice's warm body, for half an hour until he felt his eyelids begin to get heavy and his head start to droop. He was in danger of dropping off with her in his arms so he slowly tried to extricate himself, cradling her body to him for a few seconds before gently placing it down on the bed.

As soon as her skin touched the sheets and he pulled away she began to moan again, her eyes flickering but unseeing in the darkness, her head thrashing slowly from side to side.

'Hush,' he said, stroking her hair back from her damp forehead.

'Please don't do that, Bill. I didn't mean to...' she muttered, the words coming out in a gush. He was beginning to dislike whoever this *Bill* was and wondered if he was someone from her life back in England or one of the men who'd made her so distrustful since receiving her sentence.

George shook his head ruefully as he realised how little he knew about Alice. She'd given so little away about her background, her life before Australia. Perhaps this Bill was a lover or a friend or a brother. Whoever he was he sounded like trouble.

The idea of Alice having a lover sat uncomfortably with him and he had to remind himself that he should have absolutely no interest in Alice's personal life. He'd involved himself in her welfare, promised to keep her safe for the remaining few years of her sentence, but further than that he shouldn't care if she had a string of lovers.

As he stood he watched Alice begin to toss and turn again on the bed, the sheet becoming tangled around her within a couple of seconds and making her movements even more frenzied.

Carefully he pulled it to one side, eyeing the door before sitting down back on the bed and scooping her once again into his arms. This time it took five repetitions of the soothing song to calm her, and when she drifted into a deeper sleep George rested his head back against the headboard and allowed his own eyes to close. He would just rest his eyes for a few minutes, then when Alice had become calmer he could slip out before she awoke. The last thing he wanted was for her to wake up in his arms and think he was as bad as she'd first feared, ogling her while she was dressed only in her nightgown.

Alice's first thought was of fire. It felt as though her whole body was aflame, her skin prickling with heat. It was unbearable and even before her mind was fully conscious she felt a low groan escape from her lips.

Uncomfortably she shifted, wondering why she was quite so hot, then forced her eyes to flicker open. Sunlight streamed into the room, blinding her momentarily and forcing her eyes to half-close until she adjusted to the light, and even when she did so everything remained blurry for a few seconds.

For a moment she thought she was back in her childhood room, the one at the top of the house with the big windows that was always filled with light. She'd shared it with her two sisters and there had always been a warm body pressed up against her on one side or the other when she'd woken in the mornings.

Only as her vision cleared and the room took shape before her eyes did she remember where she was. Mountain View Farm. Australia. Her thoughts were sluggish and her main preoccupation was the dryness of her mouth and the pounding in her head, so much so that it took her nearly a minute to register the arms wrapped around her body.

Alice stiffened, her whole body on edge as she slowly turned her head.

Of course it was Mr Fitzgerald. Who else would it be? As she looked into his peaceful face she felt some of the panic that had threaten to overwhelm her seep from her body. His head was resting against the metal headboard, twisted to the side at an uncomfortable angle. He held her loosely, his arms wrapped around her middle and she realised she must have slept with her body resting against his chest.

Trying to remember why he was there, she felt the fog descend again. Her thoughts were fragmented, her senses dulled, and before she could summon the energy to speak she felt herself slipping back into the darkness, once again consumed by the fire that burned on her skin.

George awoke to the sound of a door opening downstairs and felt panic instantly begin to well up inside him. It would be Mrs Peterson, arriving from her little cottage to start work for the day, getting the breakfast ready and the kitchen scrubbed and shining. He had to suppress a groan at the thought of her finding him here with Alice.

Of course it was all innocent. He'd comforted Alice in her delirium, that was all, but it didn't look that way. Not with his arms wrapped around a scantily clad woman while they half-reclined in her bed. Mrs Peterson might be his housekeeper, his employee, but the woman had a strict set of morals and values, despite her shady past, and wouldn't hold back from giving him a piece of her mind if she thought something was wrong. She wouldn't look kindly on him spending time in Alice's bedroom whatever the motivation and probably would find some way to blame Alice for it.

Carefully he shifted, laying Alice down on the bed, seeing her eyelids flutter open, but the effort was too much and she fell back into a restless slumber. With soft steps he padded over to the door, watching as she pushed the golden-red locks from her forehead in her sleep, before he slipped out in the darkness of the upstairs hall.

He was back in his bedroom before Mrs Peterson started bustling around downstairs and had pulled on his clothes within thirty seconds.

'Alice is burning up,' he said without any preamble as he walked into the kitchen a few minutes later. 'She's delirious.'

'You've seen her?' Mrs Peterson's eyes narrowed ever so slightly.

'She was crying out in her sleep so I went to check on her,' he said, leaving out the details of how he'd held her warm body all night, his embrace the only thing keeping her demons at bay during the worst of the fever. 'I'm going to take her some water, see if she can drink something.'

'I should come, too,' Mrs Peterson said, wrap-

ping her apron strings around her waist and resolutely stepping forward.

'I'm not going to take advantage of the poor
girl, especially when she's in such a state,'
George said with a frown.

'I know that, Mr Fitzgerald,' Mrs Peterson said
with an earnest expression. 'It's not you that I'm
worried about.'

'Alice can hardly jump on me in her present
condition, not that she'd want to anyway.'

'You've never been good at seeing the bad in
people,' Mrs Peterson mumbled. 'Or the good in
yourself. You're probably the most eligible man
in Australia and you're nice to boot. Of course
a down-on-her-luck convict girl is going to see
if she can snare you. What has she got to lose?'

George didn't bother arguing. Mrs Peterson
had been in his life for almost as long as he could
remember and he knew she viewed him like the
son she never had. It was only natural for her to
be protective of him.

He patted her on the shoulder, picked up the
glass of water and made his way back upstairs,
hearing his housekeeper's determined footsteps
shadowing his.

Softly he knocked on Alice's door, not expecting a response. Already he dreaded going inside and finding her in a worst state than when he'd left her only a few minutes ago. Fevers were unpredictable. One minute someone could be seeming to recover, their mind clear and their body strong, the next the fever had taken over again, plunging then back into confusion and pain.

Inside, the room was already hot from the sunlight streaming in and George could see the beads of sweat forming on the exposed skin above Alice's nightgown, ready to trickle down beneath the cotton.

'Alice,' he called softly, not wanting to startle her. Her eyes flickered open, but there was no recognition behind the look. The normally sparkling blue of her irises even looked dulled, as if the fever was affecting every little part of her.

Crossing to the bed, he sat down, looping an arm around her waist and helping her into a sitting position. She reacted to his touch just as she had the night before, first stiffening and then relaxing into him.

'Come away, sir,' Mrs Peterson said, her voice tight. 'It's not right, not with her just in her nightgown.'

Ignoring his housekeeper's words and disapproving expression, George lifted the glass of water to Alice's lips and gently coaxed her to open her mouth a little, pouring some of the cool water inside. She swallowed, the sip seeming to revive her slightly, and opened her mouth for more.

'So hot...' she murmured after the third mouthful of water.

'It's the fever,' George said, using his free hand to sweep the thick hair from her shoulders in a bid to cool her even slightly.

'Mr Fitzgerald...' Mrs Peterson said.

He turned to her and shook his head, an admonishing expression on his face. 'The poor girl is ill, Mrs Peterson. And it is not like she's got her mother to nurse her, or some other well-meaning female relative.'

'Mr Fitzgerald...' Alice croaked, and for the first time since he had slipped into her room the night before her eyes seemed to focus as they came up and met his. He saw the relief in her eyes and in that moment he vowed he would stay with her until she recovered. He was the reason she was in this state, the reason she'd slipped and slid in that muddy pond, so he would be the one to stay by her bedside until he knew she was re-covering. It was the least he could do.

'Hush, Alice, you're safe,' he said as gently as he could.

She held his gaze for a few seconds before her body relaxed and she drifted back to a feverish sleep.

'I'll get some water in a bowl and a sponge,' Mrs Peterson said, her face unreadable, but her voice a little softer than before. 'A freshen up will make her feel better, I'm sure.'

Left alone once again with Alice, George looked down at her sleeping form. He'd only known her a short while, time that had slipped by so fast, and so much was still a mystery about her, but he felt a connection with this young woman. They might be on opposite sides of the wheel of fortune, him riding the top and her stuck at rock bottom, but there was an affinity between them, something that seemed to transcend their circumstances. He thought of her slipping and sliding in the mud to come and rescue him after he'd become trapped in a particularly muddy spot. About her determination and strength when he'd first met her, sore from the whipping, but still resolved to stand on her own two feet. About the slow trust she was beginning to show him, the glimpses of her true personality she'd kept suppressed for so long, but was gradually allowing to come out.

'Get better for me, Alice,' he murmured, leaning forward and planting a soft kiss on her forehead. 'You've got so much life to live yet.'

Chapter Eleven

Alice felt as though she were living in a night-mare. Days seemed to pass in a blur, with occasional moments of lucidity, but mostly filled with nightmares and hallucinations. People she knew couldn't be there appeared by her bedside. Sometimes her mother and sisters, welcome visitors who made her feel an acute homesickness even in her dreams. Sometimes more unwelcome visitors. Bill appeared a few times, that charming smile on his face that had once made her go weak at the knees, but now she knew hid a multitude of sins. Mostly she remembered him as he was during their time in London together. Smooth talking, charming to anyone outside looking in, but with an undercurrent of violence.

Once he appeared in an altogether different form. More disturbing even than the Bill that had stolen her dreams and her future. He'd appeared bloated and black, his eyes unmoving and glassy and a vibrant red ring around his neck from the noose that had killed him. Then she'd shouted out, screamed as his foul body had come towards her, only to be pulled back to reality by strong arms and soothing words.

She couldn't understand why Mr Fitzgerald was spending so much time on her. He wasn't there every time she opened her eyes, but he was at her bedside a lot. Some time in the last few days he'd moved one of his comfortable arm-chairs from his study up to her bedroom and spent much of his time sitting there beside her, ready to offer her a sip of water or pull her from the worst of her hallucinations. Alice didn't know any other employer who would be quite so caring, but even in their short acquaintance she had begun to realise Mr Fitzgerald was the rarest of men.

'Good afternoon,' he said as she shifted in the bed.

'Afternoon,' she managed to croak. Her throat felt as though it had been stuffed with sand and her tongue felt too big for her mouth.

Carefully he brought the glass of water to her

lips and let her take a long sip. It felt wonderfully cool and refreshing.

'How are you feeling?' he asked after giving her a moment to gather her thoughts.

'Awake,' she said, feeling foolish at the answer. But it did describe exactly how she felt. After sleeping for days on end she finally felt ready to be awake. 'Properly awake. Not just drifting into consciousness.'

He grinned, that smile that even in her weakened state managed to make something inside her tighten and squeeze.

'You've had me worried, Alice, but I think you might just have broken the fever.'

'What day is it?' she asked.

'Tuesday.'

Five days. Five whole days that had just passed in a blur.

She looked down at her hands resting on the clean white bedsheet, then at the freshly laundered nightgown she was wearing. Definitely not the same one she'd put on a few days ago when the fever had first caught hold.

'Mrs Peterson,' Mr Fitzgerald clarified, holding out his hands as if to ward off an attack as he watched the direction of her gaze. 'She helped you get changed yesterday and changed the sheets at the same time, I presume.'

'I shall have to thank her.' She felt the blush of embarrassment colour her cheeks at his reaction. Of course he would not be the one to change her, to bathe her body.

Thinking of bathing, she raised a hand to her hair and grimaced as she felt the matted locks. Five days of feverish tossing and turning wouldn't have done much for her appearance.

Why do you care? the little voice in her head asked and she glanced involuntarily at the man sitting beside her. The man who had taken time out of his busy schedule to stay with her when she was at her most vulnerable.

'I must look terrible,' she said, pulling the sheets up to almost her chin to cover herself.

'No,' Mr Fitzgerald said, shaking his head, 'Not terrible. Surprising when you've been so very unwell.'

'Do you think…?' She trailed off, unable to finish the question.

'That the fever has really broken?'

She nodded her head. Alice knew that her life had hung in the balance the past few days. It had taken all her energy, all her strength, to fight the fever. Her body had been unable to function in any other way, but now she was awake and lucid and felt cautiously optimistic.

'I think so,' Mr Fitzgerald said slowly and she saw the relief in his expression. She appreciated his concern for her, really she shouldn't matter to him, being just a convict worker, but she knew he truly wanted her to recover and not just so she could get back to work. 'I shall send for the doctor today—he can have a look at your wounds.'

Alice nodded. He wouldn't be able to *do* anything, but at least the man would be able to give an opinion on whether the infection was improving.

'Now I should leave you to rest. You've had a draining couple of days.'

He stood, hesitating for a moment, before reaching out and giving her hand a quick squeeze. 'I'm happy you're recovering, Alice. You gave us all a scare.'

Alice looked up at him and gripped his hand just a little harder, stopping him from pulling away immediately.

'Thank you,' she said. 'For staying with me. I know you didn't have to, but it gave me comfort.'

He smiled at her, his eyes twinkling in the sunlight, 'Just don't tell Mrs Peterson, she thinks you've ensnared me somehow and I've been spending too much time with you.'

'She's right.' Alice reddened and quickly corrected herself. 'Not about the ensnaring, but you shouldn't have spent so much time in here, I'm sure you've got much better things to be doing.'

'What could be more important than looking after someone who draws comfort from you?' he asked.

Alice felt a little pang of sadness. His words confirmed it; he saw her as one of his stray and injured animals, needing rescuing and nursing back to health. Soon he would be ready to set her back into the wild.

Chiding herself for the vague hope she was repressing that there might be something more to his care, she smiled at him and let his hand slip from hers. It wasn't just their stations in life that separated them, there were so many other reasons he would never see her for anything more than a girl who'd needed his help. With anyone else she would embrace the lack of interest, but Mr Fitzgerald was a hard man not to care about and Alice knew she would have to guard her heart very carefully if she didn't want to get hurt.

* * *

George paused outside Alice's door, balancing the tray in one hand as he knocked quietly. Since waking this morning Alice had been much more alert, sleeping for some of the time, but her waking moments were lucid and clear. The doctor had visited and declared her to likely be over the worst, but needing to rest and recuperate to build up her strength.

'Come in,' Alice called, her voice sounding stronger than it had done earlier in the day.

George opened the door and felt his breath catch in his chest. Alice was propped up in bed, her hair draped over one shoulder, a book open in her lap. The late evening sun streamed through the window, bathing everything in a golden light and picking out the red tones of Alice's hair so it glinted and shone. She was looking over to him with a genuine smile, one that widened when she saw what he carried on the tray.

'I brought dinner,' he said, shutting the door behind him.

'I'm starving.'

'I thought you might be. Five days without any food and anyone would be hungry.'

'You'd think you'd get used to hunger,' Alice

said, shaking her head. 'On the ship we were always hungry, always fighting for scraps of food. But even after all those months of hunger I'm still not accustomed to it.'

George was surprised at her candour and the unasked details of her past. Everything else he knew about her was from his questioning; Alice didn't offer much up voluntarily.

'Mrs Peterson brought me something at lunchtime…' she said, trailing off, her eyes flickering to the bowl that sat beside the bed.

'Let me guess…a nice hearty bowl of broth?'

'I couldn't stomach it.'

George pulled a face. He remembered the broth from his childhood, the thin soup his diet every time he was ill. 'For some reason she thinks it speeds recovery.' He grinned. 'I used to get creative in where I'd empty the bowl out when I was a lad. Killed a potted fern my mother was particularly keen on once. I think it was the salt.'

'What have you got there?' Alice asked, her eyes straining to see what he had on the tray. 'Not more broth?'

'No, I sneaked a few little bits past Mrs Peterson.' With a flourish he brought the tray closer and showed her the plates of bread and cheese with a few cold cuts of meat.

'That looks heavenly.'

Placing the tray on the floor by the bed, George dragged over the little writing desk to act as a table, then set about making Alice a plate up. He watched as she took her first mouthful, her eyes closed as she savoured the taste.

'Much better than broth.'

'Just don't let Mrs Peterson hear you say that.'

Alice took another bite before speaking. 'When I was unconscious,' she said slowly, 'I had awful dreams—hallucinations, I suppose.' Her eyes came up to meet his and he saw the fear there. George began to reach forward, to pull her into his arms, but remembered himself just in time, changing the movement to reach out and take a slice of bread. 'There was no one else here besides you?' she asked.

'No one.'

He saw the tension seep from her shoulders, the relief flood her face.

'You did talk a lot, though,' he said.

Her eyes flickered up to meet his and he saw the panic rekindle.

'Mainly about someone called Bill. I got the impression he wasn't a particularly nice man.'

The silence stretched out for so long George wasn't sure Alice was going to answer at all.

'Bill is the reason I'm here,' she said eventually.

'The reason you were transported?'

She nodded, then laughed a little bitterly. 'I know my decisions were my own, I know ultimately *I* am the reason I am here, but if that lying scoundrel hadn't come into my life I'd be tucked up safe in my bed in Yorkshire right now, with one of my sisters on either side.'

'He led you astray?'

She nodded. 'In so many ways. You know when you meet someone and they sweep you away? They're so unlike anyone you've ever met before. Bill was like that. He waltzed into Whitby, swept me off my feet and convinced me to run away with him.'

George sat back in his chair, imagining the ensuing scandal. Alice might not have been from the very upper echelons of society, but the same rules applied to everyone. No fraternising with men until you were married and certainly no running away with someone so unsuitable.

Alice shook her head as if she couldn't quite believe her own naivety. 'At first everything was wonderful. He treated me like a queen, but then the cracks began to show. The money ran out, the shine wore off and Bill began to show me his true personality. It wasn't very nice.'

He could just imagine a younger version of Alice, scared and trapped within her own choices.

'We started working for a gentleman out in Hampstead,' Alice said, her voice low and sombre, 'and although most of the money we earned went to fund Bill's drinking or his ill-advised schemes, I managed to squirrel enough away to buy food and pay our rent. Each week I would try to hide just a little something, to save up for the coach fare back home.'

'Your parents would have taken you back?'

George saw the tears in her eyes as Alice nodded. 'They were good people. I know I hurt them, caused them to suffer because of my behaviour, but they would take me back, I know they would. At least...'

It was two very different things taking back a daughter who'd made a few foolish choices about the young man in her life and taking back a convicted criminal.

'I suppose it doesn't matter much now. I'm on the other side of the world and it's unlikely I'll ever go back.'

'How did you get here, Alice?' George asked.

'It was a particularly bad week. Only Wednesday and Bill had spent all our money on drink. There was nothing for food and our landlord was threatening to throw us out if we didn't come up with what we owed. Bill suggested we make a midnight trip to the house where we worked to *liberate* a few choice items.' Alice shook her head at the memory. 'I begged him not to go, followed him all the way to Hampstead.'

'But you went in with him?'

'Not at first. I refused to sink that low. Whatever else I'd become I was not a criminal. I would not take something that did not belong to me.' There was a momentary flash of fire in her eyes, then it dwindled and died. 'I started to walk away, then I heard the scream.'

Alice bit her lip, shaking her head at the memory.

'I raced inside, thinking Bill had been hurt.

Stupid girl that I was still cared for him despite everything he'd done to me.'

'But it wasn't him?'

She shook her head.

'It was Mr Havers, the gentleman we worked for. He was lying in a pool of blood when I got there.'

'Bill had hurt him?'

'Hit him over the head with the hammer he carried in his bag of tools. Mr Havers was dead, I could see that from the first moment I entered. Bill thrust the trinket box he'd been in the process of stealing when he'd been disturbed into my arms and told me to run. We didn't make it out the door.'

'Mr Havers's servants caught you?'

She shook her head. 'Well, in the end I suppose they did, but I told Bill I wasn't having any part of it. I stopped still and refused to move. He told me I'd be hanged and when I still refused he went to leave without me. By that time the rest of the household was up and they caught us easily.'

'You weren't charged for the murder, though?' George asked. Murder would carry a much harsher sentence—if Alice had been convicted of that she would have been swinging at Tyburn many months ago.

'No. Bill was covered in Mr Havers's blood and he had a reputation as a dangerous man. The courts were pleased to see him sentenced to hang for the murder. Me, they just charged with theft for the box Bill had shoved into my hands. Luckily there wasn't much of value in it so it wasn't a capital offence.'

'So you were sentenced to transportation. And Bill, did he hang?'

Alice grimaced. 'I don't know. He escaped prison when I was still in England—it was the talk of the city. Who knows if they've caught him now, if his sentence has been carried out.'

'It's a different life to the one you imagined, I'm sure,' George said quietly. 'And it was this Bill that visited you in your dreams?'

Alice nodded and he saw the fear in her eyes again. Even though they were half a world apart this man still held her in his dreadful thrall. There was no way he could be here in Australia, no way he had visited Alice while she lay feverish and hallucinating, but still she was afraid of him.

'I know he wasn't really there, but still...'

'He wasn't here, Alice, I promise you. It was just a dream. A nightmare.'

She closed her eyes for a minute, her breathing slowing, and for a moment George wondered if she had fallen asleep. Just as he was about to get up and quietly gather the dinner tray she opened them again, looking at him with a renewed intensity.

'I'm sorry,' she said quietly. 'Babbling on about my life. That's the last thing you want to hear.'

She was wrong. He was interested in her life, from her early years to what had brought her to Australia as a convict. No doubt she'd left much of the story out, but now at least he understood a little about the haunted look in her eyes, a little about her deep distrust of men. It wasn't only her time dodging the violent advances of her fellow convicts on the transport ship that made her mistrustful, but these earlier experiences, too. How awful it must be to fall in love and then to slowly realise the man you'd fallen for was a monster.

'Get some rest,' he said, standing and placing a hand on her shoulder. Her skin was cooler now, it didn't have that feverish heat of the past few days, and he could feel the softness even through the thin cotton of her nightgown. 'I'll come and see you in the morning.'

As he left he paused by the door, looking back over his shoulder at her recumbent form. He knew she would never be free from this man who scared her so much, not while she didn't know if he was still alive or not. Perhaps he could write to his aunt in London, ask her to make some subtle enquiries to see if this Bill had been caught and hanged. Only once Alice knew for sure could she be free.

For a moment he watched her, the subtle rise and fall of her chest, the flickering of her eyes behind her closed eyelids. He'd spent a lot of time in this room the past few days and he felt as though he was beginning to get to know the woman hidden underneath the protective shell she'd covered herself in.

A woman you like a little too much.

He tried to quiet the thought. George wasn't entirely sure why he'd spent so long at Alice's bedside—much of it was guilt, he was certain. Guilt for being the one who'd been the reason her wounds had become covered in mud, but deep down he knew there was more to it than just penance for his mistake. He liked Alice, liked her courage and her ability to stand for what she believed was right no matter the opposition. He liked the way her lips curled into a smile when she was amused and the quiet thoughtfulness as she pondered something he'd said.

There was guilt, but there was certainly a whole lot more, too.

Quietly he closed the door, trying to suppress the memory of Alice's body pressed against his in the muddy pond. The soft curves, the red-gold hair that tumbled over her shoulders, the brilliant blue eyes that seemed wise and vulnerable at the same time. There was something about the way she moved, the way she looked at him. All of it made a deep and primal instinct stir somewhere deep inside him and with every passing day he was finding it harder and harder to pretend it wasn't happening.

'Guilt,' he murmured to himself decisively. 'That's what you feel.'

Chapter Twelve

The sweltering heat continued without any break and the cloudless sky still promised no rain. George had taken to rising early, to getting out on his land for a few hours immediately after the dawn, then returning home for the heat of midday before heading out as the coolness of dusk approached. He was worried—not that he'd voiced his concerns out loud yet—as the wells all around his properties were drying up and the land was becoming cracked and hardened. The cattle were having to travel further to find anywhere suitable for grazing as the land became dusty and barren.

'You look serious.' Alice's voice startled him from his reverie. George had been looking out of the dining-room window at the dusty enclosure where the kangaroos hopped in the shade of a few trees around the perimeter. It was past ten o'clock, but he was still finishing his breakfast, having risen before five to ride out to a patch of grazing land a few miles east of the house and returned as the sun rose higher in the sky.

'Should you be up?' he asked, eyeing her with concern.

'If I look at those four walls of my bedroom for any longer, I swear I'll go mad.'

George knew the feeling. He couldn't bear to stay inside for any length of time, let alone the week Alice had been recuperating after waking up from her delirium. By this point he'd be climbing the walls.

'Come join me,' George said, motioning to the seat beside him.

'I shouldn't…'

'Nonsense, sit down.'

She hesitated for a moment longer before giving him a hesitant smile and sitting down beside him.

'Tea?' he asked. 'Or perhaps some toast?'

She glanced longingly at the thick slices of toast set neatly in the rack in the centre of the table with the block of butter alongside.

'I can't.'

'You can.'

'I'm not your guest.'

'No, you're not,' he agreed. 'You work for me. I own this house, I buy the bread and the butter, I can invite whomever I like to sit at this table and share my meals.'

She blinked and he knew he had been a little too forceful. She was right, of course, her place wasn't at the table beside him, it was working in the kitchen or cleaning the house. Although nothing like as strict as England, even here in Australia the social order was important to people. Convict workers shouldn't sit at their master's tables, sharing their master's food. Still, George had never felt comfortable with the divide. Both Robertson and Crawford had been convict workers when they'd come to the farm. After the fateful afternoon when they'd saved his life his father had welcomed them into the Fitzgerald home as if they were members of the family. Perhaps it was this example that meant he had never been able to rule with an iron fist like some landowners who took on convict workers. Or perhaps it was just his nature.

'The toast does look good,' she said, sliding into the seat next to him. He watched as she buttered a piece of thick toast and took a bite. 'Delicious. So why did you look so serious before I disturbed you?'

'I was thinking about the farm. We still haven't had any rain while you've been convalescing.'

'Is it normally this hot?' Alice asked, looking out of the window, following his gaze from minutes before.

'No.' He laughed. 'Everyone thinks of Australia as this hot, desert-ridden country, but they're wrong. It's so big it has a multitude of climates. In the centre it's hot, with rolling dunes and red earth, but the south of the country is cooler, much more like England. And here we get the warm summers, the hours of sunshine, but it isn't tropical or arid by any means.'

'You've been to the centre of the country?' Alice asked, her eyes widening.

'When I was younger. My father loved this country, even back then when it was just a fledgling colony. He thought it was important for me to experience not just this small pocket of Australia, the area the English have claimed as their own, but to explore further afield. To see what it was like before we settled here, to understand the land and its people.'

George thought back to the six months they'd

spent travelling deep into the interior, a time when he'd still respected his father, held him in awe even. Before that he'd not thought much about the country he lived in, having spent his entire life in Australia, but after that trip he had realised why his father never wanted to return to England. There was something captivating about the ever-changing landscapes and the tribes as different as people from England and Russia were to each other.

'Wasn't it dangerous?' Alice asked.

George shrugged. 'The people were mainly very peaceful. Cautious of us more than we were of them. The Bathurst War was still very fresh in their minds and we were given a wide berth even though we were venturing deep into their territories.'

'You love this country, don't you?' Alice asked softly.

'I do. One day I'm sure you will, too.'

'I don't know. It's different when you've been forced to live somewhere. My life was in England. My home, my family...' She paused, popping the last of the toast into her mouth as she got lost in her memories. 'I suppose I'll find out. It's unlikely I'll ever go back to England.' She smiled, although there was sadness in her expression. 'Perhaps ask me in twenty years, when I've had time to forget the harshness of my journey here and the first few months. Perhaps then I might feel differently.'

'You could go back to England. Some do.'

'Very few. The price of a ticket is so expensive. And it seems that even those who are determined to save up take so long to do so that by the time they've gathered enough funds they've made a life for themselves here. People they don't want to leave behind.'

They fell silent. George could see Alice was contemplating the uncertainty of her future. It must be strange not to know even vaguely what your life would be like in five, ten, twenty years. Even though he wasn't sure of the smaller details, George knew the general direction his life would take, he always had. In twenty years' time he'd be running his farm, expanding it slowly over time. He'd have a wife, a brood of children, hopefully strong and eager to take on some of the more physical aspects of running a large farm. Alice didn't have any of that certainty. She was stuck in a country she would never have imagined she would end up in, her future nothing like the dreams she would have had as a child.

'I don't want to think about the future,' Alice said suddenly. 'A week ago I was lying delirious in bed—things could be so much worse.'

It was wonderful to watch Alice slowly relax into herself. When he'd first brought her back to Mountain View Farm she had been negative all the time, thinking the worst in people. Now he was beginning to see flashes of positivity.

'Would you care to take a little stroll around the garden?' George asked. 'If you're feeling strong enough.'

'That would be lovely. You can show me all the native plants.'

She stood, leaving the room for a few seconds to retrieve her bonnet that had rested on a hook in the hall since their last trip out together. That fateful afternoon when they'd ended up slipping and sliding through the mud.

'Shall we?' he asked, offering her his arm.

She hesitated for just a second, looking around her as if to check no one was watching, no one judging her too presumptuous for slipping her delicate hand into rest in the crook of his elbow.

Outside it was sweltering, the sun high in the

sky and giving off a brilliant white light. They walked quickly across the small exposed area until they were under the shade of the trees.

'This is a eucalyptus tree,' George said, pausing to take one of the leaves between his fingers and stroke it gently. 'See how the leaves hang down towards the ground. All species of eucalyptus trees do that—it is an easy way to recognise them.'

They moved on, with George pointing out rather beautiful specimens of gymea lily and banksia.

'This is one of my favourites,' he said, pausing beside a delicate flower made up of a stem and six bell-like flowers drooping from it. 'They're called Christmas bells,' he said. 'My mother planted them many years ago and the hardy little flowers have flourished, despite their delicate appearance.'

'You really love all of this, don't you?' Alice asked quietly, a look of wonder on her face.

'I know it probably seems terribly dull...'

'No,' she said forcibly. 'Not dull. Being passionate about something is never dull.'

'Even when that something is botany?'

'My father used to collect coins. He would

search in curiosity shops and go to house clearances. The look of excitement on his face when he found a coin to add to his collection was heart-warming.'

'What is your passion, Alice?' he asked.

A darkness passed over her face and George regretted the question. Of course she hadn't been allowed to indulge her own interests these past couple of years and it was cruel of him to remind her of the fact.

'I don't think I have one,' she said, resting her hand on the bark of another eucalyptus tree, her fingers caressing the rough surface.

'One day you will, Alice, once this is all over. I know it seems like your sentence lasts for ever, but in ten, twenty years' time it will just be a distant memory, a small part of an otherwise happy life.'

'That's a very nice way to look at it,' she said softly, her eyes coming up to meet his. George felt the ground lurch under his feet as she held his gaze. She looked beautiful in the sunshine, her hair curling in red-gold waves around her shoulders and her skin flushed in the heat. His eyes flickered to her lips, rosy and full and so inviting. In that moment he wanted to kiss her more than he'd ever wanted anything before in his life.

He saw her lips part ever so slightly, saw the subtle sway of her body towards him and he knew that she was thinking the same thing, feeling that irresistible pull.

George stepped forward, knowing there were a hundred reasons he shouldn't reach out and touch Alice, but knowing he would do it all the same. He took her hand in his own, his eyes never leaving hers, and their bodies swayed together in unison. There was only a hair's breadth between them now. It would be so easy to gather her in his arms, so easy to cover her mouth with his own and taste the sweetness of her lips.

Closing his eyes, George took control of himself. This was Alice. The one woman in Australia he shouldn't be having these sort of thoughts about.

'Mr Fitzgerald,' Alice said quietly, reminding him of the position of power he held over her. Immediately he dropped her hand as though he'd been burned.

Quickly he turned away. He'd come so close to doing something foolish. So close to being the man Alice had feared he would be.

'I'm sorry, Alice,' he said, his voice unusually gruff, 'I was caught up in my thoughts.'

Even as he stepped away he saw the flush to her cheeks, the increased rate of her breathing and knew that on some level she wanted him.

That doesn't matter, he told himself. Alice was vulnerable, afraid and alone. He would not take advantage of that.

'You should get back inside, Alice,' he said as kindly as he could. 'This heat will do nothing for your recovery.'

For a moment he thought she might refuse, might demand an explanation from him, but after a few seconds she just nodded and turned away, heading back towards the house.

George watched her leave, watched the subtle sway of her hips as she walked away, unable to tear his eyes from her.

Chapter Thirteen

'How do you normally spend Christmas?' Alice asked, slicing the apple in front of her with care. Mrs Peterson like things done *just so* and Alice was quickly learning not to argue over the small things with the housekeeper. If she wanted the apples for the pie chopped into inch-square chunks, then Alice would do just that, even though she knew the apples would bake better in thinner strips.

'Mr and Mrs Fitzgerald, the old Mr and Mrs Fitzgerald, always made a big fuss over Christmas,' Mrs Peterson said, pausing for a moment with her floury hands resting on the top of the rolling pin. 'Presents everywhere, the drawing room decorated with flowers and plants, a sumptuous meal for the family to share. It was always young Mr Fitzgerald's favourite time of year.'

Alice felt a smile spread across her face at the

picture of Mr Fitzgerald as a young lad, tearing around the house in excitement.

'Since his parents died he's still celebrated of course, but the house has never seemed quite so full.'

'He stays here on his own?' Alice asked. As far as she knew he had no other family in Australia, the rest of his relations still living half a world away in England.

'Not on his own, Mr Robertson and Mr Crawford used to come. Although with them having their own families now I don't know what will happen.' She sighed and shook her head. Alice waited for her to go on, but the housekeeper went back to rolling out the pastry for the pie.

'You think that will upset Mr Fitzgerald?'

'Good Lord, no. If you haven't worked out he's the kindest man on this earth then you must be blind. He would never begrudge his friends their happiness with their families. But whatever he says he will miss his friends at Christmas, just like he'll miss his dear parents, too. I just wish he would find someone of his own.'

For all her prickliness with Alice there was no denying that Mrs Peterson loved the man she worked for, even saw him a little like a son. She thought of Mr Fitzgerald, his kindness, his generosity, and resolved that she would do her very best to make it a special Christmas for him.

'Why hasn't he settled down, do you think?' Alice asked mildly. She couldn't help remembering the moment in the garden a few days earlier where their eyes had met and their bodies swayed together. If it had been down to her, she wouldn't have been able to stop herself from reaching up and kissing him, but Mr Fitzgerald had hesitated, had pulled away, and now he was avoiding her as though she were infected with the plague.

'I wish I knew. He had the girls falling over him, of course. He's rich and handsome and successful. And they don't even know how kind and loving he is. But I suppose there's just not been anyone who's caught his eye.'

'No one?'

'No one worth talking about,' Mrs Peterson said as she laid the pastry into the dish. 'Now you get those apples boiling.'

Alice placed the apple chunks into the pan and added the boiling water, trying to keep her hands busy all the time. These last couple of days had been torture. Despite doing her very best to be busy every waking moment she had been unable to stop her mind wandering. Thinking about Mr Fitzgerald, about the way his eyes crinkled up when he smiled, how the sun glinted off those green-blue eyes and golden hair. How his face lit up when he talked of botany or the animals he rescued. And how she'd felt whole again when he'd looked at her with desire in his eyes.

Alice had never expected to feel anything like this again and especially not after knowing someone for such a short time. After Bill she had sworn she would never let another man into her life, sworn she would never place herself in that vulnerable position again. And then the deplorable behaviour of the men on the transport ship and the archaic claiming of women that happened once they'd landed in Sydney had strengthened that resolve.

Then Mr Fitzgerald had come in and knocked it down with his kind gestures and chivalry.

Closing her eyes, Alice tried to force herself to remember the pain she'd felt inside when he'd pulled away instead of kissing her. There had been desire, a heat coming off him that was unmistakable, but he'd remembered himself, remembered their respective positions, and he'd stepped away. That had hurt, but the rational part of her brain kept trying to tell her it was for the best. There were hundreds of reasons even a single kiss would be foolish, no matter how much she longed to feel his arms around her body and his lips brush against hers.

'Don't jeopardise things,' she muttered, reminding herself how lucky she was to have ended up here rather than in one of the dreaded factories back in Sydney. Those places were grim and the conditions little better than a prison.

'Pardon?' Mrs Peterson said, reminding Alice she wasn't alone.

'Just telling myself to be careful, I don't want to drop any apple pieces,' Alice said breezily.

'I hoped he might come home from England with a wife. Some pretty little aristocrat wanting an adventure, like Mr Robertson's and Mr Crawford's wives,' Mrs Peterson said, pulling Alice out of her reverie completely.

'I'm sorry to disappoint.' Mr Fitzgerald's deep voice came from the doorway. He was leaning against the wood casually, his arms folded over his chest and a smile playing on his lips. Alice felt something lurch inside her and had to grip on to the work surface to steady herself.

'It's high time you found some respectable girl to marry and started producing some cherubic children,' Mrs Peterson said, seemingly not fazed at being caught out gossiping about her master. 'This house is too big for you to be rattling about it on your own. And those good looks of yours won't last for ever.'

'Ah. Mrs Peterson, you think I'm good looking,' he said, stepping into the room and taking the housekeeper by the hand. 'If only you weren't a married woman.'

'Hush,' Mrs Peterson said, her cheeks turning red, 'Stop fooling around. You could have your pick of the girls—you just need to choose one.'

Alice was watching him as his eyes skimmed over her as if he were unable to stop glancing in her direction.

Mr Fitzgerald shrugged, as if he'd heard this a hundred times before, and turned to Alice. For a moment it was as if the world slowed down. Alice could feel every beat of her heart in her chest, every prickle of heat on her skin, every butterfly in her stomach. It was unnerving.

'Excuse me?' she said, realising he had started speaking and she had no idea whatsoever as to what he was saying.

He gave he a slightly bemused look, but started again. 'I'm going into town,' he said, 'I've got to sort out the paperwork to confirm I'm taking you on as a convict worker and I need to visit my tailor. Do you feel up to accompanying me?'

It was more than a week now since she'd recovered from her infection, enough to start getting up and about around the house, although she hadn't ventured further than the kangaroo enclosure yet. Still, her wounds were healing nicely and the good food and kindness she was receiving here at Mountain View Farm meant she felt stronger than she had in years.

She nodded, feeling nervous at the prospect of going back to Sydney. It held bad memories for her and, even though she knew it was irrational, she had a fear that one of the guards might grab her and pull her back to the whipping post to finish off her punishment.

Mr Fitzgerald stepped closer and Alice caught a hint of his scent, a mixture of the honey from his soap and something earthier she couldn't quite put her finger on.

'I'll be right there beside you,' he said quietly so only she could hear. 'There's no need to feel nervous.'

Alice swallowed, taking a moment to compose herself before she looked up. It still wasn't enough. He was standing close, although not so close as to be considered inappropriate. The look of concern on his face was mingled with a smile of reassurance and Alice wondered what he would do if she just threw herself into his arms.

Nodding, she bit her lip, but then forced herself to smile. As he smiled back she wondered exactly what it was about him that had her feeling like a lovesick sixteen-year-old. Perhaps after her bad experiences it was his kindness she found so attractive, but as he turned away to address Mrs Peterson she knew there was the physical pull as well. It had been a long time since she'd imagined a man's arms wrapped around her, but now she was finding it hard to think of anything else.

'We'll leave in half an hour,' he said. 'Do you feel up to riding or shall we take the cart?' Before she could answer he shook his head. 'If you don't mind, we'll take the cart—I've got a few bits to pick up in town that will be easier to bring home that way.'

The cart would be slower, of course, more time in close proximity with him. Alice nodded, of course she couldn't protest. It would be a good practice for her to control herself while sitting next to the man she couldn't stop thinking about.

'Would you pick up a few bits from town for Christmas? I need some dried fruit for the cake and see if those crooks down by the harbour have any nutmeg in, but don't pay more than sixpence a measure. And we need some more of the good wine, that red you like.' The housekeeper ticked off the items on her fingers, nodding her head in satisfaction when she had thought of everything. 'I'll make you up a parcel for lunch,' Mrs Peterson said as Alice watched Mr Fitzgerald walk from the room. 'It'll take a few hours to get into Sydney on that old cart so you'll be gone most of the day.' She paused, then ushered Alice to the door. 'You go get ready—and the master is right. Don't you fret about going into Sydney. He wouldn't let anything happen to you.'

Half an hour later Alice steeped outside into the sunshine. It was another scorching day with no let up in temperature in sight. Still they'd had no rain and she knew Mr Fitzgerald was becoming increasingly anxious about the lack of water down the wells and the dryness of the earth. Carefully she adjusted her bonnet to stop the sun pinkening her face and walked around to the side of the house. Mr Peterson was there with the horse and cart, loading on a basket that no doubt contained the feast Mrs Peterson had packed. As she got to the side of the cart she felt movement in the air behind her and a soft touch on her arm.

'Ready?' Mr Fitzgerald asked.

Alice nodded, feeling a crackle of energy between them as he took her hand to help her up on to the bench at the front of the cart. He settled in beside her, took the reins from Mr Peterson and they set off at a sedate pace away from the farm.

For a while they rode in silence, the swaying motion of the cart lulling Alice into an almost trance-like state. It was only when Mr Fitzgerald shifted beside her that she came back to the present, realising they must have been travelling for a good while as the scenery had changed a little.

'That's cooler,' she said, loosening the straps of her bonnet. They were passing through a small forest, the road shaded by the tall trees, and with a sigh of relief Alice slipped the bonnet from her head, shaking out her hair so it fell about her shoulders.

She became aware of Mr Fitzgerald watching her as she settled the bonnet in her lap and felt the colour rise in her cheeks.

'It's unbelievably warm in those things,' she said, wondering how long she would feel such a rush of heat whenever he looked at her. Two years was a long time—surely by the end of her sentence she'd be able to look him in the eye without feeling like a thousand butterflies were trapped inside her stomach.

'I can only imagine,' he murmured. As usual he was dressed in a simple pair of trousers and pristine white-cotton shirt. On any other man it would look ordinary, but he managed to draw the eye as if he were wearing evening wear made by the finest tailor. 'Shall we stop for lunch?'

It was still an hour's ride into Sydney and suddenly Alice was keen to stretch her legs and enjoy the shade for a while.

'That would be lovely.'

They continued for another couple of minutes, the cart trundling slowly down the dusty track. Somewhere above them two birds called to one another, a sweet, high-pitched conversation in song that reminded Alice of the fat wood pigeons they used to get in her garden back home.

'Here should do,' Mr Fitzgerald said, pulling gently on the reins to slow the plodding horse.

Quickly he hopped down and held out his hand, as always treating her more like a lady of his class than the convict worker she was. Then he grabbed the basket Mrs Peterson had filled with food, offered her his arm and led her through the undergrowth.

'You've been here before,' Alice said as he picked his way through on an invisible path.

'I have indeed. It's my favourite place to stop on the way to Sydney.'

She was about to ask why when she looked up, her breath catching in her chest at the view in front of them. The space between the trees opened out to reveal a small lake of sparkling blue glinting in the sunshine. The bank was shallow and shaded, tapering gently down to the still water. Even here there was evidence of the drought, with a dusty, exposed foot of dried mud surrounding the lake that normally would have been underwater.

'I can see why.'

From the basket Mr Fitzgerald took a blanket and laid it out, sitting down on one side and waiting for Alice to sit on the other.

'Mrs Peterson is a good cook,' he said, dipping into the basket again, 'and she makes a fantastic dinner, but you can't beat her picnics.'

He set out several dishes and packets, unwrapping each to reveal tantalising scents. He was right—it did look like a perfect picnic. Sandwiches and scones were set out next to not one, but three types of cold meat. There was a cake, a collection of apples and even a bottle of wine hiding in the bottom.

'Let me get this cooling,' he said, getting to his feet.

Alice watched him with interest as he tied a piece of string around the bottle and set it into the lake, tucking the other end of the string under a good-sized rock.

'What would you like first?' he asked.

She took a sandwich, biting into the fresh bread and feeling her stomach give an appreciative rumble.

'How was your dinner with your friends last week?' Alice asked. It had been the dinner party she'd been invited to, the one she hadn't known whether to accept the invitation to or not, but her delirium from the fever had stopped her from needing to make the decision.

'I didn't go,' he said.

'Oh?'

'You were unwell. I didn't want to leave you alone.' He looked at her for a moment, an amused expression on his face. 'Don't worry, I sent a note.'

'Good,' Alice said, unable to summon any other words. He'd cancelled. For her.

'The dinner has been rearranged for later this week. This time Robertson and his wife are going to host. If you feel well enough.'

Alice shook her head in disbelief. She should be serving at the table, not invited to sit around it with his friends. It was intoxicating, this kindness he was showing her, something she hadn't experienced in such a long time. If she wasn't careful, she would get used to it and she needed to remember this wasn't how the world really was. It wasn't how people really were.

'You don't feel well enough?' he asked.

'It's not that,' she said quickly, not sure how to explain how she was feeling.

'They don't bite,' Mr Fitzgerald said with a smile. 'I know it seems daunting, socialising when all you've known for so long is work and punishment, but I think you would enjoy it.'

'It doesn't seem right,' Alice said, looking down at her hands. 'I'm a convict, a servant. They're… You're…'

'Have I told you how I came to know Robertson and Crawford?' Mr Fitzgerald asked, reclining back and kicking off his boots.

'You mentioned they were convicts.'

'They were. Transported as very young lads. They came to the farm as convict workers when my father was alive. They were quiet and sullen and scarred by their experiences.'

Alice shifted, making herself comfortable before taking another sandwich.

'A few months after they arrived it was harvest time and we were all out in the fields. Even my mother used to lend a hand back then. I was working alongside Robertson and Crawford, even though we hadn't really spoken before. It was hot and everyone was getting tired. I'd just turned around when Robertson sprang on top of me and I saw Crawford leap to one side, flinging himself on the ground.'

Alice watched as he got lost in the memory. It should have been a scary experience, but by the look on his face all he could see was the good that had come out of it, the friendships it had formed.

'They saved me from a poisonous snake. Robertson tackled me out of the way and Crawford jumped on it before it could spring. They saved my life that day.'

'That was very brave for two young boys.'

'It was. My father brought them into the house and realised they were good lads, just held back by their circumstances. They still had a few years of their sentences to serve out, but Father moved them into the house, educated them beside me, treated them like sons.' Mr Fitzgerald shook his head. 'They are the two most generous and courageous men I know and that is partly because someone showed them some humanity during their time here.'

'Your father sounds like a wonderful man.'

'He was. In some ways, at least.' He paused, looking over at Alice, and she sensed there was some deeper emotion he was concealing about his father, something painful and personal. 'Do you know what he would tell me to do if he were here?' he asked eventually.

She shook her head.

'He'd tell me to remember every single person

is worthy of time and attention, every single person deserves to be treated as the best version of themselves.'

'I think your father would be very proud of you.'

He shrugged, then grinned. 'What I was trying to say was that Robertson and Crawford share my view that no one should be suppressed due to their background. They would welcome you at their tables, they know what you've been through and they know that is not the entirety of who you are.'

'And their wives?'

'I don't know them well, but Robertson and Crawford wouldn't marry anyone who believed someone to be inferior purely because of their circumstances.'

Alice played with a loose thread of wool on the blanket, wrapping it around her fingers before releasing it and repeating.

'Did you ever feel jealous?' she asked after a moment. 'Of your father treating them like sons?'

'I was just pleased to have someone to share my lessons with, to run wild in the fields with. We're quite isolated out at Mountain View Farm and even more so back then. Sometimes we might go for weeks without seeing an outsider.' He sat up, waiting for her to meet his eye. 'So will you come to dinner?'

At his words her heart beat harder in her chest and her skin flushed. She *knew* he was only asking to be kind, he'd said as much a few minutes earlier. Just like his father had shown Robertson and Crawford there was good in the world, that was what he was doing for her. Still, some part of her felt as though he were asking her to accompany him to dinner. To go as his guest, to ride alongside him, to walk in on his arm.

'If you're sure it would be appropriate,' Alice said, suppressing the gushy *yes* that had threatened to spill from her lips.

'Wonderful.'

He lay back again, stretching out, and Alice had visions of lying down beside him, resting her head on his chest as he gathered her to him.

'I know we should continue our journey,' he said after a couple of minutes. 'But it's so damn hot.'

He wasn't wrong. She felt uncomfortable in her dress and for a moment she wished she could slip out of it and slide into the cool lake for a swim.

As the thought popped into her mind she saw Mr Fitzgerald sit up and eye the water as if thinking the same thing.

'I'm going for a swim,' he said decisively.

'What?' Her voice came out in a half-strangled squeak, but Alice was too distracted to notice. A swim. In the lake. Right in front of her. Presumably without many clothes on. She swallowed, already images of him stripping naked and striding into the water filling her head.

'A swim,' he said. 'I would invite you in, but I know you need to keep your wounds clean and dry.'

She nodded. Unable to form a single coherent sound. *Invite her in*, as if it were to have tea with an elderly relative. She glanced sideways at him. He had absolutely no clue as to how much he affected her.

Alice could only watch as he stood and pulled his shirt over his head. She had to stifle the sharp intake of breath with a hand over her mouth. The memory of him holding her tight to him as they slipped and slid in the muddy pond came crashing back.

'Get a grip,' she muttered to herself.

'Pardon?'

'Don't slip,' she said, managing to summon a smile.

'I won't. Thanks.'

He waded into the water with his trousers still on, pausing when he was almost waist deep before diving under the surface. It was a good thirty seconds before he surfaced again, just long enough for Alice to feel a prickle of concern.

'It's glorious in here,' he called, kicking on to his back.

She did feel a little jealous, sitting in the sweltering heat while he must be wonderfully cool, but Alice knew if she went into that water with him she might lose control and do something she would only regret.

'He's your employer,' she muttered, planning on listing all the reasons even dreaming about Mr Fitzgerald was foolish. 'He is far above you in social class. You swore never to let a man into your heart or your life again.' She paused, closing her eyes and feeling the tears building as the biggest obstacle to her future happiness came to the surface. 'You're still married,' she whispered.

Unless Bill had been caught and his death sentence carried out she was still legally Mrs Alice Fillips. Trying to suppress the tears, she thought back to the rushed wedding he'd talked her into when she'd first run away with him. Of the heady feeling of coming out of the church a married woman. And the months that followed as she realised what a momentous mistake she'd made in tying herself to a man who disregarded her feelings and even sometimes her existence entirely.

By the time they'd been hauled away to face the magistrates, her for theft and him for murder, there were none of the feelings of love or excitement left for the man she'd married, only resentment for the lies he'd told her, the stories he'd spun and the promises he'd never meant to keep.

Now she was in a perpetual limbo. On the other side of the world, unsure if she was still a married woman or if her husband had been executed. At that thought she felt a lump form in her throat. No matter how cruel Bill had been in the end she never wanted to see him hanged. Once they'd been happy, for a short while, and it was that man she mourned, not the one who'd come after their marriage.

Glancing up, she felt her chest constrict. Mr Fitzgerald was the total opposite of Bill. Kind and generous and not at all violent. But no matter how much she might want him to gather her in his arms and promise her a happy future, she knew it could never be.

As she watched he stood, the water flowing from his body as he rose up out of the lake. She knew she should look away, knew he could see her staring, but it was as though her eyes wouldn't obey. As he waded through the water the sun glinted off the droplets on his skin and gave him a golden glow, as if he were a Greek god come to visit her.

'*That* was the most refreshing swim I've had in my life. And I didn't get eaten by a crocodile. Today is going to be a great day.'

'What?' Alice asked, wondering if she'd heard him wrong.

'You know we have crocodiles here in Australia?' he asked, looking at her with a bemused expression.

She did, but only vaguely. It was one of those facts that someone had told her on the voyage out here. Like tales of spiders the size of dinner plates and venomous snakes hanging from every lamppost. They'd talked of a gigantic man-eating lizard with a mouthful of razor-sharp teeth.

'Not here, though?' she asked, her eyes darting across the surface of the water.

Mr Fitzgerald shrugged. 'Probably not. I've swum here plenty of times and survived to tell the tale. It is the sort of place they might live, though. A clean, shady spot with shallow banks and deep water. A crocodile's paradise.'

'Why on earth would you swim here if there's even the slightest risk?' Alice shuddered at the thought of a crocodile fastening its huge jaws around an arm or a leg.

'We have sharks off the coast,' he said with a shrug, 'and crocodiles in some of the freshwater lakes, it's one or the other.' He sat down beside her, his wet trousers clinging to his thighs, little droplets flying off him as he touched the ground and showering Alice in a cool spray. 'You can't spend your whole life afraid.'

'Of a crocodile you can.'

He smiled at her, propping himself up on his elbow.

'So if you're not afraid of crocodiles and you're not afraid of sharks, what does scare you?' Alice asked, checking the undergrowth one last time to rule out the possibility of an overgrown lizard hiding among the shrubs.

'Do you want the truth?' he asked, lowering his voice.

Alice nodded, leaning in a little so her face was close to his. It was so tempting to reach out and touch him, to trail her fingers over his cheek. There was an intimacy between them, a closeness that she wished could last, but she knew that as soon as they got up from the blanket and continued their journey to Sydney the spell would break.

'I'm not afraid of venomous snakes or spiders that can kill with one bite and I'm not afraid of the crocodiles or sharks that terrorise the waters,' he said, his voice low and melodious and his eyes holding hers with a warmth and intensity that made an unbidden smile blossom on Alice's lips. 'But I am a little afraid of you, Alice.'

'Of me?' she spluttered. It was not the answer he was expecting.

'Of you...' He paused and she wondered if he was going to elaborate or leave her guessing as to his meaning.

'I'm not dangerous,' she said eventually.

'Not in the conventional sense.'

'Not in any sense.'

He sat up, the movement bringing them closer together, and Alice was momentarily distracted by the heat of his body so close to hers.

'I think you're dangerous to me,' he murmured, reaching out and tucking a stray strand of hair behind her ear, his fingers lingering for a few seconds.

Alice felt the air being sucked from her body. Here was the man she had spent the last few weeks trying not to fall for admitting he was attracted to her, even though he knew it would be best for them to keep things strictly platonic. Her heart soared and she silently urged him to do something more. To trail his fingers down her cheek, to pull her to his body, to cover her lips with his own.

Instead he shook his head and sprang to his feet, pulling his shirt on in one swift movement, and started to gather the lunch things up.

Alice couldn't move. She was poised to be kissed, her lips moist and her body willing. Slowly she closed her eyes, forcing herself to focus. He was right to not take things any further, of course he was, but that didn't mean it didn't hurt. Swallowing the lump in her throat, she fixed a sunny smile to her face and stood, busying herself with packing the basket so Mr Fitzgerald wouldn't see quite how disappointed she was.

Chapter Fourteen

George felt his whole body tense as Alice rubbed against him. They were nearly in Sydney now, the road was growing busier despite the heat of the day and there was plenty that should be able to distract him, but all he could think of was the woman next to him.

He'd seen how she had watched him as he swam, seen the naked desire in her eyes and wished he could sweep her from the bank and into the lake. He would strip off every item of her clothing until she was naked under the water, then lift her on to the shore to dry in the sunshine.

His mind had been imagining similar the entire journey. Two hours of wonderful torture, of images of things that could never be, but that he wanted so much. A kiss, a touch, a night of pleasure.

Glancing at her, he shook his head, trying to rid himself of the glorious images that had plagued him the past couple of hours. For a moment he wondered about how she looked at him. The affection he saw growing in her eyes day by day and the attraction, the desire. It was at odds with her determination not to be touched by a man again. He knew the memories of what she'd endured on the transport ship and since arriving in Australia would torment her for a long time to come, but he wondered if she was realising not all men were the same. Not all men would abuse their power and their strength. And if she was, what did that mean for him?

George was distracted from his thoughts by a shout from somewhere to his left, and a smile sprang to his lips as he saw Ben Crawford cantering towards them on horseback, his shirt billowing out behind him. Following at a more sedate pace was his wife, Francesca—a woman George had grown to respect and like during their stay in London.

'Fitzgerald,' Crawford called, leaning down and clapping him on the back when he reached the cart. 'And Miss Alice.'

George felt the warmth he always did when he was with Crawford or Robertson.

'Living the life of a simple farmer, I see,' Crawford said, motioning to the cart.

'Aye. Simple folk, simple times, simple cart,' Fitzgerald said, putting on his best country accent.

Bowing as best he could from his position on the cart, he greeted Francesca.

'Mrs Crawford, it is a pleasure to see you again.'

She waved away his formality, instead leaning down from horseback and kissing him on the cheek. 'I'm so happy to see you again,' she said, her eyes shining. 'And you must call me Francesca, everyone does.'

She looked very different from the poised and formal widow of a viscount he'd known in London. Her eyes shone with happiness and there was a healthy glow on her cheeks and a hint of a tan on her arms. Her dress skimmed out over the swelling of her belly and one of her hands rested protectively on the bump.

'Francesca, this is Alice. She's working for me,' he said, making the introduction.

Alice was sitting up straight beside him, looking a little uncomfortable.

'Oh, my dear, I heard about the awful time you've had of it. Are you quite recovered?' Francesca asked, moving her horse around so she could talk to Alice directly.

'Yes, thank you, Mrs Crawford.'

'I'd like to take a whip to some of those guards,' Francesca muttered through gritted teeth. 'They've no humanity.'

Crawford grinned. 'I keep having to pull her away whenever we see a red coat. It wouldn't be pretty.' He looked them over, his eyes narrowing as he noted George's slightly dishevelled appearance. 'Where are you off to?'

'We need to visit the Governor's office, to make Alice's position in my household official.'

'Good,' Francesca said with feeling. 'While you're there you should complain about those awful men who nearly cost Alice her life.'

'They'd probably have me up against one of the whipping posts for causing a disturbance,' George said, although he knew he would find it difficult to hold his tongue if he saw the guards responsible for the gashes on Alice's back.

'Hardcastle is a good man,' Crawford said

slowly, 'but he's still an Englishman, looking to solidify his reputation before returning home to some higher position. What Australia needs is someone who loves the very earth it is built on. Someone who would dedicate their life to making it a better place to live. Someone with links to England, but who is Australian through and through.'

'You don't really get the concept of subtlety, do you?' George asked, shaking his head.

'You're the perfect man for the job.'

'They would say I'm too soft.'

'You're kind. There's a difference.'

George shrugged. Sometimes he did feel like storming into the Governor's residence and demanding scores of changes as to how they ran the colony. Slowly things were evolving, slowly Australia was beginning to see itself as more than a place to dump those not wanted in England any more, but there was a lot of work to be done.

'One day the colonies of Australia will unite,' he said softly, 'and we will become a country, a commonwealth, whatever the phrase is. People will *want* to live here—they will come voluntarily for the life this beautiful land can offer.'

George shrugged. 'But there is a lot of work to do first, but I do not think the English are ready to let their control slip just yet.'

One day the population of Sydney would be big enough, the free-men would outnumber the guards a hundred to one, and the colony would slowly transform from a place to send convicts to a proper working town that just happened to have been built by convicts. Then would be the time for someone like him to step up. To show that they weren't just a dumping ground, that Sydney had grown into so much more.

'Mr Fitzgerald is right,' Francesca said quietly. 'The colony isn't ready yet. The people still see themselves as English, many would return to England in a flash. Once they've had children, once they've built a life they don't want to leave behind, then things will change.'

He saw Alice watching Francesca closely, saw the flicker of admiration on her face. It must be hard to be surrounded by men the whole time.

'Do you have time for a drink?' Crawford asked.

George looked up at the sun. It was already getting late, but he wanted nothing more than to spend an hour chewing over the political ins and outs of the country he loved with Crawford.

'Please do, I am eager to take a stroll with Alice, if you'd care to accompany me. I promise we will stick to the shade,' Francesca said, smiling sweetly.

Next to him Alice stiffened. She wasn't used to kindness, to someone showing an interest in her.

'Of course,' Alice murmured.

'Wonderful.'

George stepped down, taking Alice's hand and helping her from the cart. As she stepped off she stumbled, her foot catching on the hem of her dress, sending her crashing into his chest. George instinctively caught her in his arms, steadying her, holding on for a few seconds until he knew she wasn't going to overbalance. As he did so he caught a hint of her scent, the honey from the soap she used and, if he wasn't mistaken, a little jasmine from the flowers in the garden. It made something tighten inside him and he had to set his face into an unreadable expression before he stepped away.

He and Crawford watched the two ladies walk away arm in arm before they continued through the streets to tavern they had frequented for years before their trip to England. Once the cart and horses were safely stowed away they entered, pleased to be out of the sun even though the interior was stuffy.

'You're smitten,' Crawford said as they sat down with their tall glasses of ale.

'What?'

'You're smitten,' he repeated, no hint of doubt in his voice.

George didn't reply. Crawford was an astute man and had known him for a long time. Any protestation would sound weak and untrue.

'She's pretty,' Crawford said slowly. 'Nice smile, lovely eyes, curves where they should be, but we've known plenty of pretty young women in our time and I've never seen you look like this before.'

George took a slow sip of ale, swallowing the cool liquid before speaking.

'How do I look?'

'You look at her like I look at Frannie.'

Crawford had been head over heels in love with his wife for years and it would appear marriage had only increased that affection.

'I do feel something for her,' George admitted.

Crawford grinned, clapping his friend on the

back. 'Struck down by love, isn't it a wonderful feeling. Terrible, of course, but wonderful, too.'

'I'm not sure it's love,' George said slowly. 'I barely know her.'

Crawford shrugged. 'You will.'

'Nothing can happen.'

'Why ever not? You like her. She likes you. You're both consenting adults. Sounds pretty straightforward.'

'When she first came to the farm she was rather jumpy. In fact, the first thing she said to me when I rescued her from that whipping post was that she wouldn't be my whore. She doesn't trust men. She doesn't trust anyone.'

For a moment Crawford's eyes became distant as they always did when he was remembering his own time on the transport ship as a convict.

'She wouldn't have had it easy,' he agreed, his fingers drumming on the table. 'But already I can see she trusts *you*.'

'Exactly. She trusts me. I can't break that by doing the one thing she expected of me when we first met—taking advantage of her. She's had enough people treat her badly.'

'But you wouldn't be taking advantage of her,' Crawford said.

George ran a hand through his hair, then rubbed at the stubble on his face. 'I would. I'm her employer, she's my convict worker. It's not an equal relationship to start with.' He thought with a pang of nausea of his father and the inappropriate relationship with the convict girl that had destroyed both him and George's mother, in more ways than one. He didn't want history to repeat itself. Not that he could tell Crawford that. Both Robertson and Crawford thought George's father had been a saint and in many ways he *had* been kind and generous. But he hadn't been perfect. George wasn't about to wreck his friend's memories of the man who'd saved them from a life of drudgery, so the less moral of his father's actions he kept to himself.

'You think she would feel obliged to pretend feelings that weren't there.'

He thought of her fire, her feistiness, the way she'd stood up to him when they'd first met.

'No,' he said slowly. 'But I find myself not wanting to ruin her opinion of me. I want her to feel safe at Mountain View Farm, to have a refuge there for the next few years. If I push forward and make an advance which is unwelcome, it is hardly a safe haven for her.'

'But if you don't you risk losing the woman who could be the one for you.'

He thought of her smile, the way sometimes she fought it as if she didn't think she deserved to be happy. He thought of those brilliant blue eyes and the way the sun glinted off her red-gold hair. He thought of how she hugged her arms around herself when she was uncertain and how she'd strode into that muddy pond without a second's hesitation to rescue him.

'After what she's been through I doubt she wants any man to touch her again,' he said with a shake of his head.

Crawford took a long gulp of ale, placing the glass down on the table before speaking. 'You might look at her as I look at Frannie,' he said with a smile. 'But she looks at you like Frannie looks at me.'

George felt the pulse of his blood beat a little faster around his body. He'd noticed the long looks, the soft blushes that coloured her cheeks, the way she sometimes lingered when he touched her, but he hadn't let himself believe that they were all signs of her desire for him.

'Perhaps...' he said, wondering if soon he might be brushing her hair from her face and covering her lips with his own. It was a heady fantasy.

'Of course there's the obstacle of how she sees herself to overcome,' Crawford said, motioning for the landlord to bring them over another ale. 'Do you remember when Robertson and I were first taken in by your father?'

George nodded. They had been youths, worn down by the relentless grind of the manual labour and the cruelty they'd experienced from the guards and fellow convicts. They'd begun to believe they were worthless, that they didn't have futures, that they deserved to be punished. It had taken time for George's father to show them their worth, to make them believe in themselves again, and it would be the same for Alice.

'I would never have believed I could have the life I do now if you'd told me I would back then. I'd have laughed you from the room.'

'She doesn't see herself as anything more than a convict at the moment,' George agreed.

'The guards are very good at demoralising you.' He clapped George on the back. 'But what man doesn't like a challenge? Get your Alice to see she is still a woman, still a person worthy of love and affection, and everything else will fall into place.'

'What did I do without you for almost two years, Crawford?' George murmured.

'Probably lived your life with much less interference.' Crawford shrugged with a self-deprecating smile.

They drank their ales in silence for a few minutes while George contemplated his friend's advice. They were wise words, all true, and he felt a flicker of hope and anticipation inside him.

For a moment he wondered if his attraction to Alice was just a reaction to his friends both having paired off and found their soulmates. The last thing he wanted to do was force something that wasn't there because he felt lonely or left behind, but then he thought of Alice's smile, her quiet contemplation of the problems of the farm and how it felt as though the earth shifted beneath him whenever their bodies came into contact, and knew what he was feeling was very real.

'How are you finding Australia?' Francesca asked, linking her arm through Alice's as she spoke.

'It is different to back home,' she said politely, 'but I'm told everyone gets used to it.'

'And your new position?'

'Mr Fitzgerald has been very kind.'

'What about Mrs Peterson?' Francesca asked, lowering her voice conspiratorially.

Alice glanced sideways at the woman next to her. She didn't know what to make of the woman she knew had once been married to a viscount, but was chatting away to her as if they were long-lost friends.

'She can be a little bit of a dragon,' Francesca said with a smile. 'She loves the *boys* so much, but she still thinks they are exactly that: boys. I know she took a while to warm to both Georgina and myself, and we didn't have to live with her.'

'She's been kind,' Alice said slowly, wondering how much to reveal. The warmth and kindness coming from Francesca was enveloping her and it reminded her of chatting to her sisters back home. The memory was a comforting one. 'Although she is rather protective of Mr Fitzgerald.'

'I suppose she's even more fond of him,' Francesca said. 'Ben and Mr Robertson only arrived at the farm when they were young lads, but Mr Fitzgerald has been there his whole life.'

'It's nice he has someone who cares for him, seeing as his parents passed away a few years ago.'

Francesca nodded. 'That's very true. Although he is such a wonderful man that I doubt he will ever lack having people care about him.'

'Did you know him well?' Alice asked.

'Not well, not in London. But he was instrumental to me marrying my husband. He pushed for Ben to follow his heart even if society disapproved and to make me realise the same. And of course Ben talks about him all the time. They're very close, you know, as close as brothers.'

They walked along in silence for a couple of minutes. Alice felt herself relaxing a little. It was hard not to like Francesca. She was open and honest and had a ready smile on her face.

'I was sorry to hear about your treatment before Mr Fitzgerald took you in,' Francesca said softly.

Alice winced as she recalled the sting of the whip on her back and the feeling of her skin ripping open.

'You probably don't want to talk about it, or about anything else you've suffered,' she continued, squeezing Alice's arm, 'but if you do I've always got a friendly ear. And plenty of tea.'

'That's very kind,' Alice said, feeling a lump form in her throat. Almost three years she'd been surrounded by cruelty and hardship and now there were all these people looking out for her well-being.

'Ben, my husband, doesn't talk much about the convict ship or the first few years he spent building roads in Sydney, but sometimes I look at him and he's far away with a pained look upon his face...' she paused and dropped her voice even lower '...and it must be worse for a woman.'

Alice remembered the rough hands on her, the ripping of her clothes, the hot breath on her neck and grimaced.

'Well, the offer is there. And even if you don't want to talk you must pop by very soon. Mr Fitzgerald isn't working you too hard, I hope.'

'Not at all. In fact, I feel a little lazy. He has asked me to arrange things for the Christmas celebration, but aside from planning the menu with Mrs Peterson and searching the garden for the plants I will use to decorate the room, there really isn't much to be done.'

Francesca clapped her hands with delight. 'Oh,

I do love Christmas. Do you know we never really celebrated much when we were in England? But I understand it was an important time of year at Mountain View Farm when the boys were growing up. Ben loves Christmas and I have to admit some of his enthusiasm has been rubbing off on me.'

'Mrs Peterson told me they always used to celebrate together, Mr Fitzgerald and his friends.'

'Yes. Ben has been talking non-stop about finally being back at Mountain View Farm for Christmas. I hope Mr Fitzgerald wasn't planning on having a quiet celebration this year as Ben has already invited himself round in his mind.'

Alice smiled. It was lovely to hear of the affectionate way Francesca spoke of her husband and the bond between the three men Alice had glimpsed at herself.

'So what have you got planned?'

'We've got the dinner planned, down to every last detail, and a few days before will be decorating the drawing room with plants and flowers from the garden. I've ordered a large number of candles to light up the room as it gets dark and next week I'm going to venture up into the attic to find the music for some carols for the piano.'

Francesca clapped her hands with delight. 'I'm looking forward to it already. You must let me know if I can do anything to help.'

They were walking down a wide street towards the sea, Francesca's parasol shading them both from the sun, when Alice stopped abruptly.

In front of them the sea glistened a brilliant blue in the curve of the harbour, but this wasn't what had made Alice turn pale and stiffen. In the distance there was a ship, large and battered, bobbing on the gentle waves.

Alice knew it was too far away for her to smell the stink of the hundreds of unwashed bodies or hear the pitiful cries of the convicts who were seeing dry land for the first time in months, but she felt every bit of despair and relief all the same.

'I always wish I could do something to help,' Francesca murmured as she followed her gaze. There was nothing to be done, though. The convicts were under the control of the guards and would be closely guarded for the first few months. Only once it had been determined who could be trusted and who the troublemakers were would the better-behaved prisoners be allowed to take up positions in the town, with those with a trade often faring better than the unskilled convicts who were set to ship building or road digging.

'You there,' a voice called out, hostile and loud, making everyone turn to look.

Alice felt the blood drain from her face as she recognised the guard who had been responsible for the welts on her back. He'd been the one to catch her taking the extra piece of bread, the one to drag her to the whipping post and to wield the whip. Her wounds burned at the memory and for a moment she had the urge to run. It was a primal instinct, one to protect herself, even though she knew it would be futile. There were thousands of guards in Sydney, the town teemed with them. She wouldn't get further than a few paces without being seized.

Telling herself she hadn't done anything wrong, she straightened her back and raised her chin a notch. It helped, but only a little, and she felt herself cowering inside as the man approached.

'What do you want?' Francesca asked beside her, and for the first time Alice glimpsed the persona of the daughter of the nobility. Her tone was supercilious and her expression impatient.

Alice saw the guard hesitate for a moment as if not used to being challenged.

'And you are?' the guard asked, giving Francesca a leery look up and down.

'Mrs Crawford. What is your name and who is your supervisor?'

The guard stepped closer, as if thinking to intimidate them both with his proximity, and Alice couldn't believe the expression on her companion's face.

'I'll ask you to step back,' Francesca said, waving a hand in front of her nose. 'Your body odour is not something I wish to inhale.'

Alice watched as the guard's face reddened and he looked around quickly to see who might have overheard the insult.

'You're coming with me,' he said, gripping Alice's arm tightly. 'We have unfinished business.'

'Take your hands off me.' Alice's voice was loud and clear, surprising even herself. It felt as though a thousand butterflies were trying to burst out of her stomach and she could feel the minute tremor in her hands, but none of that was visible to the guard.

The guard paused, blinking a couple of times in surprise, then pulled at her arm again, hard enough to dislodge her from where Francesca was gripping the other arm tightly.

'You have no right to manhandle me,' Alice said, trying to keep her voice calm. The guard wasn't adhering to the rules and Alice needed to make him remember his duty. The guards here in Sydney might be a vindictive bunch, but they were kept in line by their commanders. They weren't allowed to be violent towards the prisoners unless it was a sanctioned punishment and mainly this rule was upheld. Alice knew in some prisons the guards had free rein to beat and humiliate the men and women they guarded, but it wasn't the case here. This man could get into trouble, perhaps even lose his job, if he were to drag her off with the intention of hurting her.

'There's no *gentleman* to save you now,' he said, spitting on the floor, his saliva only narrowly missing Alice's feet.

'I don't need anyone to save me,' she said, propelling her body forward and using the momentum to swing her fist around, catching the guard on his left cheek. Alice yelped as her knuckles struck bone, the pain travelling all the way up her arm to her shoulder. The guard yelled out, loosening his grip on her arm and allowing Alice to pull away. 'You have no right to touch me,' Alice said, taking a step back as she saw the anger flare in the guard's eyes.

'You'll pay for that,' the man said quietly and Alice felt the first slither of dread bite into her stomach. He looked beyond angry.

Alice continued to back away, only to find herself backing into the wall. The guard loomed over her, reaching out and taking her by the wrist, holding her so tightly she felt the blood pulse against his fingers.

'This time I'll whip you until you've no skin left,' he murmured into her ear.

'Take your hands off her.' Mr Fitzgerald's commandeering voice came from a little way away.

Alice felt the relief flood through her, then pulled herself up. She couldn't rely on Mr Fitzgerald to save her every time she got into a fix. One day he wouldn't be there any more and she'd be all alone in this country. Then she would have to fend for herself. Still, that was not today, and for now she was just grateful he wasn't being dragged back to the whipping post.

'I'll have you reported,' Mr Fitzgerald said calmly. 'Now if you value your health I would step away from the ladies and get out of my sight.'

'She's no lady.' The guard laughed, but there was a nervous edge to it now as if he knew he'd overstepped.

Alice watched as Mr Fitzgerald took a couple of steps towards the man, stopping only when they were within touching distance. He was calm, but there was an iciness about him that she hadn't seen before.

'You have no idea what she is,' he said, shaking his head in disgust at the guard.

The guard looked as though he would say something more, but then glanced up at Mr Fitzgerald's figure towering above him and turned and hurried off, looking back over his shoulder to check he wasn't being pursued.

'What a horrible man,' Francesca said.

Alice couldn't speak. Her heart was thumping inside her chest and her legs felt as though they might give way any moment.

'He's gone,' Mr Fitzgerald said quietly, moving to her side. He looped an arm around her waist just as Alice's legs buckled.

'I'm sorry,' she said, wishing she wasn't so weak. The man had scared her more than she liked to admit. It was a reminder of what her life could look like right now if Mr Fitzgerald hadn't stepped up and given her a home at Mountain View Farm a few weeks earlier.

'Don't apologise,' he said and his voice had a hard edge to it. 'Never apologise. You have nothing to be sorry for.'

Alice looked up into his eyes and felt the warmth she saw there spread through her.

'Thank you,' she said quietly.

For a few seconds the rest of the world seemed to fade away as if they were the only two there. The sounds and smells of the town became muffled and fainter and all Alice could think of was the man in front of her. She tilted her head up, her lips opening just a little, and wished more than anything else in the world that he would kiss her.

'We'll take our leave,' Mr Crawford said from somewhere behind them. It was enough to break the spell, even though the Crawfords were subtly backing away.

'We'll see you at Robertson's dinner,' Mr Fitzgerald said, waving to his friends. They waited until the Crawfords had left, then Mr Fitzgerald looked back down at her.

'Come,' he said, offering her his arm. 'Let us get this wretched paperwork completed, find the items Mrs Peterson requested, then we can get out of Sydney and go back home.'

Alice nodded, her head still spinning from the intensity of the feelings of just a moment before. She wished she'd been brave enough to rise up on her toes and kiss him, no matter who might have been looking.

Chapter Fifteen

It was getting dark and already the temperature was dropping as the sun dipped over the horizon. They should have found somewhere to stay in Sydney, but after Alice's encounter with the guard earlier in the afternoon George had a strong urge to get her home.

He felt her shift closer to him as she shivered and reached into the back of the cart to find one of the blankets he kept there for exactly this eventuality.

'Here,' he said, passing two woollen blankets to her. 'Put one round your shoulders and the other across your knees. It'll keep you a little warmer at least.'

Alice wrapped herself in the first blanket and then spread the second across her lap, reaching over so it covered his knees as well. As she straightened the blanket out her hand brushed against his thigh and out of the corner of his eye he saw her hesitate before continuing on with the movement.

'I'm glad everything is official,' she said. 'I was worried they might have changed their minds and wanted me to be punished further.'

'You thought they wouldn't allow you to come to me as a convict worker?'

Alice nodded. 'I know it was unlikely, but I was worried they might refuse, say I had to be taken to one of the factories.'

'I wouldn't have let that happen.'

'Even you can't go up against the whole establishment.'

'I would…' he paused, looking down at her '…for you.' Crawford's words were swirling round in his head and George knew soon he would have to decide how he felt about Alice and perhaps, more importantly, what he was going to do about it.

He watched as she bit her lip, worrying the delicate skin, before looking up at him.

Gently he pulled on the reins, waiting for the cart to come to a stop before turning his body so he was angled towards her a little. While all the things he wanted to say ran through his mind he busied himself adjusting the blanket on her shoulders.

'Alice,' he said softly. Even in the moonlight he could see the beautiful blue of her eyes, although they looked inkier in the darkness.

'Yes, Mr Fitzgerald?' she said when he didn't continue.

'Please, call me George,' he said, hating the reminder of the chasm that stood between them.

'George,' she whispered.

She was looking up at him with affection in her eyes, affection and something else, something hotter and more primal. He knew he *had* to touch her and lifted his fingers, running them softly down her cheek.

There was something pulling him to her, something that he couldn't deny any longer.

Softly he kissed her, feeling the instant response of her lips, the softness, the heat. She looped her hands behind his neck, pulling him closer to her, and George felt as though something had been unleashed inside him. Something he'd been holding back for a very long time.

He tangled his hands in her silky hair, wanting to make this moment last for ever. Everything about Alice was drawing him in, bewitching him further. For a second he pulled away, peppering kisses down the line of her jaw and on to her neck, loving the gasp that came from her lips as he teased the soft skin. He was at risk of being swept away and he wanted to check Alice was completely on board with what they were doing.

'Don't stop,' she murmured, the words lighting a fire inside him.

He captured her lips again with his, kissing her until he thought he might forget his own name. Somehow Alice had slipped on to his lap and was pressed tight against his chest, her hair falling down over his neck as he pulled her even closer to him.

'Alice,' he murmured, running a hand down the length of her back. 'You don't know what you do to me.'

She pulled away slightly and in the moonlight he saw her give him an uncertain smile.

'What I do to you?' she said with a laugh, shaking her head and kissing him again.

Through her back he could feel her heart pounding in her chest, her skin warming under his touch. He knew he had to stop, had to put some distance between them before he found himself laying her down in the back of the old cart out under the Australian sky. That wouldn't be fair to Alice, no matter how much they both might want it.

'We should go home,' he said, trying to control his desire. If her response to his kiss was anything to go by, there would be plenty more opportunity to enjoy one another.

She nodded, slipping off his lap and on to the seat beside him. George waited until she had covered herself with the blankets again before picking up the reins and urging the horse forward.

'Alice,' he said quietly after a few minutes of silence, 'You did want to…?'

There was fire in her eyes as she turned to him.

'How can you doubt it?' she asked.

He thought back to the scared and defiant woman of a few weeks ago, the one that had kicked up a fuss because there wasn't a lock on her bedroom door. Back then he would never have imagined they would be like this with each other, that she would warm to him quite so much or he would feel so much more than the purely protective instinct that had ben there at the start.

As the cart trundled through the night Alice

rested her head on his shoulder, her breathing deep and even, and George felt more contented than he had for a long time. Thoughts of the future, infinite possibilities, began streaming through his mind and he had to remind himself nothing was certain. It had only been a kiss.

They were almost home, at most another half an hour to go and George could feel Alice growing heavy on his shoulder. Her breathing had become deep and regular so he carefully slipped an arm around her waist to ensure she didn't slip from the cart. As he did so he looked away from the road for a second. When he looked back he almost jumped in his seat. There was a man in front of them, staggering on to the dirt track, holding up something metallic that glinted in the moonlight.

'Stop,' he shouted, his voice ragged. 'Stop or I'll shoot.'

George pulled on the reins of the cart, slowing the horse down, but making sure not to spook it unnecessarily. As he drew closer he could see the man was in a dishevelled state, his clothes filthy and ripped and his face covered with dust. Even in the moonlight George could see the man's lips were cracked and bleeding and from the sound of his hoarse voice he hadn't had anything to drink for days.

'Here,' George said, throwing down a full waterskin. The liquid would no longer be cool, but the man in front of them didn't look as though he would be fussy.

Alice stirred, lifting her head off his shoulders. Her eyes widened as she saw the man in front of them, holding out what he'd professed to be a gun.

The dishevelled man looked at the waterskin suspiciously before his thirst got the better of him and he picked it up, taking great gulps of the water.

'Not so fast,' Alice said, her voice calm. 'It'll make you sick.' She'd spotted what he had: the 'pistol' was nothing more than a polished metal rod, the same size as the barrel of a pistol, but much less deadly.

The man was most likely a runaway convict. There were a couple a month who decided to take their chances in the wilderness rather than serve the remainder of their sentence doing hard labour. Most were foolish, unrealistic in their expectations. The Australian countryside could be dangerous, especially if you didn't know the terrain. The wild animals weren't used to people in the most part, especially the further you travelled from Sydney, and he'd heard of more than one escaped convict who'd perished before they'd been recaptured.

Most were recaptured. The guards seemed to take it as a personal affront when one of the convicts escaped and no effort was spared in scouring the countryside. After a week, perhaps two, the convicts were usually found much more emaciated and weary from their attempt at freedom.

'Where have you come from?' Alice asked, her voice light as if she were making small talk to an acquaintance in the park.

The convict looked up at her, as if deciding whether to answer the question, his legs buckling at the knees for an instant before he regained his balance.

'The barracks,' he said eventually.

George could picture the huge stone building that housed many of the male convicts at least for the first few years of their sentence. They were locked up there overnight, only being allowed out to go to whatever job they were assigned to during the day. Despite its decorative arches and imposing architecture, the barracks were nothing more than a prison really, a place to keep the convicts under lock and key.

'What work were you assigned?' Alice asked.

'Stone yard.'

From the man's appearance you wouldn't believe he worked twelve hours a day breaking down rocks into smaller pieces. His physique wasn't suited to the job and George could see why day after day of the monotonous, back-breaking work might get to be too much for the man.

'How long have you been out here?' Alice asked.

'Four days.'

It wasn't all that long, but with the drought no doubt the man had struggled to find any water.

'And what do you plan to do now?' George asked.

He had an urge to help the man, even though it would be against the law. To help an escaped convict carried a penalty of its own.

There was desperation in the man's eyes as he looked up at them. 'You'll give me your cart,' he said, 'and any money you have.' He brandished the metal rod at them, but George could see his heart wasn't in it.

'You could give yourself up,' George said as gently as he could muster. It wasn't an appealing option for the convict. At best he'd be whipped, at worst his sentence might be extended or he could be sent to one of the less civilised colonies to serve out the remainder of his time.

'No,' the man said sharply, taking a step towards them.

Beside him George felt Alice stiffen for the first time, her hand clutching his. He would do well to remember the runaway convict was a desperate man and desperate men could be the most dangerous of all.

Quickly George slipped from the cart, putting himself in between the convict and Alice. The man stopped instantly, looking George up and down, then seemed to decide against advancing any further.

'We can take you back to Sydney,' George said, trying to keep his voice reassuring and even.

'No.'

For an instant he thought the convict might lunge for him, try to grab the reins of the cart and make his escape, but instead he looked at

George forlornly, turned and loped off into the night.

A minute passed and then another. When he was sure the man wasn't coming back George hopped back up to his seat beside Alice.

'Poor man,' she murmured.

'It's horrible seeing someone so desperate.'

They rode in in silence for a few minutes, George keeping vigilant in case the convict decided to return, but there was nothing but the open road ahead of them.

'You look troubled,' Alice said.

'He could die out there tonight,' George said eventually.

Alice shifted on the seat beside him, slipping her hand into his free one and giving it a squeeze.

'You can't save the whole world,' she said. 'It was his choice to run away. Just like it was my choice to steal that bread that led to my whipping.'

'But the punishments don't fit the crimes. How desperate must he have been, how completely unhappy, to risk everything by venturing into the unknown.'

Alice nodded silently. 'The stone yard is a grim place to be assigned,' she said quietly. 'Hour upon hour of cracking rocks in the sweltering heat of the sun. I know some men can't stand it.' She looked at him, waiting for him to lift his eyes to meet hers before continuing. 'You saved me, though,' she said quietly, 'and I'll always be grateful for that.'

George felt a crackle of guilt flare inside him and creep from his centre until it was almost consuming him. She was *grateful*. Grateful that he'd saved her. Grateful that he'd given her a chance to change her life. That wasn't what a relationship should be built on.

Glancing sideways, he took in her serene smile and wished he could work out exactly what she thought of him.

Chapter Sixteen

Alice paced nervously backward and forward across the length of her small room. It only took her ten steps, small ones at that, to go from one wall to the other, but she couldn't seem to stop herself.

He'd kissed her. Mr Fitzgerald—no, George, she corrected herself—had taken her in his arms and kissed her. Alice felt her heart soaring and knew there was a huge smile on her lips. Even though everything was complicated she couldn't help but be happy.

Glancing at the door handle, she steeled herself to venture out of her room. She needed to face George, needed to see how he would be with her, to see how things had changed. He wasn't the sort of man to just kiss a woman and then pretend nothing had happened, but last night he'd just given her hand a little squeeze as he'd helped her down from the cart, aware of the Petersons bustling around unpacking everything.

'Courage,' she whispered to herself. Today she would tell George about Bill. She would confess that she was married, or at least had been when she'd sailed from England. Alice wasn't sure how he would take it, what his reaction would be. She hoped if she explained that Bill most certainly no longer possessed her heart and hadn't done so for a very long time he might understand, that he might at least give her a chance to show him what they could have together.

What could we have together? All night she'd lain awake trying not to let her hopes and dream spiral out of control. George was a good man, a man she would be lucky to have any sort of relationship with, but they couldn't ignore their differences in circumstance. And Alice knew that however much she liked him, however much she felt the warm stirrings of desire when he looked at her, she didn't want some short fling. She wanted so much more.

With a deep breath to settle her nerves she opened the door and marched out into the hall, deflating a little as she began to search through the house, only to find it completely deserted.

'You look like a woman with a purpose,' George said as he came in through the kitchen door, wiping his hands on a cloth. It looked as though he'd been tinkering with some machinery as the skin of his hands held a hint of the oil and there were a couple of splatters on his shirt.

Everything Alice had been determined to say flew from her head as he smiled at her. It was a smile filled with warmth, but she could see a hint of hesitation there, as if he were holding himself back.

'Ah, you're up, Alice.' Mrs Peterson's voice. 'I hope you're not too tired. Mr Fitzgerald always comes back far too late from Sydney. I've told him time and time again it's not safe, not in these modern times.'

Alice glanced at George and saw him shake his head almost imperceptibly. They both had kept quiet about the escaped convict they'd encountered the night before. The man might have threatened them, but he'd been desperate and neither of them wanted anything to do with his recapture and subsequent punishment.

'I feel well, thank you, Mrs Peterson.'

'Good. We've got a busy day today. I'm just going to add some more brandy to the Christmas cake and then we need to get started on the jams. And we can put that nutmeg you bought yesterday to good use, too.'

Glad of the distraction, Alice began pushing up her sleeves, but before she could start gathering the bowls they would need for the jam George stepped forward.

'I just need to borrow Alice for few minutes,' he said lightly. 'I'll have her back to you shortly.'

Mrs Peterson frowned and Alice had to laugh at the older woman's expression. Although she was eager to keep the divide between master and servants, Mrs Peterson wasn't afraid of telling her employer what she thought.

'You can come instead if you want,' George said with a shrug. 'It's just I know you aren't keen on gardening...'

'Go on, then,' Mrs Peterson said to Alice, 'but no dallying. We've got a full day ahead of us and I'll need all the help I can get.'

With a pounding heart Alice followed George outside, wondering if he did really need help with the gardening or if it was just a ploy to get her alone.

'Come here, you little rascal,' George said, sweeping the baby kangaroo up into his arms

to avoid stepping on him. They'd named him
Lucky and already the little animal was thriving
on the milk and love he was receiving. He carried him through the gate into the little garden
at the side of the house, setting him down in the
shade to have a little explore.

Alice followed them into the garden, closing
the gate behind her. For a moment she watched
as George stroked the baby kangaroo, then felt
her breath quicken as he rose and faced her.

'Good morning, Alice,' he said, taking a step
towards her. In the sunlight his eyes sparkled
and his skin seemed to glow with a golden tan.
She had the urge to throw herself into his arms,
then remembered the reservation she'd seen in
his eyes when they were in the kitchen and instead hugged her arms around herself.

George stepped closer, one hand rising up
slowly to rest on her waist. It was an intimate
gesture and as his hand came in contact with the
material of her dress Alice felt her hopes soaring again. She swayed towards him, tilting up
her chin, seeing his smile before their lips came
together and she was lost in the kiss. This morning he was gentle, kissing her softly, cupping her

face, running his hands softly down the length of her back, but there was no mistaking his desire.

'I dreamed about you,' he said as he pulled away.

'Oh?'

He grimaced. 'It was a good dream. A very good dream. Perhaps too good.'

She felt the smile forming on her lips and some of the tension leaving her body. He hadn't changed his mind, hadn't realised what a mistake this would be in the light of day.

'Come here,' he said, taking her hand. 'Out of view of the house. I have something I want to talk to you about.'

He led her down the winding path through the garden to the little shed he kept at the end. She hadn't been inside before, the garden being very much his private domain, but she knew he kept seeds for growing in there and clippings of plants he'd collected.

For a moment he disappeared inside, then re-emerged with a few pots and thin wooden stakes in his hands.

'Do you mind if we work while we talk?' he asked, 'I've always found it easier.'

Shaking her head, Alice knelt down next to

him and watched as he began filling the pots with soil. She waited until she was sure of what he was doing and then began to fill one of her own. The soil was dry and crumbly, another reminder of the last of rain these past few months.

'I need to know something, Alice, and I need you to be completely honest with me,' he said as he patted down the soft soil.

'I promise.'

'I know you feel grateful to me, for saving you from the whipping post and giving you a job here,' he said slowly and Alice realised the direction his mind was travelling.

'No,' she said sharply.

'No?'

'I know what you're going to say and the answer is no. No, I didn't kiss you out of gratitude. I kissed you because I wanted to. I *want* to.'

He glanced up then, as if wanting to assess the truth of her words.

'I know things are not equal between us, Alice...'

'No. They are not. But I'm not the sort of woman who thinks I need to repay a debt of gratitude with intimacy.' Alice spoke firmly—it was a subject she was passionate about. All throughout the voyage on the transport ship and during those first few months in Australia she'd seen women giving themselves away just because a man had done something for them. As if it were some sort of payment. She'd hated witnessing it, hated seeing other women value themselves so low.

George began pressing tiny little seeds into the soil, passing her a handful to do the same.

'I don't know what *this* is between us,' Alice said more softly, 'but please believe that I want it. If we were two people, two free people of the same circumstance, I would still want it. It's not your status or your wealth that I see, it's *you*. Your kindness, your warmth, your...' She trailed off, blushing as she realised what she was about to say out loud.

He looked up at her, a smile creeping on to his lips. 'I want you, too,' he leaned in and whispered. Alice felt a heat rise up from the core of her body and saw the same desire reflected in his eyes.

'I think I need to explain,' he said after a few seconds. Carefully he covered the little seeds over with soil and rose to get some water. Alice waited for him to return and give the newly planted seedlings some water, seeing he was trying to put into words what he was thinking.

Only once the seeds were tended to did he rise, taking her hand and leading her over to a bench near the shed. From here they had a beautiful view of the garden, the flowers blooming and the trees a verdant green, and beyond the rolling hills of the countryside spread.

'I haven't ever told you much about my parents,' he said eventually.

'You said they came to Australia, dreaming of building a better life.'

'They did. My father was the youngest son of a destitute baron. He had no land, no money and no real prospects, but when he married my mother he promised her the world. They emigrated here soon after they were married and bought the land and built the farmhouse just as I was born.'

Alice thought for a moment of her own parents, their smiling faces and warm hearts, and felt a pang of homesickness but pushed it away. Whatever George wanted to tell her had been playing on his mind so she was determined to focus.

'They always seemed like the perfect partnership,' George said, looking out into the distance as if remembering the good times. 'My father was a strong man, with strong beliefs, and my mother always quietly got on and *did* things. She wasn't one to sit back and keep to what others might have viewed as her place.'

Gently she slipped her hand into his, giving him an encouraging squeeze.

'I always thought my father was a saint. He was so *good*. So kind. So generous. He was always talking about making a difference in the world, about helping those more in need than ourselves...' He trailed off and shook his head. 'He was a good man, he did care about those things, but of course no one is perfect.'

Alice felt the weight of George's disappointment and wondered what had made him realise his father was only human, only a man, and a man who made mistakes like everyone else.

'When I was fifteen we had a young convict worker girl come and work in the house. My father had taken Robertson and Crawford in by then and our family had almost doubled in size. We needed a little more help and my father said this would be the answer, while saving one convict from the factories at the same time.' George paused, looking out over the garden to the countryside beyond.

'She was young, no more than eighteen, and shy and willing to do whatever was asked of her. Her name was Mary and she worked hard, but other than that I can't say I noticed her very much.'

'What happened?' Alice asked.

'One night I couldn't sleep and I went downstairs. I caught my father being intimate with her.' He shook his head as if the memory was too much and he wanted to banish it completely from his mind. 'He wasn't forcing himself on her,' he said slowly, 'but I could see by the look in her eyes that she wasn't particularly enjoying it. That she felt obliged.'

It was an awful thing to learn about his father, especially of a man he'd looked up to so much.

'I'm sorry,' Alice said quietly. His fierce protection of her made sense now and his hesitancy in pursuing anything even when he clearly desired her.

'He saw me,' George continued, his voice hollow, 'and the next day he came to me and begged me not to tell my mother.'

'Did you?'

Slowly he shook his head. 'For weeks I couldn't make up my mind, couldn't decide if telling her would be selfish, to share the knowledge and unburden myself, or if she had a right to know. In the end I told myself I was protecting her, told myself the right thing to do was keep my father's dirty little secret.' The pain in his eyes told Alice that he now thought it had been the wrong decision.

'Did she find out?'

'Eventually. Father got rid of Mary almost immediately and I know Mother was suspicious of whatever explanation he'd cooked up, but she didn't know for sure until many years later...' he paused, looking out into the distance '...not until she was told by the doctors her health problems were caused by advanced syphilis. Syphilis my father had caught from Mary and later passed on to my mother.'

Alice's hand flew to her mouth in shock.

'That's terrible.'

George grimaced. 'I'm told it is more common than you would think. The silent killer. A disease that slowly ravages your organs until something fails. With my mother it was her heart.'

'And your father?'

'I'm not really sure what killed him. He died suddenly, only a few months after my mother. He had ulcers, which I'm told are common in people with the disease, and he'd started coughing up blood, but I don't know what killed him.' He ran a hand through his hair, letting out a low sigh. 'He was still my father, I still loved him, still looked up to him, but after that day I caught him with Mary it was as though a spell had been broken. He was no longer perfect, no longer my idol.'

'Many young boys would have hated their fathers after catching them like that.'

'For a while I thought I did hate him. But as time passed I realised it was disappointment rather than hatred. I had thought of him as infallible and that belief had been smashed into tiny pieces.'

'You friends don't know, do they?' Alice asked, picturing Crawford and Robertson's awe-struck and admiring faces whenever Mr Fitzgerald senior was mentioned.

'No. They needed a hero. Someone to believe in. To them he was still perfect, the man who had rescued them. I wasn't going to be the one to take that away from them.'

Alice smiled up at him, feeling the warmth radiating off him. 'Sometimes I wonder if you're too good to be true,' she murmured.

He turned to her, the sun glinting off his hair and making it look golden, and Alice found herself swaying towards him. The pull she felt was irresistible, the attraction overwhelming. She knew she should stop herself, should take this opportunity to tell him about Bill, to make sure there were no secrets between them. George had just let her glimpse into the most intimate and painful moments of his life, now was her chance to do the same.

Alice opened her mouth, but the words wouldn't come. She felt a panic rising up inside her. What if he heard about her past and decided it was too complicated? What if it highlighted the huge gulf between them, made him see that they weren't supposed to be together?

She knew she should say something, that he'd just told her he hated secretes, but still she couldn't bring herself to make a sound.

'You know everything about me now, Alice,' he murmured, reaching up to run a finger down the length of her cheek, dipping behind her ear and caressing the soft skin of her neck.

Alice felt her tongue stick to the roof of her mouth and her throat go dry. She *needed* to say something, to confess her marriage, the foolishness of her youth.

Before she could summon up the courage Alice saw the spark of desire in George's eyes and felt every rational thought leave her. As his lips met hers the regret and uncertainty left her and she was swept away by the warmth of his kiss.

Chapter Seventeen

Whistling, George looped his cravat around his neck and tied a loose knot. He didn't have a valet like most men of his wealth and status would back in England, preferring to dress himself, but that did mean some of the intricacies of formal dress looked a little haphazard when he attempted them. Still, it was only Robertson and Crawford and their wives, no one would mind if his cravat looked as though it had been tied by a heavy-handed child.

There was a hesitant knock on the door and George glanced over. Mrs Peterson wouldn't knock like that, hers was a firm rap, which meant one thing only. Alice was standing outside his door.

He glanced at the bed, the setting for many of the vivid dreams he'd had featuring Alice in the past few weeks: Alice in various states of undress, Alice looking at him with inviting eyes as she lounged back on the pillows. Alice underneath him, Alice on top of him…

The knock came again and George was jolted back to the present.

'Come in,' he called, perhaps a little too tersely, but he was busy trying to rid his mind of the vivid images that were far too distracting.

The door opened slowly, hesitantly, to reveal Alice standing looking beautiful in a deep blue dress. It complemented her colouring, the blue making the red-gold of her hair seem even more vibrant than usual.

'Alice,' he said, unable to stop himself from taking a couple of steps towards her. 'You look ravishing.'

She glanced down, using her hands to smooth the silky material of the full skirt, a delicate blush rising in her cheeks.

'It's the most beautiful thing I've ever worn,' she said, biting her lip. 'It doesn't feel right.'

The dress had apparently been his mother's, not that he could ever remember her wearing anything so fine. They had found it packed away in a box in the attic while searching for the music sheets for the Christmas songs. Alice's eyes had widened as her fingers had caressed the fine stitching and the luxurious material and she'd shaken her head in protest when he'd suggested she wear it for the evening they were about to spend with Crawford and Robertson.

'Who else is going to wear it?' George asked.

Her eyes flew up to meet his and she opened her mouth, closing it abruptly almost immediately as if trying to keep the words inside. Unspoken they still hung between them. *Your wife.* That was who should be slipping into the beautiful blue dress. But he didn't want a wife, at least not one of the daughters from the other wealthy farming families. He wanted Alice.

Taking a step closer to her, he reached out and took her hand, lacing his fingers through hers.

'Alice,' he said, feeling something catch in his chest as she raised her eyes to meet his. They were still sparkling, still the same brilliant blue, but there was a shadow in them as if she was worrying about something. 'There is no one else in the world I want to see wearing that dress.'

'It doesn't feel right.'

'It is a gift. I'm giving it to you.' He shook his head as she opened her mouth to protest. 'No arguments. I would much rather you got to enjoy it than it sits up in the attic gathering dust for years.'

'Does it make me look too pretentious?' Alice asked.

He laughed—she was the least pretentious person he'd ever met.

'No. It makes you look beautiful.'

George was having a hard time keeping his eyes still. They wanted to roam over her figure, to take in the swell of her breasts, the curve of her waist, to imagine the slender legs under the swathes of material. She looked beautiful in the dress, but he had the sudden urge to want to get her out of it, to strip her completely naked and spend the evening showing his appreciation of every inch of her skin.

'I don't want your friends to think I have ideas above my station.'

'Alice,' he said, cupping her cheek, 'stop worrying. They won't think anything of the sort.'

Although her worries were completely unfounded he found it endearing that she cared so much what his friends thought of her. He realised he did, too. He wanted them to like her, wanted them to see what he did.

'I didn't know whether to put up my hair,' she said, twisting a strand around her fingers.

'Don't,' he said quickly. Although it was convention for a woman to wear her hair neatly done up on her head he loved how Alice's fell down her back. Every time he saw the soft waves of red-gold it made him smile and he didn't want her to tuck it away even for a dinner party. 'Stop worrying,' he said, leaning forward and placing a gentle kiss on the furrow between her eyebrows. As he pulled away he saw a flash of movement out of the corner of his eye. He turned, but there was no one there.

'Did you see something?' Alice asked, looking over her shoulder.

'No, at least I don't think so.' Not that it mattered really. The only people in the house were the Petersons and although Mrs Peterson might have a few choice words to say if she saw him kissing Alice it didn't much matter. He was her employer and, more than that, she cared for him as though he were a son. She might tell him she thought he was being unwise, but she couldn't do much else.

Unwise, the word stuck in his head. Was he being unwise? Every day he spent with Alice he discovered something new about her that made him like her even more. Every day she gained a little more confidence and her smile shone a little brighter. At the moment he was trying not to get ahead of himself, trying to just enjoy each and every day, but the inevitable thoughts about the future would assail him every now and then. And right now he couldn't really imagine a future without Alice in it.

'I've got something for you,' he said, stepping away and crossing to his desk. There was a little parcel in the top drawer, something he'd been saving for this occasion. He'd bought it when they'd gone to Sydney, slipping away for a few minutes after it had caught his eye in a shop window.

He passed her the package, watching as her fingers deftly untied the ribbon.

'You shouldn't buy me gifts,' she said, something catching in her voice.

'Why not?'

She shook her head and he glimpsed the scared, undervalued young woman she had once been. He cursed the man who had done this to her, who had taken her goodness and vibrancy and worn her down so she expected to be treated so poorly.

George wondered when the last time was she'd received a present. He would wager it wasn't for a good few years.

Alice's face lit up as she opened the box and her eyes fell on the dainty necklace. It had a silver chain, thin and snaking, with a tear-shaped pendant on the end. The pendant was made out of amber, the stone a smoky orange colour, perfect in its imperfection.

'It's beautiful,' she said, running her fingers over the smooth stone.

George reached in and took the necklace from the box, motioning for Alice to turn around so he could loop the chain around her neck. Once the pendant was securely fastened he moved around to face her, giving his nod of approval.

'See if you like it.'

She moved to the mirror, a smile on her lips as she admired the necklace. It sat perfectly at the base of her throat, glinting in the sunlight that poured through the windows.

'It's lovely,' she said, biting her lips again, 'but I can't accept it.'

Raising her hands to the clasp at the back of her neck, she began to run the chain through her fingers as if trying to take it off. George placed his hand over hers, stopping the movement.

'Why not?' he asked, coming in close so his voice was barely more than a whisper.

'I…' she said, hesitating as she tried to put into words why she felt quite so unworthy. 'It wouldn't be right. I don't deserve it. You shouldn't buy me gifts.'

Gently he spun her to face him, kicking the door to his bedroom shut at the same time. This conversation needed privacy.

'Alice, do you doubt I'm a level-headed man, a man who knows his own mind?'

She shook her head, her breathing quickening as he stepped closer.

'Do you doubt my ability to make my own decisions?'

Again she shook her head.

'I *choose* to give you this gift. I believe you do deserve it, and I want you to have it.'

'But…'

He smiled then, loving how she still managed to protest even in the face of the strongest argument.

'Alice, if you don't stop protesting I'm going to have to kiss you to shut you up.'

'But…'

He grinned, swooping down and kissing her, feeling his body respond to the velvet softness of her lips. He wrapped an arm around her waist, pulling her to him, desire mixing with happiness, and she sighed and sank into him.

'We should go,' he said reluctantly as he pulled away. Taking a step back, he put some distance between them—another minute and he would have tumbled Alice on to the bed. He wanted nothing more than to lie down on the bed with her and spend the entire night getting to know her intimately, but he knew it was too soon. Perhaps one day…but not today, however much he wanted it.

Alice felt the tension seep back into her body as they neared the Robertsons' farm. Although she had met Mr Robertson and Mr Crawford, as well as Mrs Crawford when they had taken the trip into Sydney, she hadn't yet met Mrs Robertson. Although George reassured her that Mrs Robertson was friendly and kind Alice knew the woman had been the daughter of an earl and while living in London had been known by the title Lady Georgina. She seemed so far above

Alice's station it was daunting, even if George said she was not what you would expect from a daughter of the nobility.

'Horsey,' was the shout from a young boy as he came speeding from the house, his little legs carrying him much faster than Alice would have believed possible.

'James,' Mr Robertson bellowed as he came running out of the front door at speed, too. The little boy took no notice of his father, too intent on reaching the horse he'd spied.

George reined in Kareela, who had good naturedly allowed himself to be harnessed to the cart despite normally being reserved for riding.

'Horsey,' James repeated, coming to a stop by Kareela's hooves.

Mr Robertson caught up with him, scooping the young boy into his arms.

'Never known a child move so fast,' he said, breathing heavily as he shook his head. 'You'd think he would be fed up of horses.'

Alice knew Mr Robertson owned the largest stud in Australia and was almost single-handedly responsible for providing the settlers and military alike with their mounts.

'He's like you,' George said, leaping down

from the cart. 'I can't imagine you ever getting fed up of horses.'

'True,' Mr Robertson murmured, stroking Kareela's nose, allowing his son to reach out and mimic his actions.

'He can't be your son,' George said, shaking his head in disbelief. 'Far too handsome.'

'Thankfully the boy takes after his mother,' Robertson said with a grin, although Alice could see the resemblance between father and son.

'Good evening Miss Alice, welcome to Low Wealden Farm.'

Alice hitched up her skirts and hopped down from the cart, smiling uncertainly. From behind him a beautiful young woman emerged with a sunny smile on her face. She was heavily pregnant, her gait elegant still, but Alice could see the effort it must have taken for Mrs Robertson to cross the short distance towards them.

'Mr Fitzgerald,' she said warmly, taking his hand. 'I can't tell you how happy I am that you've come home.' Her eyes sparkled as she spoke and Alice could see the warmth in her expression. Her voice was soft and refined, exactly how Alice had always imagined a lady would sound.

'Sam talks of you so much I feel as though I know every part of your life.'

'May I introduce Miss Alice Fillips,' he said, taking Alice's arm and guiding her forward.

'I'm delighted to meet you, Miss Fillips,' Mrs Robertson said, linking her arm through Alice's just as Mrs Crawford had a few days earlier during their walk through the streets of Sydney. 'Come inside out of this heat, I've got some lovely cool lemonade to take away the taste of the dusty road.

The Robertsons' house was wood-clad and pretty. It was a fair bit smaller than the Mountain View farmhouse, but the rooms were well proportioned and beautifully decorated. Everywhere there were little reminders of the Robertsons' son James: abandoned toys, a little jacket hanging over the banister, a framed portrait on the wall. There was no doubt that he played a central role in family life.

'You have a very beautiful home,' Alice said as she looked around her.

'Thank you. You wouldn't believe the state of the place when I first arrived here a couple of years ago.' She looked teasingly at her husband. 'There wasn't a single picture on the wall, there was only one usable chair and the windows were so thick with grime you could barely see out.'

'I didn't spend any time indoors,' Mr Robertson said with a shrug.

'I half-expected to see a horse strolling out of a bathroom,' she said in an exaggerated whisper.

'It was never *that* bad,' Mr Robertson protested.

Mrs Robertson arched an eyebrow and for the first time Alice could picture her commanding the attention of every eligible bachelor in a crowded ballroom.

'It was *that* bad,' Mrs Robertson murmured to Alice.

They made their way through to a pretty drawing room, the late-evening sunlight reflecting off the bright wallpaper and giving the room a warm glow. On a low table there were three abandoned oranges and a pile of cloves, bright ribbon waiting to be tied around the pomanders when they were finished. This must have been what young James had been doing before he'd been distracted by the arrival of the horse. The scent of the cloves took Alice back to Christmas at home, sitting at the kitchen table with her sisters meticulously decorating their own oranges.

As Alice perched on the edge of a comfortable sofa she felt a warm contentment settle inside her. Despite all her worries and misgivings these were good people. People she could be comfortable around.

As soon as she'd had the thought she stiffened. It wouldn't do for her to get too comfortable here. She needed to remember her place. These were George's friends, his equals, and when she shattered the trust he'd placed in her by revealing she might still be married they would gather round him and shut her out.

Misreading the expression on her face, George gave her hand a surreptitious squeeze while the Robertsons were distracted by their son barrelling into the room. Alice felt the tears pricking in her eyes, wishing she'd had the courage to tell him earlier, wishing that Bill wasn't still such a dark shadow in her life.

Chapter Eighteen

George leaned back in his chair and grinned. It was the perfect evening. He was surrounded by the people he loved the most, the food was fantastic and the wine was flowing. The years he'd spent in England and voyaging home without his friends had been wonderful, but he'd missed their joking and their camaraderie. And he was pleased that his two closest friends hadn't changed despite getting married and starting families in the time he'd been away.

'Has he told you of the time he fell down the well near Rabbit's Corner?' Robertson asked, addressing his question to Alice. His two friends were having a great time retelling all their youthful exploits to a new pair of ears.

'No,' Alice said leaning forward. 'Although he did fall down a well a couple of weeks ago on my first day on the farm.'

Robertson and Crawford turned to him, their eyes shining at this piece of information.

'I told you, he hasn't changed since he was fifteen years old. Most people become more careful…' Crawford said, shaking his head. 'Tell us *exactly* what happened.'

'Was he trying to rescue something?' Robertson asked, 'He's normally trying to rescue something.'

'Not that time,' Alice said. 'Although he did get stuck in a muddy pond later the same day rescuing a koala.'

Crawford and Robertson looked at each other and burst out laughing.

'Tell us about the well,' Robertson prompted.

'We were riding out to check on the farm and Mr Fitzgerald was worried the wells were dry. He looked down it, leaning on the stone wall around it, but wasn't satisfied by simply looking.'

'I wanted to make sure it was actually dry and not just appearing so by something covering the bottom,' George murmured good-naturedly.

'I begged him not to lean too far, told him he'd fall in, but he just seemed to lean out further.'

'Showing off,' Crawford murmured with a shake of his head.

'He was holding on to the wooden strut above

the well and suddenly it cracked. I thought he would plummet to his death, but he managed to grab hold of the wall, after flipping himself over.'

George shrugged. 'What can I say, I'm a natural acrobat.'

'It would have been easier to heed Miss Alice's advice and not put yourself in that situation in the first place,' Crawford said.

'Don't pretend you're the epitome of sensibility,' Francesca challenged him with raised eyebrow. She turned to the rest of the table, 'Only last week I found him balancing an almighty bundle of tools on his back as he climbed up the ladder to the hayloft. A *sensible* man would have made three trips, but you risked slicing your arm off for the sake of a few minutes.'

'Extra minutes I got to spend with you, my sweet.' Crawford winked at his wife, making her cheeks blush a deep pink. 'The time he fell down the well at Rabbit's Corner was even more impressive,' Crawford said, steering the conversation back to George.

'We were about sixteen years old, sent out by Fitzgerald's father to check on the wells around the property, see if any of the covers needed repairs, if the stone walls were in good condition,' Robertson said, swinging back on his chair only to be abruptly pulled back down to the floor by his wife. 'When we got to the well at Rabbit's Corner he peered down and was convinced there was something stuck down there.'

'It *looked* like an animal had fallen in,' George said, remembering the day as if it were yesterday.

'Before we knew what he was doing he took a length of rope, looped it around his waist and instructed us to lower him down.' Robertson grinned, shaking his head as Crawford took up the story.

'What he hadn't done was check the rope was in good condition.'

'It was damn unlucky a mouse had chosen that particular rope to chew through,' George murmured.

'He hopped over the edge of the well, began his descent and as we braced ourselves to hold him the rope gave way,' Crawford said with a shake of his head.

'He should have died,' Robertson said quietly, 'but this man has the luck of the devil and on his way to the bottom of the well managed to grab hold of a tree root that was sticking out of the wall of the well.'

'We looked down, expecting him to be lying at the bottom with a broken neck, but instead we saw his face grinning up at us about eight feet down.'

It had been a hair-raising few seconds. By rights he should have died that day, but some-one had looked kindly on him and somehow he'd caught hold of the only protruding tree root in the whole well shaft.

'How did you get out?' Alice asked.

'Crawford and Robertson tied together the horses' reins and made a rope long enough to reach me, then they pulled and I climbed.' He could still remember the burning of his muscles, the creeping fear that he was going to slip and the relief when his friends' hands had reached over the lip of the well and pulled him to safety.

'Tell her the best part,' Robertson said with a wry smile.

'I couldn't just leave whatever it was stuck at the bottom of the well...' he said as Alice groaned.

'You didn't go back down there?'

'We rode back and fetched a decent rope and half an hour later we tried again.'

'Tell her what was at the bottom. What we made all that effort for.'

George grinned, remembering descending into the darkness for a second time, unable to walk away even though the well had almost claimed his life.

'It was a bundle of old clothes,' he said. They'd never worked out how the bundle had made its way to the bottom of the well, but George had just been relieved it wasn't an injured animal. He had climbed back up brandishing the clothes and spent the journey home listening to his friends' jokes with a smile on his face.

He glanced at Alice as she laughed at the story, noting the flush of her cheeks and the sparkle in her eye. She'd been nervous about coming tonight, her whole body held tense on the way over here. If he was honest, he'd felt nervous, too. Every day that passed he felt as though he were drawn closer to Alice and he knew that somehow their futures would be intertwined. It was important for him that she like his friends and that they liked her. All the important occasions were spent with the two men he'd grown up with, it would be horrible if Alice felt awkward around them. Catching her eye, he smiled at her, watching as she popped the last of the spiced gingerbread dessert into her mouth while she listened to the flow of the conversation.

He knew he had nothing to worry about. Robertson and Crawford and their wives had worked to put Alice at her ease. As the conversation had swelled he'd seen her relaxing until she was actually enjoying herself. Now she was laughing as freely as the rest of them and he hoped that for this evening at least she would forget her label of convict and see herself just as a normal young woman surrounded by friends.

'How about the time Fitzgerald almost got trampled by a stampede of cattle?' Robertson asked, pouring more wine into all the glasses. 'Has he told you about that?'

'I can't work out if you're just really unlucky or if you throw yourself into dangerous situations,' Alice said. As she spoke their eyes met and George felt the spark of desire he always did when he looked at Alice, but something more passed between them as well. Something deeper, something warmer, something that made George want to gather her in his arms and make her promise she would be his for ever.

'Both,' Crawford and Robertson said together.

'I'm sure everyone has had one or two brushes with death,' George said, trying to tot up how many near-death experiences he'd had over the years.

'One or two,' Robertson agreed, 'but yours must number in the dozens.'

'The venomous snake, the well at Rabbit's Corner, the stampede of cattle, the time you fell off the roof of the barn, the crocodile at Turber's pond, the wild dogs on old man Hunter's farm, the angry mob in that tavern in Sydney,' Crawford reeled them off.

'Stop—' George laughed '—you make me sound like the most careless man in Australia.'

'Not careless,' Crawford said a little more seriously.

'Never careless,' Robertson agreed. 'I think if anything you care too much. You go rushing in to do the right thing, to save the wounded animal, to ensure someone else doesn't get hurt, but you don't always think of yourself.'

'Apart from when you fell off the roof of the barn. Now *that* was just careless.'

'I wish I could have known you all then,' Mrs Robertson said, looking from one to another.

'In some ways we've barely changed,' her husband said. 'But in others I don't recognise the boys we used to be.'

'I have a sneaking suspicion that when you are back together you revert to the boys you once were,' Alice said with a laugh.

All three men nodded in agreement, grinning like naughty children, but unable to help it.

'Shall we move next door?' Mrs Robertson suggested.

George stood, offering his arm to Alice as they walked back through to the comfortable drawing room.

'Do you mind if we steal away Alice for a few minutes?' Mrs Crawford said, linking her own arm through Alice's and steering her away.

'We won't be long,' Mrs Robertson confirmed.

As he watched Alice being swept out of the drawing room and out of view he felt a protective instinct, even though she was being hustled away by two of the kindest women in Australia.

Chapter Nineteen

'You look radiant tonight, Alice,' Georgina said as the three women settled down on to the chairs in the airy room. The doors out to a wide veranda were open, letting in some of the cooler evening air, but still Alice felt her skin was prickling from the heat.

'You do, my dear,' Francesca agreed.

'Thank you.' Alice looked down at her dress. It was in perfect condition, but it did feel a little strange to be wearing someone else's clothes. At least someone she hadn't known. She and her sisters had always shared clothes growing up, passing things backward and forward as their likes and sizes changed, but this felt different. Perhaps it was the beautiful material or the quality needlework, or perhaps it was because it was a dress a woman like her should never even dream of wearing.

'We found it in the attic, packed away in a trunk,' she explained.

'It's a perfect fit, almost as if it were made for you,' Francesca said, smiling.

'There is a modiste in Sydney, a very talented woman who seems to know the perfect material and cut for everyone who walks through her door,' Georgina said, stroking her bump softly. 'She even managed to find something that flatters my shape while I'm the size of a whale. Next time you're in Sydney you should ask Mr Fitzgerald to take you there.'

'Oh, I couldn't,' Alice said quickly. It was one thing borrowing a beautiful dress for an evening, but quite another to have one made for you. 'It wouldn't be right,' she added quietly.

For a few hours she'd allowed herself to forget that she didn't fit in here. Everyone had been so kind, so welcoming. They'd treated her like a friend, not a convict worker on a neighbouring farm. Both couples had done everything in their power to put her at ease and Alice had felt her spirits soar. Just as George made her feel worthwhile again, so did his friends. They listened to her opinions, included her in their jokes, made her part of their intimate little group. The two women had even insisted she call them by their first names, bringing her into their close and intimate group.

'I'm just a convict worker,' she murmured, trying to inject a note of levity in her voice, horrified when it came out sounding as if she were going to cry.

'No,' Francesca said quietly, 'you're not.'

It took half a minute for Alice to compose herself to look up from her hands. Both Georgina and Francesca were looking at her with a mixture of sadness and encouragement.

'I shouldn't have come here. I forgot my place.'

Francesca reached out and placed her hand over Alice's. 'You have no predefined place in the world, Alice, look at me and Georgina. If we had followed what people expected of us, if we'd taken up the roles everyone expected of us we wouldn't be here, blissfully happy with the men we love.'

'It's not the same,' Alice protested quietly. She wanted part of this world, wanted the warmth and the friendship and the civilised conversation as they sat round the dinner table. But no amount of wanting could change her circumstance.

'Of course it is. It's about having the belief, the

conviction, to follow your heart,' Georgina said. 'At the time I met my husband I had received a proposal from a duke. It was everything my family had ever wanted for me, everything I had been taught to strive for.' She closed her eyes and shook her head. 'And he was a lovely man, very kind. He would make someone a good husband. I almost married him, Alice. It would have been the easy path, the path of conformity, but I knew it was the wrong thing to do.'

Georgina looked at her and Alice thought she would see condescension in the woman's face, but instead there was just concern.

'I haven't spent much time with Mr Fitzgerald,' she continued, 'but where Sam talks about him all the time I feel like I know him. I know his kindness and his loyalty. I know his willingness to put everyone else above himself. I know how hard he works and how invested he is in not only the success of his farm, but the success of Australia.'

'He is a very special man,' Alice murmured.

'And he looks at you in a very special way,' Francesca said bluntly.

'I suspect you do not feel worthy of him, Alice,' Georgina continued more gently, waiting for

Alice to give a minute nod before saying more. 'But *he* obviously thinks you are. He sees something in you and sometimes you have to trust the person you love to see something you are blinded to.'

'She means your worth,' Francesca clarified.

'I'm just a convict worker...'

'No,' Georgina said sharply. 'You're so much more than that. Convict worker is a label you've been given, it is a short period in your life, but it is not who you are.'

'Why are you being so kind to me?' Alice asked, feeling the tears building in her eyes.

'Do you know what I've learned from my husband?' Francesca asked in reply. 'The value of a good friendship. The three of them know that no matter what they have the others to rely on, to be there whatever the hardship. It is a very powerful thing.' She smiled at Alice and took her hand. 'I never had that, not before I came here. My late husband wasn't a particularly pleasant man and he isolated me from all of the friendships I did have, leaving me lonely and without anyone to help when things were going wrong.'

Georgina smiled at Francesca, a warmth passing between the two women that Alice realised she badly wanted a part of.

'I know we don't know you well, Alice, but we'd like to. And what is more important is that Mr Fitzgerald cares for you. Ben tells me Mr Fitzgerald is an excellent judge of people and if he cares for you so deeply after such a short time then you are someone worth investing in.'

The tears slipped out of Alice's eyes and on to her cheeks. Immediately both women were at her side, Georgina wrapping her arms around Alice and Francesca leaning in and patting her back.

'He doesn't know everything about me,' Alice said quietly once she'd regained her composure. She thought of Bill, of the hurried wedding and the months afterwards living as husband and wife. As always when she thought of her husband she remembered his face as he struck Mr Havers, of the emotionless act of violence that had finally confirmed what manner of man she'd allowed to seduce her.

'Sometimes the few days or weeks before you admit exactly what you feel for one another can be the hardest,' Georgina said. 'You have to iron out all the little complications, clarify what is really important. But if you're meant to be together then it will all work out in the end.'

Alice bowed her head, wondering if what the other women were saying was true. She desperately hoped it was. For weeks she had been trying to deny that all she dreamed of was a future with George. A future filled with happiness and children and blissful domesticity. Never had she admitted so much out loud, most of the time she wouldn't even admit it to herself.

George did care for her. It was obvious in the way he treated her, how he looked at her, the passion in his eyes as he kissed her. Every day he showed her he cared for her. Even bringing her to dinner with his friends hinted that their relationship was something he wanted to nurture and grow.

Perhaps Georgina and Francesca were right. Perhaps Alice just needed to tell him the truth and deal with the consequences, and if they were meant to be then it would all work out in the end. For a moment she panicked, her heart squeezing at the idea that her secrets might be enough to keep them apart, but quickly she rallied. It wasn't as though she could keep Bill secret for ever. She should have told George about him long ago, but the best thing she could do now was reveal the truth as soon as possible and explain her reasons for not telling him sooner.

'Sam told me once that it took years for him to stop doubting himself,' Georgina said softly. 'Even when he had finished serving his sentence and started to run his own farm he still found himself thinking he wasn't worthy.

'The guards and the officials spend so long making sure you understand how worthless you are, how low on the ladder of society, that it is hard to think anything else. But it does improve. Now he certainly doesn't suffer from any lack of confidence.'

Alice wondered if she would ever be the same. She thought it would probably depend on her future. Mr Robertson and Mr Crawford had been lucky, they'd had George's family to champion them, to give them opportunities to flourish and allow them to see themselves in a different light.

'I think I need to tell George—Mr Fitzgerald,' she corrected herself quickly, 'about my past.'

'And try not to worry too much,' Francesca said with a note of reassurance in her voice, 'I'm sure it can't be that bad. It's not as though you've killed someone, or are ~~married~~ with a brood of five children.'

Alice smiled weakly, her breath catching in her throat, wondering all the time if her revelation might be the end of the most wonderful thing that had ever happened to her.

'When will you ask her?' Robertson asked, leaning back in his chair and loosening his cravat.

'Ask her what?' George asked mildly, even though he knew what his friend was referring to.

'To marry you. You're completely besotted so there's no point holding off.'

'Soon,' he said, knowing it was pointless to try to be evasive with his friends. They knew him better than he knew himself sometimes. 'If she wants to we can wait until she's finished her sentence to marry, or we can do it in the next few months.'

Slowly he was beginning to let go of the feeling he was doing something wrong. Alice might be a convict worker under his protection, but he hadn't taken advantage of her. They were just two people who had fallen for each other. She was a strong woman, a woman who had spent the last couple of years striving to remain independent, refusing to take the protection of a man even though it would have made her life a lot easier. It told him that it wasn't just obligation or gratitude that made her sink into his arms.

George tried to suppress a grin, but wasn't quite successful.

'You're thinking about her,' Ben murmured. 'I've never seen you look like this before.'

It was true. He was thinking of how Alice looked at him, how her whole body swayed towards him whenever they stood close, how she let out those little sighs of contentment when their lips met. All of those things told him how she really felt about him.

George shrugged. 'What can I say, I'm besotted.'

'That's not a bad thing,' Sam said. 'I'm still besotted with my wife three years down the line.'

'And I've been besotted with Frannie since we were ten years old,' Ben added quietly.

'I think she'll say yes…' George said, allowing the slight doubt to creep into his voice. He knew Alice cared for him, desired him, but he felt as though she were holding something back.

Whatever it was he was sure they could work through it, but only if she let him in.

'Do you doubt it?' Crawford asked.

Slowly George shook his head. 'There's something she's not telling me, something about her past perhaps, something that plagues her. I don't want to push too much...' He was afraid it might be something to do with her time on the transport ship, she'd told him a little about the hardships she'd endured, but he was worried there was something worse, something that still scarred her to this day.

'Ask her about it,' Robertson said. 'It is always best to have complete honesty in a relationship.' Ruefully he shook his head. 'I nearly lost Georgina because I wasn't honest with her. It makes me feel sick to think of it.'

'I don't want to make her relive parts of the last couple of years she'd rather forget.'

'I suppose she doesn't need to tell you the details,' Crawford said. 'Just tell her you feel like there is something that is making a barrier between you, ask her to tell you what it is in general terms. If she doesn't want to go into the details she doesn't have to, but it can put your mind at rest that there is no great awful secret between you.'

It was a sensible suggestion. Perhaps even just acknowledging that there was a feeling she was holding something back would be enough to ease his mind.

'Just think, in a few months you'll probably be married with a baby on the way.' Robertson shook his head. 'How strange it is to think of the lads we once were and how different our lives are now.'

'To success and domesticity,' Crawford said, raising his glass in a toast.

They all drank, and George felt a warmth and contentment wash over him. Here he was surrounded by his closest friends, about to embark on a future with the woman he loved.

The thought was sobering. *The woman he loved.* He hadn't said the words to Alice yet, but it was what he felt. There was no other way to describe the crashing emotion that almost overwhelmed him every time he looked at her. Feeling buoyed by his friends, he allowed himself a moment to picture the future. A future with Alice by his side. Whatever it was Alice was keeping from him, surely it couldn't be anything that could shatter the happiness they felt when they were together?

Chapter Twenty

Alice looked over her shoulder, waving at the figures silhouetted in the doorway. It had been a lovely evening. Alice hadn't ever attended a dinner party before and she knew that the evening at the Robertsons' home had been an informal affair, but she'd enjoyed it immensely. All her misgivings about not fitting in, about not being of the right social class, had been swept away by the warmth of George's friends.

No doubt she had picked up the wrong cutlery or drunk from the wrong glass at the dinner table and probably she had stood too soon after dinner or sat in the wrong way in the drawing room, but now she realised that none of that mattered. Everything she'd been so worried about now seemed trivial.

'Did you have a nice evening?' George asked, wrapping an arm around her.

'I did. Your friends are wonderful.'

'Don't let them hear you say that, Robertson and Crawford have enough self-confidence already,' George said with a smile on his face.

'Georgina and Francesca are very kind, too. I've never met women quite like them before.'

She thought of the spirit of sisterhood the women had emanated, that desire to see her happy despite only knowing her for a short time.

'Robertson and Crawford are very lucky,' he murmured. Alice glanced up at him, wondering if he felt jealous of his friends' circumstances. They were both married to women they seemed to adore, with a child each and more on the way. There wasn't any hint of envy in George's expression, though, and Alice wondered for the hundredth time how she had managed to find the most generous and selfless man in Australia.

She shivered, the wrap around her shoulders not doing enough to keep out the cool evening air. The temperature had dropped once the warmth of the sun had disappeared and Alice knew she should be grateful for the respite from the sweltering heat, but her body wasn't used to the cool air and here she was sitting shivering

in temperatures that in England would be considered balmy.

George gently pulled her closer to him and
Alice could feel the warmth of his body through
the layers of their clothes. She rested her head
down on his shoulder, allowing the rhythmic
sway of the cart to relax her body.

'I've got something special planned for tomorrow,' he said as the cart trundled along the dirt
road.

'What is it?' Alice asked.

'A surprise.'

She felt the tension back in her shoulders and
tried to tell herself to relax. Alice knew she
needed to tell George about Bill, about the man
she had married so foolishly. Only then, only
once all her secrets were out in the open, would
she be able to enjoy the time she spent with
George to the full.

'What sort of surprise?' she asked.

'Just wait and see. You'll like it, I promise.'

Part of her wanted to blurt out her secret now,
but she pressed her lips together. She needed a
little time to think about how best to word her
revelation. There would be plenty of time tomor-

row, perhaps it would be best to leave it until after George had revealed his surprise.

She knew it was cowardice making the plan to wait, but she just wanted one more day, one more memory before she told her secret. George was a reasonable man, but she knew this revelation could be enough to push him away.

Impulsively she reached out and took his hand.

'George,' she said quietly, her voice carrying in the quiet night air, 'you know I would never intentionally do anything to hurt you?'

He looked down at her, a bemused smile on his face. 'Have I got something to worry about?'

Silently she shook her head. 'I just want you to know that I would never want to hurt you. I'm grateful for everything you've done for me…' she paused, feeling her heart beat in her chest '…and I care for you very much.'

It was so much more than that. She loved him, that much she'd finally admitted to herself, but she couldn't come out and tell him yet. Not until everything was settled between them. To hear him say he loved her back, only to retract the words when he found out about Bill, that would break her heart.

The cart trundled to a stop outside the farmhouse, but George made no move to get down.

'Whatever it is you're worrying about, we can get through it together,' he said quietly. He looked at her, the moonlight glinting off his blue eyes, then leaned in and placed a kiss on her forehead.

Silently she nodded, wondering if tomorrow everything would change.

'Get some sleep,' he said as he helped her down from the cart. 'Everything will look different in the morning.'

George woke up early, just as the first rays of sun were filtering through the window. Already it was hot, the chill of the night dissipating quickly as the sun rose over the horizon. For a few minutes he lay in bed, taking time to think over his day. Today was the day, the big moment. In truth he'd been building up to this point for a while, but the conversation with his friends the night before had given him the push to go ahead and do it.

Today he was going to ask Alice to marry him.

It was the logical next step. He loved her and he knew she cared for him. Already they enjoyed the time they spent together much more than any time apart.

For a moment he felt a flicker of doubt, but pushed it away. Of course she would say yes. There was no reason not to. Even if she didn't look at him as though she could see no one else when he was in the room, the marriage was advantageous for her.

'Stop worrying,' he told himself, pulling on his clothes. He opted for a simple pair of trousers and a crisp white shirt. Many men would choose to wear something more formal, something smarter, when they proposed to the woman they wanted to marry, but George knew it would be another sweltering day and the last thing he wanted was to be uncomfortable when he asked Alice to marry him.

Downstairs Mrs Peterson was already bustling around, preparing the kitchen for the day's work. He'd asked her to make up a basket for lunch today and he saw with satisfaction it was already half-full.

'Good morning, sir,' Mrs Peterson said with a suspicious look in her eyes. 'I'm just preparing your lunch now. May I ask where you are planning on going?'

He grinned. Although they had been discreet, it was unlikely that his housekeeper hadn't picked up on the budding relationship between him and Alice.

'I'm taking Alice out to Turner's Meadow,' he said, knowing the time for secrecy was over. If all went well today he would return from the trip out engaged to be married to Alice, there would be no keeping that from the Petersons.

'Turner's Meadow? Whatever for?' Mrs Peterson asked.

At that moment Mr Peterson walked in through the kitchen door, the rescued baby kangaroo in his arms.

'I should imagine to have some peace with the woman he's going to wed,' the gruff older man said quietly.

George couldn't help but grin. Mr Peterson was stoical and quiet most of the time, but that didn't mean he wasn't observant. And he didn't seem to object to Alice the way his wife did.

'What?' Mrs Peterson spluttered.

'Oh, hush, Edie,' Mr Peterson said, placing the baby kangaroo down on the floor and letting him hop around the spacious kitchen. 'You know as well as I that when two people are meant to be together there's nothing to be done but accept it. No matter the difference in their stations.'

'It's not right,' she muttered. 'How do you know she's not using you? Seducing you?'

George took a step towards his housekeeper. He felt an enormous affection for the older woman who had looked after him and his home for so many years. He knew her words came from a place of concern, a place of love, and that when she saw Alice made him happy she would accept things easier.

'I'm thirty-one years old, Mrs Peterson,' he said softly, 'And in all my life I've never felt the way I do about Alice. It's not rushed or impulsive, but when the heart knows what it wants, there is no arguing with it.'

He saw the flare of emotion in the older woman's eyes.

'You have to trust me,' he said. 'Trust me to know myself, to make the right decision.'

'She makes you happy?' Mrs Peterson asked, the emotion making the words stick in her throat.

'She does. More than anything.'

The older woman nodded, sniffing to cover the tears that were rolling down her cheeks.

'Then I suppose that is the most important thing.'

George leaned in and kissed his housekeeper on the cheek, grinning as she batted him away like a naughty schoolboy, but seeing the blush of pleasure on her cheeks.

'Away with you. I need to finish this basket for your lunch.'

He wandered back out into the hall, unable to focus on anything, his mind in too much turmoil for him to even think of doing any work.

'Good morning,' Alice said as she descended the stairs. It was early, but she looked fresh and bright, her hair tumbling around her shoulders in bouncing waves. He caught a look of trepidation in her eyes and wondered again how he was going to get her to tell him exactly what it was that she was keeping from him. 'I should go and help Mrs Peterson,' she said.

She paused for a moment as she reached his side and he couldn't help but reach out and pull her into his arms.

'George,' she whispered in protest, 'someone might see.'

'Let them see,' he murmured. 'I'm done with pretending I don't feel anything for you.'

He felt her relax in his arms, saw the warmth in her eyes and bent his head to kiss her. Softly at first, savouring the sweetness of her lips, groaning as she wrapped her arms around his neck and pulled him closer to her. Every inch of skin her fingers touched tingled and burned and he wondered how damned he would be if he just lifted her into his arms and carried her to his bedroom.

There was a shuffling of feet behind him and guiltily Alice sprang from his arms. They turned together, just in time to see Mr Peterson's retreating back.

'He saw us,' Alice said.

'Stop worrying. The Petersons would have to be blind not to have seen what has built between us the last few weeks.'

Alice hesitated and he saw her frown as she tried to think through the repercussions, his heart lifting as she smiled at him and sank back into his arms.

'Where are we going today?' she asked, looking up at him, her eyes sparkling in the sunlight that poured in through the windows.

'Somewhere special,' he said with a smile. Turner's Meadow was always beautiful at this time of year, even when there hadn't been rain in months. Three little streams converged on the hillside, flowing down from their bubbling brooks, providing the perfect conditions for the bloom of wildflowers over the meadow. He hadn't visited since returning to Australia and even just the thought of sitting looking out at the rolling hills covered by summer flowers with the sun on his face made him feel relaxed. 'We'll take the horses. It's less than an hour's ride away.'

'Your lunch basket is ready,' Mrs Peterson said, bustling out into the hall. Alice stepped away guiltily, flashing the housekeeper a wary look, but Mrs Peterson handed over the basket without comment.

'We shouldn't leave too late,' George said, stepping closer to Alice again and speaking quietly. 'We don't want to be on horseback in the hottest part of the day. I need to leave some instructions for Mr Peterson, check on the cattle in the top field and then we can be on our way.'

He leaned in and kissed her again, seeing the passion he felt reflected in her eyes. George felt happier than he ever thought possible. Today he was going to take the woman he loved out somewhere it would just be the two of them and tell her exactly how he felt. They would be able to plan their future together, work out how they wanted to live their lives. It was going to be the start of something very special.

Chapter Twenty-One

It was hard not to be swept away by George's infectious enthusiasm. As they rode he pointed out the perimeters of his farm, the spots he played as a child or where he, Robertson and Crawford got up to mischief when they were young.

As she looked out over the rolling hills, brown and yellow under weeks of relentless sunshine, Alice realised she was beginning to fall in love with the country. Not the harsh world of convict-heavy Sydney, but out here, the true Australia. The beautiful countryside stretching out as far as the eye could see, the peace, even the heat. She was beginning to see what George was so passionate about.

It was different to the stark and striking vistas near her beloved Whitby, but stunning all the same.

'That little copse of trees over there hides a

pond and that is where my father taught me to swim,' George said, shielding his eyes as he pointed into the distance.

'There were no crocodiles there?' Alice asked, still amazed anyone would risk swimming in a country where a crocodile might be lurking under the murky waters.

'No, the pond is small and far enough from any other water to make it unlikely.' He looked at her and grinned. 'I'm guessing I'm not going to be able to persuade you to come in swimming with me?'

'Definitely not.'

'Shame,' he said, his eyes raking over her, the heat of his gaze making Alice shiver with a wonderful anticipation.

Alice's head filled with images of George stripping down and pulling her into the cool water, kissing her until she lost all rational thought. It was a tempting fantasy, even with the threat of giant hungry lizards with a mouth full of huge teeth.

'We're nearly there,' he said, motioning to a little hill in front of them, 'Just on the other side of that ridge.'

Alice felt the knot begin to form in her stomach again, a heavy, dragging sensation that she couldn't rid herself of. The closer they got to their destination, the sooner it would be that she had to tell George the truth about her past. It wasn't fair to keep it secret any longer, especially as she knew he felt the same about her as she did about him.

The rode slowly, allowing the horses to pick their own sedate pace in the sweltering heat. As they mounted the top of the ridge Alice felt her eyes widening. In front of them the countryside rolled away in gentle hills, the hazy Blue Mountains ever present in the distance. It was the closest fields that caught the eye, though, large open meadows filled with wildflowers of every colour. Bursts of yellow and red mixed in with the pinks and greens. Alice couldn't believe such a stunning display could survive the oppressive heat, but somehow the little oasis of beauty was flourishing.

'It's beautiful,' she said, unable to take her eyes away from the view.

'I thought you would like it here.'

George led the way to a spot in the shade, underneath the leafy branches of a huge tree. He dismounted, tied up Kareela loosely to a low branch, giving the horse enough length to move about and sample the grass, then he turned to Alice. He gripped her by the waist, lifting her down, continuing to hold on even once her feet were firmly on solid ground.

She felt his eyes on her, darting over her face as if trying to take it all in.

'Did you know you're even more beautiful in the sunlight?' he said quietly.

Alice laughed. 'What do you mean?'

'Well, you're beautiful all the time, of course, but in the sunlight you look even more radiant. Everything shines: your hair, your eyes, your skin. You are beautiful.'

Self-consciously Alice brought a hand to her hair, feeling the heat of it after riding under the hot sun for almost an hour. George stepped closer, resting a hand on her waist.

'You're beautiful Alice,' he repeated. 'I find I can't take my eyes off you.'

Softly he stroked her hair, running his fingers through the silky locks, then continuing down the length of her back. Alice was wearing the thinnest dress she possessed, in a light blue cotton material, so she could feel the movement of his fingers as if they were on her bare skin.

As always when George touched her, Alice felt herself go weak, an almighty shiver of anticipation running through her core. She knew one more touch, one more kiss, and she would forget all reason. Already she was finding it hard to focus on anything but the man standing in front of her and how she felt as his fingers ran over her body.

After a moment George stepped away and Alice had to suppress a moan of frustration. She watched as he lay out the blanket on the ground, smoothing it down before kneeling down, holding a hand out for her. She took his hand, squealing in surprise as he tugged hard, catching her as she tumbled into his lap.

'Hello,' he murmured as their bodies pressed together.

'Hello.'

'Did I mention you looked beautiful?' he asked.

'You did.'

'And kissable?'

'I don't think—' She was cut off by his lips capturing hers and Alice felt herself melt into George as his arms came round her back and pulled her even closer to him.

He kissed her until she had forgotten where

they were, had forgotten everything but the man in front of her. Alice felt as though her whole body was on fire, begging to be touched, begging for attention.

'You don't know what you do to me,' George whispered, his words tickling her ear.

Shifting in his lap a little, she ran her hands through his hair, down his back and George tightened his grip on her in response. For a moment they pulled apart, a look of understanding, of mutual desire passing between them, then they were kissing again.

Alice giggled as George tipped her from his lap, laying her down on the soft wool of the blanket, never stopping kissing her for more than a couple of seconds at a time. She watched as he shrugged off his jacket, leaving him just in his thin white shirt and trousers. Her hands grasped the bottom of his shirt, pulling it up over his head, revealing the tanned, taut muscles. She paused, running her fingers over his skin before she finished pulling off his shirt and deposited it on the blanket behind her.

'If only your dress was so easy,' he murmured as his fingers started on the fastenings that ran the length of her back. It was true she hadn't dressed for this, hadn't thought about ease of getting undressed, when she'd woken up this morning.

As he worked to reveal inch after inch of skin he peppered kisses down her spine, making her shiver in anticipation. When he neared the bottom of her back he pulled her to her feet, pushing the material of the dress down past her hips so it pooled on the blanket beneath them. Underneath her dress she was wearing the thinnest of shifts, an almost sheer garment that reached her mid-thighs.

'You're beautiful,' George said, gripping the hem of her shift and pulling it up over her head.

For a moment he just looked at her, then with a fiery passion in his eyes he tumbled her back down on the blanket, his body on top of hers. Alice felt herself being swept away, able to think of nothing but the jolts of pleasure as his hands caressed her skin, as his body brushed against hers.

'I could kiss you for ever,' he said as his lips left hers and he started to trail kisses down her neck and on to her chest. Alice almost cried out as he took one of her nipples into his mouth, arching her back and closing her eyes, savouring every wonderful moment. She felt her skin burn as his fingers trailed down lower, dancing over her abdomen, then continuing on down even lower. She gasped as his fingers grazed her most private of places, responding instinctively as he dipped inside, clutching him tighter to her.

Alice felt a wonderful tension begin to build inside her, increasing with every rhythmic movement George made. Her hips were thrusting up to meet his fingers, her back arching, her skin tingling, then suddenly there was a wonderful release and wave after wave of pleasure crashed over her.

'George,' she cried out, pulling him even closer, and when she opened her eyes he was smiling down at her.

There was a fierce desire in his eyes as Alice gripped the waistband of his trousers and pushed them down, moaning in pleasure as she felt his hardness against her. With a swift thrust he was buried inside her, Alice gripping him, pulling him to her. Again and again their bodies came together until Alice felt everything tense before her body was overtaken by a crashing climax. Above her she heard George moan, felt him push inside her one last time, then collapse down on top of her.

They lay entwined for thirty seconds before George gently rolled off her, moving so he was next to her, one arm looped across her waist.

'I've been wanting to do that for a long time,' he murmured after a while.

Alice smiled. She felt content lying here in the heat with the man she loved beside her.

'Me, too,' she said.

As they lay there, their breathing slowly returning to a normal rate, George trailed his fingers softly across the skin of her abdomen. It felt intimate, wonderfully so, and Alice wished they could stay like this for ever.

'I hope no one rides past,' she said, making no move to cover her naked body. It seemed an isolated spot and they hardly ever met anyone when they were out and about around the countryside anyway.

'They won't,' he said, kissing her neck. 'This is my land and there are no roads nearby. Someone would have to be quite off track to come across us.'

Alice nestled her head into his shoulder, inhaling his familiar scent, and closed her eyes.

Right here, right now, she felt as though everything was perfect, and she didn't want time to move forward. She wanted everything to stay as it was right now.

It was another hot day, even under the shade of the tree, and Alice felt her eyelids drooping. Giving in to the contented fatigue she felt, she allowed her mind to empty and her body to relax. She felt safe in George's arms, safe and happy.

Chapter Twenty-Two

George awoke slowly, stretching his legs out on the soft blanket. Alice was still in his arms, still curled up next to him, her skin warm against his. He took a moment to watch her, to see the rhythmic rise and fall of her chest, the creamy white skin that never saw the sunlight, the beautiful curves that made up her figure. He felt happier than he had done in a long time, perhaps happier than he ever had before. All he needed now was for her to agree to marry him and he would have everything he'd ever wanted.

She stirred, her eyes blinking open, her mouth stretching into a smile as she focused on him.

'Good afternoon,' he said, leaning down and kissing her, feeling his desire for her surge again.

'I can't believe I slept,' Alice said, sitting up and looking around.

She looked so wonderfully bemused that he

couldn't help but gather her in his arms and kiss her until they tumbled back down on to the blanket, their bodies coming together again. This time it was slower, less frantic, and George was able to savour every wonderful second. He felt his body tense as Alice cried out underneath him, her hands clutching him to her.

'Sorry,' he murmured as they lay in one another's arms afterwards. 'I couldn't help myself.'

Alice smiled, 'I wasn't complaining,' she said, kissing him again.

'We should get dressed, have some lunch.' His mind was already flitting to the proposal he had planned, the question he had brought Alice out here to ask.

Slowly they dressed, George helping Alice to fasten her dress, taking the opportunity to kiss the smooth skin of her shoulders, carefully avoiding the healing scars on her back. Once he had pulled on his shirt he sat down again, motioning for Alice to take the spot beside him.

'Shall we eat?' he asked, opening up the basket Mrs Peterson had packed for them. Together they unpacked the lunch that could have fed six, setting out the little packages of food on the blanket in front of them.

As they began to eat George ran through what he wanted to say to Alice. He was almost certain that she would accept his proposal. He loved her and he thought she felt the same for him. Surely that was the main thing they should focus on. He knew she was still keeping something of her past from him, but hopefully one day she would find she wanted to tell him, either that or it would stop being so significant as she relaxed into her new life.

'I've got something to ask you Alice,' he said, turning to face her.

She looked up and he saw a flash of panic in her eyes.

'Something very important.'

She shook her head quickly, almost frantically. 'No,' she said her eyes fixed on his, as wide as a baby koala's.

'No?' He felt his own panic begin to rise. Was she saying no to the proposal he hadn't yet made or no to the idea of him asking her a question?

'No,' she repeated, shaking her head quickly. 'Don't ask me. Not yet.' She looked away, biting her lip.

George felt all his hopes and dreams begin to deflate. Had he read the situation so very wrong?

Surely he hadn't imagined the feelings they had for one another? Alice had fallen into his arms so willingly just a few minutes earlier—what could have changed so drastically.

'I love you, Alice,' he said quietly but firmly, feeling his heart break a little as she shook her head again.

'I love you, too,' she said. The words should have made him shout for joy, but the desolation in her voice took all joy from the declaration.

'Marry me. I love you. I want to spend the rest of my life with you.'

'George…' she said, her voice cracking with emotion. The silence seemed to stretch on for an eternity, until she said the words he hadn't ever considered a possibility. 'I can't.'

'You can't?'

She shook her head, tears falling from her eyes on to her cheeks. His first instinct was to take her into his arms, to comfort her, but as he reached out he hesitated. Perhaps he had got everything wrong, perhaps he had been building up a fantasy, thinking he detected emotions in Alice that were never there. He felt sick, wondering if he *had* forced her, not physically, but by using her gratitude to him for saving her.

He backed away a few feet, putting the distance between them as he tried to work out exactly what was going on. His head was spinning, his thoughts all over the place.

'I can't,' she said, taking a shuddering breath. 'I'm married.'

George felt the admission hit him with the force of ten galloping horses. She was married. She had already given her heart to someone else.

'Married,' he echoed, unable to say anything else.

Alice nodded, reaching out her hand towards his, but hesitating at the last moment and letting it drop on to the blanket instead.

'Then this…' he said, shaking his head in disbelief '…this was all a lie?'

'No.' Her protest was loud and immediate. 'No. Everything between us, everything I've said and done, everything was real.'

'Except you're married.'

'Yes. Well possibly…yes.'

He couldn't bring himself to look at her, he knew every awful emotion he was feeling would be reflected on his face.

'I love you, Alice. I've told you things I've never told anyone else before.' He shook his head. 'And you couldn't even tell me you were married.' Closing his eyes, he saw flashes of all the moments they'd spent together, happy and laughing. He couldn't quite bring himself to believe it had all been a lie. 'What do you mean *possibly*?' he asked, his mind only just catching up with her statement.

Alice sighed. 'I don't know if my husband is still alive.'

'So you're hedging your bets with me.'

'No,' she said, her voice hard. 'Don't say that.'

'What else is there to say, Alice?' he asked. 'You're married. However much I love you I can't change that.'

She reached for him, a pleading look in her eyes.

'George, please.'

He felt her hand on his arm, that warm touch that just a few moments ago he'd revelled in. Closing his eyes, he stood, backing away.

Alice scrambled to her feet, her hands reaching out in supplication but he just shook his head. She was married. *Married.* All this time, all the chances she'd had to tell him.

He pushed her hands from his arm, gently but firmly. He needed some space, needed to put some distance between them. He walked away, not stopping until he had reached the edge of the meadow, leaning his head against the trunk of a tree.

Married. He hadn't ever imagined that could be her secret. Alice who had seemed so wary of men, so scared, and she'd been married all along. His mind flashed back to when she'd been delirious, to the fear in her voice as she spoke of a man called Bill, the man she said had led her astray. He had assumed Bill had been her lover, no more than that. Bill had been the man to get her into this mess, the one responsible for her being sentenced to transportation. What sort of husband did that to his wife?

Taking a deep breath, he calmed himself. Alice had said she loved him. She had kept her marriage from him, but that didn't void all that had happened between them. Not all marriages were happy—the fact she was a married woman didn't mean the last few weeks had meant nothing.

'Alice,' he said, his voice ragged as he turned around. He thought she would be still sitting where he'd left her, looking desolate as she stared down at the blanket, but the spot was empty. Her horse was gone from where it had been tied and as George looked across the meadow he could see her disappearing into the distance.

'Alice,' he shouted, knowing he had to stop her. She might have kept a huge secret from him, but that didn't mean he didn't love her. Somehow they could work this out, if only he could get her to stop and talk to him, to explain everything.

Breaking out into a run, he crossed the meadow to Kareela in half a minute, untying the horse and leaping on to his back in one swift movement. He set off in pursuit of Alice, covering the ground quickly. With a few minutes' head start Alice had the advantage, but George was the faster rider so he hoped he would be able to catch her.

He galloped over the meadow, leaning low on Kareela's back, urging his horse to go faster down the gentle slope. When they reached the edge he had to pause, trying to work out what direction Alice had taken. Here the rolling hills and copses of trees made his task more difficult as Alice had already disappeared from view. There wasn't even a dust cloud to show her progress.

Cursing loudly, he looked from one side to another, shielding his eyes from the bright sunlight.

He had to hope she had returned home, that she had memorised the way from their journey out here and was heading back to the sanctuary of the farm. Nudging Kareela to the left, he pushed on, praying that Alice would be waiting for him at the house.

It was getting dark as George jumped down off Kareela. He'd been out looking for Alice all afternoon. After he returned home when he'd lost track of Alice, his worst fears had been realised when she wasn't there waiting for him. With Alice out on her own he'd quickly remounted, calling for Mr Peterson to ride out and ask Robertson and Crawford for their help in searching.

His two friends had found him near Turner's Meadow later in the afternoon, both their faces clouded with worry. He'd told them the bare bones of what had happened and between them they'd divided up the routes Alice could have taken. For hours they'd searched, only calling a halt when the light had begun to fail.

'We will find her,' Robertson said as he came out of the house to greet George.

Shaking his head, George tried not to give in to his despair. The nights could be harsh in the wilderness if you were not used to them. He hated thinking of Alice cold and scared, all alone because of his reaction to her.

'I hope so,' George said, running a hand through his hair. 'We need to find her before anyone else, or she could be branded a runaway.'

Robertson grimaced. It was a horrible possibility. If Alice was picked up by someone else and handed back to the guards in Sydney, she would be classed as a runaway and punished as such. The penalty for running away could be another public whipping or it could be being sent to one of the more inhospitable penal colonies, somewhere no one would show her any mercy.

'We will,' Robertson said resolutely. 'We will go back out at first light and search until we find her. I'll gather all the men I can and I'm sure Crawford will do the same.'

George nodded. He knew it was all they could do, but still he felt a crushing panic seize him. Alice was out there all alone. His Alice. The woman he loved. The woman he should be taking care of.

He closed his eyes, wished he could go back to the moment Alice had revealed she was married. His reaction had been poor, accusatory even, al-

though in his defence the news had been shock-
ing. For a moment he had mixed up the facts,
had assumed that her marriage meant that she
couldn't love him. Now he'd had time to think
things through he knew that wasn't the case.
Alice loved him, she'd told him so. And from
what he had learned of her husband, the snippets
she had let slip, he hadn't been a very pleasant
man at all. He wished he could go back, ask her
calmly to explain the circumstances, and somehow work through it all together.

'Get some rest,' Robertson said. 'You'll need
all your energy for tomorrow.'

Nodding, George traipsed inside the house,
knowing that he wouldn't sleep at all until Alice
was safely back with him.

Chapter Twenty-Three

Alice shivered. She was lost and cold and miserable. Dismounting, she stroked her horse's neck, taking some comfort from the calmness of the animal.

'Where are we?' she murmured, looking around, hoping to see a landmark she recognised. Although she'd been out and about with George many times over the last few weeks the countryside was still not familiar and she knew that she was completely and utterly lost.

'Foolish girl,' she muttered, sinking down against the trunk of a tree. She hadn't planned to flee as she had, it had been an impulsive action, one fuelled by the pain on George's face as she'd told him she was married.

Now she had no idea where she was or what she was going to do.

Alice closed her eyes and rested her head back

against the rough bark, trying to swallow back the sobs that were threatening to break free. Earlier that morning she'd been so happy, swept away by passion and contentment, and now everything had changed.

She thought of the moment George had told her he loved her, then asked her to be his wife. It was everything she wanted, that was what made it all so cruel. Alice wished for nothing more than to have never met Bill, to be free to become Mrs Fitzgerald.

George's face when she had said she couldn't marry him had been a picture of devastation. She knew she should have stayed, should have tried to explain more about her past, but she'd seen the distance in his eyes and felt her heart break. She'd deceived him; of course he would want nothing more to do with her. So she had fled, taking the horse and riding until her legs ached and the tears blurred her vision.

Since then she had been trying to work out where she was. None of the rolling hills seemed familiar and the burnt yellows and browns of the fields all merged into one. There were no landmarks to orientate herself, she could be only a couple of miles from the farm and not know, or she could be closer to Sydney.

Shivering in the chill of the night air, she felt her heart sinking at the thought of the city. Alice knew she was in a dangerous position. If anyone came across her, she would be branded as a runaway, punished for abandoning her position. The best thing for her to do would be to go back to George, no matter how difficult it would be to see him.

'I love him,' she murmured to herself. She loved him with a ferocity she'd never experienced before. It was heartbreaking to know that after today he would never look at her in the same light again.

Wrapping her arms around herself in an attempt to keep warm, Alice closed her eyes again and tried to sleep. Tomorrow she would have to decide if she was running away from or back to Mountain View Farm and the man who had thawed her once-frozen heart.

Her eyes had only been closed for thirty seconds when she heard the low murmur of voices. Her first thought was that George had found her, but as she scrambled to her feet she knew the voices in the distance didn't belong to anyone she knew.

It could be a farmer, of course, but equally it could be a guard—perhaps sent from Sydney to search for the runaway they'd seen desperate in the wilderness the previous week.

Alice was frozen with indecision. Part of her wanted to stay where she was, make herself as small as possible and hope whoever it was passed on by without noticing her. The other part of her wanted to run, to get as far away from the danger as she could.

Standing slowly, conscious of every rustle and swish of material, she moved slowly towards her horse, not daring to look in the direction of the voices. She used the tree to help her mount, pulling herself up into the saddle as quietly as she could. Only once she was on horseback did she dare look over her shoulder.

Alice's heart began to pound in her chest. There in the distance were five men dressed in the distinctive red coats of the guards' uniform. They were mounted, their horses trotting along slowly. None of them had spotted her yet, she could tell as much by their relaxed posture and the quiet murmur of conversation between them.

If she moved, they would see her. Of course she would have a head start, but these were men used to spending days in the saddle, whereas she was hardly an experienced rider.

They might not follow her, that was a possibility, but Alice had spent long enough as a convict to know if the guards saw something they thought suspicious they would investigate. And if they caught a woman alone in the middle of the countryside... It didn't bear thinking about.

She shifted in the saddle, guiding her horse closer to the tree, hoping the guards would pass by without noticing her. A minute passed and then another. They were only twenty feet away now, riding along the road past her position, the closest they would pass to her hiding place. The slightest movement and their eyes would be drawn in her direction. Alice found herself holding her breath, one hand resting on her horse's neck in an effort to keep the animal calm and still.

She almost sobbed when they disappeared around a bend in the road, her whole body going weak as she released some of the tension she'd been holding. Even though the guards had gone she knew she couldn't stay where she was. It was too exposed, too likely for her to be spotted by someone from the road. Carefully she urged her horse in the opposite direction to the guards, feeling the exhaustion overcome her now the immediate danger had passed. It was going to be a long night.

Alice had slept fitfully, unable to get comfortable on the hard ground and finding her thin cotton dress entirely inappropriate for spending a night outdoors. Stretching out, she bit her lip to control the cry of pain she would have made as the tense muscles slowly warmed up.

She'd slid from her horse a few hours earlier, finally acknowledging she could ride no further without risking falling asleep on horseback and injuring herself when she fell from the saddle. She'd propped herself against the thick trunk of a tree, hoping it would give her shelter from any prying eyes, and determined to rest only until the first light of dawn.

The sun was only just coming up over the horizon, but already she was glad to find it brought a little warmth with it. Standing, she took a moment to shake off the stiffness she'd acquired during the night, then crossed to where her horse was tethered.

'Good morning,' she said quietly. 'I think it is time for us to find our way home.'

Home. That was how she thought of Mountain View Farm. She might not have resided there long, but it was the only place she'd felt truly comfortable since she'd left her parents' house in Yorkshire. She knew, no matter how badly she'd damaged the trust between her and George, she would always have a home there. He was too good a man to turn her away. More than once he'd assured her she would be safe at the farm until she had served out the remainder of her sentence, Alice knew that would never change. What would change was how George would look at her. Gone would be the love and desire, replaced by that coldness she had seen the day before.

Using the tree to help her, she mounted her horse, picking a direction and hoping it would lead her back home to safety. Perhaps she could explain things to George. Even as the thought popped into her head she saw the betrayal that had filled his eyes when she'd revealed the secret she'd been keeping from him. Still, she had to try.

* * *

After riding for thirty minutes she reached a road. It was nothing more than a dirt track, the ground pitted and dusty, but it was a road all the same. It would lead somewhere. Whatever direction she chose, all roads led to and from somewhere. Turning her horse, she chose a direction and set off at a sedate pace, keeping alert for any signs of the group of guards she had spotted the night before. Once again it was a hot day; even in these early hours of the morning the sun's heat was intense.

She'd only travelled a few hundred feet when she paused, pulling on the reins to stop her horse. Alice couldn't be entirely sure, but she thought she saw movement somewhere in front of her, around the bend in the road. There was a haze to the air, the suggestion of a cloud of dust and underneath it something large moving.

Feeling panic seize her, Alice looked around for somewhere to hide. She felt vulnerable, out here alone and knew that she was in a precarious position. Cursing, she spun to look behind her—there was no shelter in any direction, no copse of trees or even low bushes to hide behind.

It looked as though she would have to face whoever was coming towards her.

Her heart began hammering in her chest. She knew there was a chance it would be someone friendly, a farmer or landowner, even a ex-convict travelling through the countryside looking for work. Equally it could be a band of convict workers, seconded from Sydney to work on the land or building roads into the interior. Or it could be the guards from the night before, perhaps sent to search for runaway convict workers.

One head rounded the corner, followed by another and another. The first man was dressed in the bright red of the all-too-familiar guards' uniform, sitting on the back of a sturdy horse. The men that straggled after him were in much poorer garb, some of which you would struggle to call anything more than rags. There were about twenty men in total and bringing up the rear were two more guards also on horseback.

'Halt,' the first guard called as he caught sight of Alice.

The convicts looked up, their eyes weary and unable to summon any interest in what was going on around them.

'Good morning,' Alice said, trying her best to mask the fear that was creeping over her body.

'Good morning, miss,' the guard said. He looked her up and down, then smiled politely. 'It's early for you to be abroad, unescorted as well.'

'Indeed,' Alice said, telling herself if she could just maintain an air of superiority they couldn't touch her. They weren't to know she was a runaway. They weren't to know she was a convict at all. Her dress was too fine to raise suspicion, even if she had slept in it the night before. 'It is a vexation, but I am hoping to reach my cousin's farm by midday. It will make the early start worthwhile.'

'Do you live nearby, miss?' the guard asked. She didn't know if it was something about her that was causing him to question her, or if he was just a naturally inquisitive man.

'I'm heading to Mountain View Farm,' she said. 'Please don't let me hold you up. It looks as though you have your hands full.'

The guard inclined his head and Alice slowly let out the breath she had been holding as his horse took a step past her.

'Mountain View Farm?' he asked, pausing and

frowning in a quizzical way. 'That must be two miles in that direction.' The guard pointed down the road in the direction she had been coming from.

Alice cursed silently, the words she'd picked up during her time on the transport ship only able to express a fraction of her fear and frustration.

Slowly she looked back over her shoulder and nodded. 'I'm sorry, it must be the early start. I'm coming from Mountain View Farm,' she corrected herself.

'And where are you heading, miss?' the guard asked, his tone less polite than it had been previously.

Desperately Alice tried to trawl through her brain for the name of the Crawfords' house. She knew the Robertsons lived much closer to George, but the Crawfords were a little further away. If only she could remember the name of their property.

'My cousin is Mr Crawford. I am going to stay with him and his wife. She's expecting a child and they will need an extra pair of hands for the birth.' Alice hoped this extra detail would be enough to convince the guard in front of her that she was on legitimate business.

'Mr Crawford,' the guard said thoughtfully. 'I know of him. These men labour near his farm. I think you must have got turned around, Miss...?'

'White,' Alice said, taking the name of the maid that had helped look after her and her sisters when they were small.

'Why don't you accompany us, Miss White, we can see you safely to your cousin's house?'

'That's very kind,' Alice said, unsure whether to feel relieved that she would soon be on familiar ground or uneasy that this guard was taking too much of an interest in her. It was clear he didn't trust her, but hopefully when he saw the Crawfords knew her then he would walk away and think no more about her.

They rode in silence, Alice feeling more and more like a prisoner as every minute passed. She tried to stop herself from taking sidelong looks at the guard beside her, tried to imagine how Francesca or Georgina would be if they were in her position, but even the idea was laughable. They never would be in this position.

'Have I seen you somewhere before, Miss White?' the guard asked after half an hour of riding.

'I think that is unlikely,' Alice said, trying not to engage in further conversation. The guard must have seen her reluctance as he fell silent again.

Every minute that passed Alice felt the tension wind tighter inside her. She glanced at the guard, wondering if this was all a ruse, wondering if any moment they would round a bend and she would see the familiar buildings of Sydney come into view and strong hands would seize her, condemn her for being a runaway.

She shuddered, remembering the ripping of the flesh on her back as the whip made contact again and again, knowing that if she was found to be a runaway she would be tied to that post once more and this time George wouldn't be there to save her.

The sun was high in the sky when the group of men were called to halt and Alice felt her hands tighten on the reins. She wouldn't be taken without a fight—at the first sign of anything amiss she would urge her horse on and hope to lose herself in the wilderness.

The men groaned and grumbled as they slumped to the floor. They must have been walking for nearly two hours, with no stops for water even though their clothes were soaked with sweat. Alice knew as a female convict she'd been spared the worst of the hard labour and, seeing some of the desolate faces of the convicts behind her, she felt thankful for that.

'Ten minutes,' one for the guards at the back called. 'Then we start again.'

'Shall we, Miss White?' the guard asked, motioning for her to ride on with him. Alice looked back uneasily, but knew she had no choice. 'It is only a few more minutes.'

The countryside was still unfamiliar with no landmarks she recognised, but sure enough in less than five minutes a pretty farmhouse came into view. Alice felt a surge of relief, tempered only by the guard's impassive face riding close by. She just hoped that Francesca or Mr Crawford was at home—the servants would quickly deny any knowledge of her.

Alice dismounted outside the farmhouse, her heart hammering in her chest as the guard slipped from the back of his horse as well. Slowly she walked over to the door and knocked. Inside she could hear footsteps, then the door swung open and revealed a cheerful, round-faced woman with wisps of wild hair sticking out from her head.

'Good morning,' she said, looking Alice up and down with a smile.

'I'm here for Mrs Crawford,' Alice said, feeling the guard take a step behind her.

A second passed and then another, drawing out for an eternity as Alice held her breath.

'I'll go see if the mistress if available,' the woman said, her eyes flitting over the guard behind Alice.

'Not expected, then,' he murmured as the woman stepped away from the door.

A minute passed, and then another. With every passing moment Alice felt the guard behind her edge ever closer. She knew he could sense her fear, knew he was beyond suspicious, and part of her wanted to flee like a cornered animal.

There was a murmured conversation from inside the house, but still no one appeared and Alice heard a low, stifled sob pass her lips. She'd come so close, only to be wrenched away now.

Her whole body stiffened as the guard placed a firm had on her arm.

'I think...' he said.

'Alice,' Francesca shouted as she came running through the hall. Francesca threw her arms around Alice, drawing her into an embrace that brought tears to her eyes in its sincerity and warmth. After a moment she stepped away, her eyes travelling to the guard standing a few feet away. 'Is there a problem?' she asked, Alice loving her in that moment for the note of aristocracy she put into her voice.

'No problem, miss,' the guard said, executing a little bow and flushing slightly, his hand slipping smoothly from Alice's arm. 'Miss White was a little turned around in the countryside and I wished to escort her safely to her destination.'

Francesca's face broke into a smile and she called back into the house, talking quietly to the round-faced woman who must be her housekeeper. The housekeeper disappeared for a few seconds, then came back and handed something to her mistress.

'Thank you,' Francesca said, holding out a couple of coins to the guard, 'for being such a kind citizen and ensuring my dear Alice came to no harm.'

The guard took the coins, gave Alice one last puzzled look, then nodded and walked away.

Alice watched him as he remounted his horse,

waiting until she was sure he had left the property before letting out the breath she'd been holding for far too long.

'Alice, we've been so concerned,' Francesca said as she took Alice's arm and led her into the house. 'Ben's been out since dawn helping Mr Fitzgerald look for you. He tells me Mr Fitzgerald was the most worried he'd ever seen him.'

'I'm sorry to have caused so much trouble,' Alice said. She hadn't imagined Mr Crawford would have gone out to search for her, and probably Mr Robertson, too.

'Nonsense, I'm just happy you're safe. I barely slept last night with worry about you out there all on your own.' Francesca paused, giving Alice a sidelong look as if deciding whether to say any more. 'What happened?' she asked as they entered a comfortable sitting room, the doors flung open against the heat.

Alice sank down into an armchair, luxuriating in the comfort and closing her eyes for a second before answering.

'I've ruined everything,' she said, feeling the weight of despair she'd been holding back the past few hours come crashing over her.

'Oh, Alice, I'm sure that's not true.'

Alice thought of George's face, the look of betrayal, how he'd walked away after she'd told him her secret.

'It is,' she said. 'I kept something from George... Mr Fitzgerald. Something I should have told him long ago.' She shook her head, the tears welling in her eyes again.

'He will forgive you,' Francesca said with a conviction Alice wished she could believe.

'I don't think he can. It was a terrible secret. And he trusted me with his confidences.'

'He will forgive you,' Francesca repeated. 'Whatever it is, he cares too much for you to let this come between you.'

Alice was silent for a few minutes, wondering if there was a chance. George was a good man, an understanding man. Perhaps given time he might be able to appreciate why she had kept her secret from him.

'I'm married,' she said quietly.

Francesca's eyes widened and she blinked a few times in quick succession as she took in Alice's statement.

'At least I was married. I might still be. My husband...' she shuddered at the word '...was sentenced to hang, but he escaped from prison before the sentence could be carried out.' It felt wrong to bring her troubles to such a lovely, wholesome household, it made Alice feel dirty and tarnished, but after so long of carrying her secrets alone she felt compelled to spill them and Francesca was so kind and understanding she knew the other woman would not judge her too harshly.

'Oh, Alice,' Francesca said, moving closer and taking her hand, squeezing in solidarity.

'He was a bad man, a cruel husband,' Alice said, closing her eyes to try to rid herself of the image of Bill, his lips curled in contempt for her. 'In the end I hated him, but I should never have kept him secret from George.'

'I can see why he would be shocked, but if you explain…'

'I'm not sure I deserve the chance to explain.' She felt utterly exhausted, emotionally even more than physically, but she knew she had to carry on. She had to find George and at least tell him the whole truth. She owed him that much.

'Of course you do. Everyone makes mistakes. It wasn't malicious, just a misjudgement. And Mr Fitzgerald will see that.'

'He asked me to marry him,' Alice said softly.

'It was everything I've ever wanted. *He's* everything I've ever wanted, but I couldn't say yes.'

Francesca fell silent, her grip on Alice's hand never weakening and sympathy in her eyes.

'I should send word to Mr Fitzgerald that you're here, safe. I think he's been going out of his mind with worry.'

Alice nodded. She both longed to see him, to tell him it was him she loved, and dreaded seeing the mistrust on his face. Mistrust where there had once only been warmth.

As Francesca stood Alice leaned back into the chair, allowing her eyes to close. She wouldn't sleep, no matter how exhausted her mind and body, but she could rest a little.

Chapter Twenty-Four

George stood outside the Crawfords' elegant farmhouse and took a moment to compose himself. He'd ridden hard when he'd received the message that Alice was at the Crawfords' house, imagining she'd had to endure all kinds of terrible hardships the night she'd spent out in the wilderness.

Now he was here he was torn between wanting to rush to Alice's side, to check she was unharmed, and a creeping caution, a need to protect himself from further heartache.

'She's in the sitting room,' Francesca said as she stepped outside. 'I'll give you some privacy.'

George nodded his appreciation, not sure he trusted his voice not to crack, then with a deep breath stepped inside.

For a few seconds after he stepped into the room he was able to observe Alice before she noticed his presence. She looked exhausted, with her head tilted back and resting against the fabric of the armchair and her eyes closed. He knew she wasn't asleep by the drumming of her fingers on the arm of the chair, a nervous movement that made him want to reach out and place his hand over hers.

'Alice,' he said quietly.

Her eyes sprang open and she sat upright in the chair, a worried expression flitting across her face. She made to rise, but George motioned for her to stay sitting, taking the chair next to her and pulling it so they were almost facing one another. He leaned back in the chair, crossing his arms across his chest, putting a physical barrier between them.

'I've been worried,' he said, trying not to blurt out every thought and concern he'd had in the past twenty-four hours since she'd gone missing.

'I'm sorry. That was never my intention.'

'What happened to you? Where did you go?' He heard the coldness in his voice, saw the hope flare and then die in her eyes as she saw the blankness of the expression on his face. He needed to protect himself and this distance was the only way he knew how to.

She shrugged. 'I'm not sure. When I rode off I was in quite a state, I didn't look at what direction I was headed. Then by the time I had calmed down I was utterly lost. In the end I just chose a direction, hoping it would take me home or at least to somewhere I recognised.'

'And last night? Did you spend it outside?' He knew they were avoiding what they really needed to talk about, but George wanted another couple of minutes before broaching the subject, time for all his thoughts to settle into some semblance of order.

Alice nodded, shuddering slightly. 'It was cold and uncomfortable, but it was only one night.'

They fell silent, both knowing they needed to have a very difficult conversation.

'I'm sorry,' Alice said quickly. 'I'm so sorry for everything.'

'Everything?' he asked sharply. His fear was that their relationship hadn't been what he thought. That everything had been a lie, the feelings he'd thought she'd had for him a figment of his imagination, a projection of what he had hoped might be between them.

'I'm sorry for not telling you the truth earlier,' she said. 'I was a coward, I didn't want to jeopardise what we had, I didn't want you to think less of me. But in keeping it secret I know I caused much more damage.'

George felt a glimmer of hope. He could understand that, the feeling that there was never quite the right moment, the uncertainty of when to reveal something so momentous. At first Alice would have wanted to keep her former life private from a man she hardly knew and then as their relationship grew it would have been hard for her to decide when to reveal such a secret.

'Tell me about him,' George said a little softer, knowing that the only way they would be able to move forward would be if she told him everything, as painful as it might be.

Alice nodded, staying silent for a few moments before speaking. 'I met him in Whitby, when he was visiting family up north and staying in the town. At first he was charming and exciting, seemingly from a world so different to my own. I'd led a sheltered life on the farm and he was offering me a glimpse of another way of living.' Alice shook her head ruefully. 'Of course he only showed me the good bits, there was no mention of the poverty in London, the hard work for very little pay. And he was charming, not like later on.'

He could just imagine a young Alice swept away by a rogue. She wouldn't be now, of course, she was too worldly wise, but at seventeen or so he imagined her sheltered and naïve. As she spoke he felt his stiffness relax a little, felt some of the tension draining out of him.

'I ran away with him, we got married almost straight away and then made our way to London. It was nothing like I'd imagined. We could only afford a small room in a less-than-desirable neighbourhood. It was filthy and dingy and no amount of scrubbing and cleaning would ever change that.' Alice sighed and George felt the urge to take her into his arms, but first he wanted to hear just a little more. 'I don't think that would have troubled me terribly if Bill hadn't changed completely. It was as if as soon as we were married he had dropped the façade he'd been projecting and I saw his true character.'

'Did he hurt you?' George asked, hating the idea of Alice being scared of anyone, let alone the man she'd put her ultimate trust in.

'Not often. He struck me once or twice, but I know many women have it worse.'

A flash of rage shot through his body. The idea that anyone had hurt her, that anyone had dared to lay a finger on her, made him feel angry beyond words. No woman should have to put up with that, especially not from the man who was meant to care for them, provide for them. *Love* them.

'How did you bear it?' George asked. He wished he could go back in time, that he could be there when this brutish bully raised his hand and could shield Alice from everything that had come next. George felt a sudden surge of protectiveness and instinctively reached out and covered Alice's hand with his own. He saw the hope in her eyes, but he needed to hear the rest of her story before he could make her any promises.

'It was my life,' Alice said sadly. 'At first I was too proud to run home, to admit that I'd been foolish and naïve, but as things got worse I knew I could swallow my pride if it meant an escape from Bill, from the terrible life he'd dragged me into.

'I was saving a little money where I could when Bill came up with his scheme to steal from Mr Havers,' Alice said, biting her lip. 'A few more months and I would have had enough for the journey back to my parents.'

George leaned forward, taking both of her hands in his and caressing the soft skin.

'If that had happened, if you'd left London, then I would never have met you,' he said quietly, his voice thick with emotion. The idea of never meeting Alice made his heart squeeze painfully in his chest. 'And I don't want to think about that. I don't want to think of a life without you in it.'

'You forgive me?'

There was a pause, a moment when George looked into Alice's eyes and instead of seeing lies and betrayal he just saw the woman he loved looking back.

'I forgive you.'

'I should have told you everything sooner, it just never seemed the right time,' she said, her eyes filling with tears. 'At first I was determined to keep you at a distance so you didn't need to know the terrible, sordid details of my past, and then I'd fallen for you and it felt as though I'd already missed my opportunity to be truthful.' Her words came out in a rush and George smiled reassuringly.

'I understand, Alice. It was a mistake, nothing more, and we all make those.'

George was thrown back in his seat as Alice launched herself at him.

'I love you,' she said through her tears. She'd settled herself in his lap and buried her face in his shoulder so her voice was muffled, but he heard the relief in her voice all the same. 'I thought I had ruined everything.'

He waited for her to look up, smoothed her unruly hair away from her face and kissed her. 'I'm rather besotted with you,' he said with a rueful grin. 'It would take more than a possibly dead husband to chase me away.'

Chapter Twenty-Five

Alice woke early, the excitement surging through her and making her want to jump out of bed. It was Christmas Day and she hadn't felt this level of enthusiasm for Christmas since she was a little girl. Then it had been a magical day, filled with food and family and the anticipation of a small gift or two, a day she remembered warmly. Now she was excited for different reasons, the main one the man sleeping peacefully next to her.

It had been almost a week since Alice had told him about Bill and now they were closer than ever. They had decided to give up the pretence of being anything other than completely in love and Alice had moved into George's bedroom a few days earlier. She'd expected disapproval from Mrs Peterson, but the older woman had slowly

warmed to the idea of a new mistress of the house
and was already talking about children.

'Good morning,' George murmured as he
slowly opened his eyes.

'Merry Christmas,' Alice said, leaning in and
kissing him.

'Well that's a welcome start to the day.' He
closed his eyes again and Alice sighed and shook
him none too gently.

'I've been preparing for Christmas for the last
month—the least you could do is come downstairs and have a look.'

'That would be polite,' George said. 'Although
I thought I might be able to convince you to stay
in bed for a few minutes longer.'

He kissed the skin of her neck and back and
Alice felt her resolve weakening. Another half
an hour in bed didn't sound like such a bad proposal.

'I'm sure the decorations will be waiting for
us when we do decide to get up,' he said, his fingers caressing her, making her lose all coherent
thought as they snaked across her body.

'I'm sure they'll look better when the sun is
fully up and lighting the room,' Alice conceded,
tumbling back on to the sheets and shrieking
with delight as George quickly pinned her down,

climbing on top of her and kissing her until she was breathless.

'I'm glad you agreed,' he murmured. 'It would have been a poor start to Christmas if I couldn't give you the first of your many gifts.'

Before Alice could gather her wits George had trailed kisses down across her breasts and over her abdomen, kissing the silky curls beneath and then making her cry out as his lips brushed against her most sensitive spot. He kissed and nipped, making Alice writhe underneath him, until she clutched at his shoulders and felt wave after wave of pure pleasure roll over her body.

As he sat up Alice gripped his waist, flipping herself over and pinning him to the bed, her hips hovering above his.

'Shall we head downstairs?' she asked, letting her hair fall around her shoulders so it brushed against George's chest.

George groaned, closing his eyes as she moved against him, the lightest of touches that she could see was already driving him mad.

'You're not that cruel,' he murmured.

Alice paused for a long moment, drawing the tension out before she sank down on top of him.

'That's very true,' she whispered as their hips came together.

* * *

Twenty minutes later Alice was lying with her head resting on George's shoulder, wondering if she could truly be this happy. They had agreed to forget about their pasts and the future for now and just enjoy what they had together, and since then she had been so much more contented.

'Now I'm ready,' George said, kissing her on the forehead and then sitting up.

'Prepare to be amazed.' Last night Alice had sent George upstairs, making him promise not to peek, straight after dinner. She and Mrs Peterson had spent the next two hours transforming the downstairs of the house with plants and flowers. It wasn't anything like a Christmas back home, but Alice had been ecstatic with the result.

Quickly they both dressed, slipping out of the bedroom into the silent house. Alice watched George's face as they descended the stairs, feeling her heart clench as he broke out into a huge smile.

'How did you do all this?' he asked.

Alice looked around her. The hall was decked in wreaths made of ferns, studded with pretty acacia and waratah flowers. Garlands of bottle-brushes added to the festive feel with their bright red flowers. She led him into the drawing room, seeing his smile as he saw the candles placed on all available surfaces ready for lighting later that evening when the Crawfords and Robertsons arrived for dinner. In the fireplace she'd made a huge bouquet of the finest specimens from his garden and she saw the pleasure in George's face as he knelt down and fingered the dainty petals.

'This is a very special Christmas,' he murmured, turning to Alice and gathering her in his arms.

'Mrs Peterson told me how important Christmas was to you growing up,' she said. 'And how your mother used to decorate the house. I wanted to give you a little of that nostalgia.'

'You've done a very good job.'

She took his hand and led him over to the comfortable armchair, motioning for him to sit before she took a parcel from the mantelpiece.

'It's not much,' she said, handing over the neatly wrapped present, 'But I wanted to give you something meaningful.'

'You didn't need to get me anything, Alice.'

'I did. I wanted to. You've changed my life, taken a cynical scared girl and transformed her into a woman who can love again. You've given me so much.'

'It's not all one-sided,' he grinned and pulled her into his lap. 'I get you, remember.'

'The better half of the deal, of course.'

Alice wriggled in his lap, impatiently waiting for him to open the present.

Carefully, he unwrapped the ribbon around the package and opened the paper. Inside was a little book, bound in leather, the pages of good quality but at the moment blank. He opened it up and out fluttered a pressed flower from the boronia tree that grew just outside the house.

'I know you collect flowers and plants, and make notes on them, but this is for you to gather it all together in one place and perhaps one day find someone to publish it.'

'I love it,' he said, his eyes shining. Alice knew that George was confident in almost every area of his life, but his dream—to publish a book on the native flora and fauna of Australia—was the one part in which he lacked self-belief. So she'd decided to believe in him in his place. This book was the first step in helping him realising his dream.

'And I love you.'

* * *

Outside it was getting dark as Alice stepped on to the dusty path. Inside the candles were flickering, casting a cheery light over the remains of the feast Mrs Peterson and Alice had spent the last couple of days preparing. The Crawfords and the Robertsons were tucking their children up into one of the beds upstairs and Alice had taken the opportunity to slip out and enjoy the balmy evening. The clouds were rolling in and Alice knew everyone was hoping for rain. It would be a welcome respite from the drought that had plagued Australia for the past few months.

'Merry Christmas,' George said, coming up behind her and wrapping his arms around her waist.

'Merry Christmas.' She felt contented, happy and loved, but also settled and safe, and for Alice that was important. For so long she hadn't known where she would end up, but now she knew whatever the future held it would be wonderful.

'I still haven't given you your present,' George said.

Alice turned around to face him, looking at the little box in his hand.

'It comes with a question,' he said quietly.

Alice glanced down, biting her lip. He flicked open the box, revealing a beautiful ring inside, a clear-cut diamond surrounded by a ring of sapphires.

'I know we said we wouldn't plan too much, but I can't imagine my future without you. Marry me, Alice. It might not be possible this year, or even this decade, but once we know you're free, marry me.'

'We may never know what happened to Bill,' Alice said softly.

'Then we shall live in blissful sin for the rest of our lives. But if one day we do know you're a free woman, then I'm asking you to be mine.'

Alice raised herself up on tiptoes and kissed him. 'Of course I'll marry you, I only wish we didn't have to wait.'

'I don't know. Living in sin gives a man a little boost in his reputation in some sectors.'

'Not a woman.'

'I promise I won't ever let anyone treat you badly because of your past or our living arrangements Alice.'

'I know.' And she did. Ever since that first day when he'd rescued her from the whipping post he'd been defending her and protecting her and loving her.

George slipped the ring on to her finger, kissing her knuckles as he did so. As he released her hand a fat raindrop fell from the sky, landing on Alice's cheek. It was followed by another and then another. As the cloud burst above them and the downpour started George took her by the hand and together they ran back to the house, their clothes already drenched.

In the shelter of the doorway he kissed her, running his hands through her wet hair, and Alice felt her heart swell.

'One day,' she murmured, 'one day I will be your wife.' It was a hope and a promise.

'You're my wife already...' he gestured to his heart '...in here.'

Epilogue

'Give me strength.'

The cultured voice came from behind the closed door and George couldn't help but smile. He was sitting on a bench, his face turned up to the sun, his legs stretched out in front of him. In less than an hour he and Alice were getting married at the church in the middle of Sydney, but Alice had insisted on stopping off to see the Lieutenant Governor first. He could just imagine her, dressed in her finest silk dress, making her demands of the man who ran the penal colony.

A minute passed and George could hear calmer discussion, then the door opened and Alice emerged, smiling triumphantly.

'For the sake of my sanity please take your wife-to-be away,' Colonel Hardcastle said as he escorted Alice out of his office. Despite his words he was still in good humour and George knew that he appreciated Alice's work for the female convicts.

'You won't forget?' Alice asked.

'I won't forget,' he assured her. 'I know you won't let me.'

'It would make such a difference to the women, a safe, dedicated place for the female convicts to live, at least for the first six months after their arrival here.'

'I won't forget,' Colonel Hardcastle said. 'Now go or you'll be late for your own wedding.'

Alice took George's arm and together they exited on to the bustling street.

'You persuaded him, then?' George asked.

'Once I showed him the initial outlay would not be very great he warmed to the idea...' Alice paused before continuing. 'He's a good man. I think he does care about the welfare of the convicts, he just needs a little help in seeing what the women need.'

Alice was now a free woman, her sentenced served in full. For the past six months she had become increasingly involved in the politics surrounding the female convicts, using her position in the community to advocate for them, to fight for improved conditions and more equality with the male convicts. She had confided in George that her aim was for no female convict to feel the need to seek the protection of a man, if she didn't want to.

He kissed her on the head, feeling the heat of the sun on her silky-smooth hair. It was another hot summer, but nothing like the one three years previously when he and Alice had first met.

'Are you ready to become Mrs Fitzgerald?' he asked.

'I've been waiting for this moment for a long time.' The news that Alice's husband Bill was dead had reached them a few months ago. George's aunt, who still lived in England, had set a man to investigate for him and after a few months the investigator had reported that Bill had been found dead, floating in the Thames. He'd avoided the hangman's noose, but it looked as though he'd lost his footing in a drunken stupor and fallen into the murky waters. Alice had been quiet when he'd told her the news, unable to feel much for the man who she had once cared for, but had caused her so much trouble.

One warm spring evening a couple of months ago George had taken Alice outside into the garden which was blooming under their joint care and asked her to marry him again. This time when she'd said yes there were no stipulations or clauses.

As they walked through the streets Alice gripped his hand excitedly and pulled him to one side, leading him to the small bookshop that had opened about a year ago. In the window, with a very fetching green and yellow cover, was *The Native Flora and Fauna of Eastern Australia.* It had taken George a year to compile his notes, which he'd sent to England, thinking he would never find a publisher, but interest in Australia was growing and his snippets of local flavour and anecdotes from his life growing up near Sydney, interspersed between the pictures and information about the plants and animals, had proved to be a winning combination. It had been published in England a year ago, the first copies finding their way to Sydney about nine months later.

They entered the cool building of the church, their eyes taking a moment to adjust to the darkness. At the very front, sitting in the pews waiting were the Crawfords and the Robertsons, both families swelled in numbers by more new arrivals, two little babies that were still so small they spent most of their time sleeping and feeding. Then, sitting next to Francesca, her brilliant blue eyes shining, her hair the same golden red as her mother's, was his and Alice's little girl, Elizabeth. She was two years old, although sometimes George felt she spoke with the wisdom and solemnity of an adult.

'Mummy,' she screeched, bolting out of Francesca's arms and throwing herself at Alice. Alice bent and picked her up, planting kisses all over her soft rosy cheeks. Then Elizabeth grinned at her father and catapulted herself into George's arms. George had once thought he could never be happier than when Alice had agreed to marry him, but he'd been wrong. When their partnership of two had become a family of three his heart had swelled even further.

Together the three of them approached the vicar, a small, jolly man who was standing waiting for them.

The ceremony passed in a blur, the vows, the blessing, the placing of the wedding ring on Alice's finger to join the sapphire and diamond one she never took off. Then finally, after three long years, Alice was his wife.

'Congratulations,' Crawford said and everyone crowded round Alice and George as they made their way out of the church.

'I don't know what took you so long,' Robertson murmured.

'Three years is a very long engagement,' Alice said, looking down happily at the ring on her finger.

'You, my darling, are worth the wait.'

* * * * *

LET'S TALK
Romance

For exclusive extracts, competitions
and special offers, find us online:

- **f** facebook.com/millsandboon
- **⊙** @millsandboonuk
- **🐦** @millsandboon

Or get in touch on 0844 844 1351*

For all the latest titles coming soon,
visit millsandboon.co.uk/nextmonth

Want even more
ROMANCE?

Join our bookclub today!

'Mills & Boon books, the perfect way to escape for an hour or so.'

Miss W. Dyer

'Excellent service, promptly delivered and very good subscription choices.'

Miss A. Pearson

'You get fantastic special offers and the chance to get books before they hit the shops'

Mrs V. Hall